praise for d[...]

"Lain's writing is unsettling, ferociously smart, and extremely addictive."
—Kelly Link, author of *Get in Trouble* and *Magic for Beginners*

"Straight out of the Pamela Zoline era of New Wave fiction, with a strong dose of nuclear paranoia and Reagan-era 'kill a Commie for mommy' reverse-nostalgia, Lain writes from the conscience."
—Jay Lake, author of *Mainspring* and *Rocket Science*

"I don't know anyone else doing quite what Lain is doing; fascinating work, moving, strikingly honest, powerful."
—*Locus*

"An intellect and a questioner of literary forms, Lain is also a husbanding, fathering advocate for the Everyman in us all. The result is curiously human and intimate—down to earth, even as the universe falls apart in our hands."
—Kris Saknussemm, author of *Zanesville* and *Enigmatic Pilot*

"To find oneself alternately pondering the metafictional importance of a *Sesame Street* book and choking back the tears induced by a surprisingly human drama is a testament to Lain's writing. I loved every sentence, every word."
—J. David Osborne, author of *By the Time We Leave Here, We'll Be Friends*, on *Wave of Mutilation*

"Lain proves himself adept at dramatizing such decidedly non-whimsical matters as autism, parent-child estrangement, and the quest for individual identity amidst political upheaval."
—James Morrow, author of *The Last Witchfinder* and *Towing Jehovah*

"*Billy Moon* is postmodern SF, powering past mere science and into a cubist world of strange...moving and profound, with a radically evanescent style. Just the thing for our new century."
—Rudy Rucker, author of the WARE Tetralogy

after the saucers landed

ALSO BY DOUGLAS LAIN

Billy Moon

Collections:
Last Week's Apocalypse

Editor:
In the Shadow of the Towers:
Speculative Fiction in a Post-9/11 World

after the saucers landed
douglas lain

night shade books
new york

Night Shade books may be purchased in bulk at special discounts for sales promotion, corporate gifts, fund-raising, or educational purposes. Special editions can also be created to specifications. For details, contact the Special Sales Department, Night Shade Books, 307 West 36th Street, 11th Floor, New York, NY 10018 or info@skyhorsepublishing.com.

Night Shade Books® is a registered trademark of Skyhorse Publishing, Inc. ®, a Delaware corporation.

Visit our website at www.nightshadebooks.com.

10 9 8 7 6 5 4 3 2 1

Library of Congress Cataloging-in-Publication Data

Lain, Douglas.
  After the saucers landed / by Douglas Lain.
     pages ; cm
  ISBN 978-1-59780-823-1 (softcover : acid-free paper)
  1. Extraterrestrial beings—Fiction. 2. Human-alien encounters—Fiction.   I. Title.
  PS3612.A466A69 2015
  813'.6—dc23

                                                                    2015009977

ISBN: 978-1-59780-823-1

Cover design by Rain Saukas

Edited by Jeremy Lassen

Printed in the United States of America

after the saucers landed

prologue

When the alien gets around to unzipping her jumpsuit it'll be impossible to see what's underneath.

I've been through this before. Her argument with Harold Flint, all the usual ways a woman has to get past indifference, none will work, and when she unzips she won't offer her body, her inhuman perfection, but rather what she'll offer is her absence, and even this will go wrong. Flint, being too busy recovering from the last disappearance he witnessed, will be unimpressed.

There have been suicides in the UFO research community since the saucers landed on June 11, 1991. Of course there have been suicides. Maybe the first one, John Mack, might have been a surprise, but a year later the bodies stacking up aren't shocking. Each death is expected, and most go unnoticed and unreported in the media.

"We believe humanity is limiting the experience and significance of contact," the alien will say to Flint. Her name is Asket and she comes across a bit like a Vegas showgirl and a bit like a Jehovah's Witness.

Flint will look at her, look her up and down, and then snort. Actually the sound he'll make at her will be a partial snort as only part of the noise will emanate from his nose. There will also be a guttural noise, something like gagging, coming from his throat.

What made the Ufologists so despondent was that the arrival of real extraterrestrials, real aliens in real flying saucers, turned out to be an empty experience. The big event played out just as the contactee and presumed hoaxer Charles Rain had predicted. It was exactly like something from a B movie from the '50s. It even happened on the White House lawn.

The whole world watched the photo op between the alien commander, a Nordic-type alien from the Pleides who called himself Ralph Reality, and the President of the United States. The smiling politician, the former CIA director in his red tie and blue suit, shook hands with the humanoid wearing a white jumpsuit adorned with red sequins, and both of them smiled for the viewers of CNN. In the end both the President and the alien came out seeming smaller and less interesting than they had at the start. The suicides, the mostly older men and women who'd been warning everyone, who'd been collecting the data, who'd been so sure that Earth was indeed being visited no matter what Carl Sagan and his ilk said, those brave souls, Cassandras all, didn't get to witness an apocalypse or live through *Childhood's End*, but found an alien invasion that was just another television program. The landing was another sequence of moving pictures set between commercial breaks.

Flint had explained it at his wife's funeral. He'd said, "Imagine your whole life taking place on Christmas Eve and then, out of the blue, and after thirty years, it's Christmas morning and Santa has left you a present. Now imagine that what you find in your stocking isn't a lump of coal, but a turd.

That's what these kitsch aliens are, a turd left in our collective stockings. It's no wonder Mack and Budd and, Carole are gone. They took their lives because they couldn't stand to watch another Pleidien interviewed on some banal cable talk show like Donahue."

Of course, lumping his wife in with the others, with the rest of the disaffected UFO community, was a bit of misdirection. Anyone who knew Carole knew she hadn't cared for UFO research. She'd had her art and her artist, and that had been enough for her until Flint had spoiled both and broken her heart.

"Mr. Flint." Asket is going to say his name at the end of the argument. "Mr. Flint," she'll say, "you've got everything backward. I'm not here as an alien at all. I'm not with them." And then she'll unzip her jumpsuit.

asket unzips

Harold Flint is out of place in the '90s. My mentor and colleague is the kind of man who holds onto things. His appearance hasn't changed much for thirty years. He's this grey-haired, thin, severe sort of man who is determined to be an anachronism: always dressed in the same tailor-made, three-piece black suits, and always with a white shirt and black tie. I assume it's not actually the same suit every day, but I can't be sure.

Myself, I try to keep up with the times. Well past thirty, I'm a bit on the round side I guess, but I've started wearing cargo pants and plaid shirts. Today I'm wearing khakis with a red and black plaid, and last week one of the other adjuncts introduced me to Soundgarden. That song about Jesus Christ? I pretended to like it.

I'm optimistic. All of the professors I know are optimistic about this young decade; certainly my colleagues in English Literature are happy, happy to have survived the Reagan administration if nothing else. We're all of us full of hope. What with Clinton and the UFOs we're all of us pledged to never stop thinking about tomorrow, all of us except for Harold that is. He's still in mourning for the '60s, especially for the year 1961. Back then his short hair and seriousness fit the scene and his sarcastic and discordant art was the weirdest thing around. He didn't have to compete with MTV or Pee-wee Herman.

From where we are I can only see the back of Harold's head. He doesn't want to turn around apparently. He's facing away from us and sitting on his stool supposedly working, but I keep tapping on the wire mesh glass window. I know he can hear me.

"You can't just leave me out here," I shout, trying to make my voice audible through the thick doors.

I do deserve better than this. Okay, so he doesn't want to meet this alien, or any alien. He made that plain, but I did tell him I was going to bring her around regardless. Now he's making us wait and I'm stuck with the Pleidien, stuck standing too close to her on the other side of the green doors to the school's art studio.

Like all the Pleidiens she's beautiful if a bit wholesome, and she's wearing the uniform, that tight jumpsuit with the red sequins that I mentioned earlier. Standing this close I can smell her clean hair. She smells like strawberries but her eyes are blank.

"I think there is something wrong with her."

"Of course there is something wrong with her," Flint yells back. "She's a moron." Satisfied with this dig he finally lets us in.

"Mr. Flint, after today I'll go away forever if you want me to, but please," she says, "just answer one question."

Flint likes to mingle with the students' work even if he's usually put out by the students themselves. He's comfortable amidst their irony and their clichés and this studio is filled with both. There's this cartoonish painting of a woman shaving her legs in a bathtub full of wild dogs, a mannequin wearing a beige cashmere sweater, and a marble pedestal to the right of the mannequin. I pause at this work though. It's an approximation of a Grecian column only in miniature, and on top of it there is a display of prescription medicine bottles. The whole thing is a tribute or monument to what I assume is some sophomore girl's slump.

What Flint is doing is making a reproduction of one of his earlier works. He's pouring hot wax into a slightly oversized version of his famous 1964 Marble Maze.

"This one is for the Whitney," Harold tells the alien.

"You're selling that one?" she asks.

"I am."

Back in the '60s Harold was part of Fluxus but it's only been recently, around '88, that his work has become known. When the MOMA published photographs of Harold's matchboxes and wooden treasure chests in the *Big Book of NeoDada* Flint became a name. After that the curators and gallery owners who mattered in New York knew who he was. I was his chance to cash in but Harold resisted the temptation at first, even protesting the MOMA's Fluxus exhibit and the attendant coffee table book by taking out an ad in the *Village Voice* denouncing everyone involved. It's only now that Ufology has stopped mattering to him that he's become cynical enough to play along with the revival.

"What does it mean?" Asket asks him. She's pointing at the Marble Maze, at the sentence "Language does not exist," and standing close to Flint. I can't quite tell, but from where I'm standing it looks like she might be pressing herself up against him.

Harold doesn't answer her question but moves the maze aside and slides an oversized box of kitchen matches into the space so that he can get a closer look. This box of matches is a reproduction of an anti-artwork he created in 1968. There is white paper taped over the original label and on the paper there are instructions printed in 16-point black Helvetica script:

"'Use these matches to destroy art.'" He opens the matchbox and pours in wax. "What can I do for you, Miss. Asket? I'm guessing that you don't want to talk to me about my art."

"Why did you quit UFOs?" she asks.

Flint looks up at her, sighs, and then turns back to his work.

When he started investigating flying saucers most of his friends in the art world, people like John Cage, Ray Walker, and Alison Knowles, thought his research was an elaborate joke, a Dadaesque prank. It wasn't. Flint was always serious. He'd seen something in the sky himself, back in the late '50s when he was a student at Black Mountain College. He didn't start investigating and incorporating saucers and abduction reports into his art and performances until the late '70s, but that early sighting was always in the background. That is, it was always in the background until it was in the foreground, or until the saucers landed.

Asket has been visiting me during office hours since the start of the semester. She's been auditing one of my intro composition classes even though she clearly doesn't care about the class. Her office visits are never about the course, she never asks about Aristotelian or Rogerian forms of argument, for example, but only visits in order to ask about Flint. She figured out that I'm his ghostwriter and started stalking me, trying to get to him.

"I think Flint can help me," she told me during her first visit. Now she's saying it again. "You can help me," she says.

There is something wrong with this Pleidien. She's got none of their usual confidence. Instead of channeling spiritual entities or speaking in aphorisms, she's standing there having a quiet anxiety attack. She's hanging on Harold's every word and really suffering under his sarcasm and indifference.

"Why don't you answer her, Harold?" I ask. "I'm wondering why too, actually. You know that we could make a bundle on it now. We're well positioned."

Harold looks up again; he starts to address me, point at me as if he's going to deliver another of his lectures, but stops himself and turns back to the Pleidien instead. "You want to know why I quit?" he asks.

She nods hesitantly.

"It's because of you. You and your friends. Your arrival ended a dream for me. I've spent my life on this dream, you know, this dream of a different world? But you people ended that."

Asket shifts her weight, takes a step back from Harold.

"Back in the '70s I worked in a dentist's office, I was a male secretary and I became accustomed to being taken as a fool, to being asked to endure every idiot colleague's opinion. I needed the work and I tried to remain stoic, but this dentist, a born-again Christian named Terry, made it difficult. He wanted to convert me," Harold says. This was a familiar anecdote, and I knew he was just getting started.

Harold has a tattered paperback copy of the *Big Book of Fluxus* open on the worktable, presumably using it as reference, a way to jog his memory on his original work. The book is open to a page with a full color reproduction of Nam June Paik's sculpture "Exposition of Music – Electronic Television." What it was was a prepared piano, a stand-up piano with an open case so the pressure bar, pin block, hammer rail, and strings were exposed. The keys were wrecked by nails, there were knickknacks and various gizmos and devices stuffed into the frame. A telephone was glued down on top, a bottle of antifreeze propped on the pedals, and eggshells were scattered here and there atop the hammers. The idea behind such a work was to disrupt the routine of music production, to break the listener's expectations, and involve the audience in a new kind of listening. Every detail, every noise, had to be caught and considered. The fact that all of the notes together didn't cohere was just an added benefit.

Harold is still deriding the notion of an immanent God.

"What the dentist wanted me to realize was that Jesus was a superhero. Jesus could save me. It wasn't a metaphor or a mystery. It wasn't a matter of faith. This was real and I was turning down a real person, a person I might actually meet."

Harold quit the UFOs after the landing for the same reason he wasn't interested in a superhero version of Jesus. If he could really meet Jesus, if Jesus was a person who could appear in his life that meant that his life, Harold's life in that office, would stay the same. If Jesus could appear right there, right then, by the Pepsi machine in the employee's kitchen, then Jesus wasn't interesting.

"You didn't want to meet Jesus by a vending machine?" she asks. "Why not?" Harold looks like nothing other than a college professor and she is dressed only so as to be unzipped. Watching them, the two of them, I feel as though I'm at a Halloween party or at a dress rehearsal for *The Rocky Horror Picture Show*. I find myself waiting for the cut away, waiting for some other more hilarious and action-packed scene, but the cutaway isn't happening, not yet.

"Any Jesus that could appear like that, in a puff of smoke, that could just show up by the Pepsi machine? He wouldn't be of any use, would he? Who would want any part of such a mundane Jesus?" Harold asks.

"Why would Jesus be mundane?" the alien asks. "Couldn't it be that the Pepsi machine would transcend? You're confusing me."

"God doesn't drink soda pop."

"But, if He did…if God drank soda pop wouldn't that change the soda pop? Why is it that the Pepsi can change God?"

Harold takes his glasses off to look at her, leaning in toward her. She seems, all at once, to be of interest to him after all.

"What exactly do you want from me? What do you Pleidiens want?" he asks.

Asket steps farther back from him. She steps away from Harold, then circles around the art, the students' art. She stops to look at the painting of the wild dogs, then pauses by the mannequin wearing a sweater. "I was wrong," she says. "It's not you that I need to talk to at all. Our souls switch around so often that it's sometimes difficult to keep track."

"Our souls switch around?" I ask.

"That's just a way of speaking. It's a physical thing."

"How do you mean? What's a physical thing?"

"The soul is physical. It's our ideas of ourselves. Your idea of yourself, your idea of Brian Johnson that switches," she says. "Our names: Brian Johnson, Harold Flint, or Asket, those are spiritual."

Harold picks up a damp towel from the worktable, wipes his hands, and then hangs the rag on a hook underneath the table. He claps his hands together, stands up, and starts for the door.

"Where are you going?" I ask.

"She doesn't need me after all," he says. He turns to look at her. "That's right, isn't it? You don't need me? I can leave?"

Asket is unsure. She doesn't want him to leave, but at the same time she doesn't appear to want to look at him. She's averting her gaze. "I don't need you here, but I do need the idea of you."

"What does that mean?" Harold asks. "You're here for my soul?"

"No. I want...I want you to give him back his idea."

She looks at him finally, a bit sternly I think, and she reaches for the zipper of her jumpsuit. Even though I've seen this before I'm a little surprised by the gesture, a bit embarrassed for her. "You don't know how to give an idea," she says. "You've forgotten how, but I'll show you. You've got everything backward. I'm not here as an alien at all. I'm not with them." And then she unzips.

But as she steps out of her clothes I find that I can't look at her. I'm unable to look in the right direction or to focus my eyes properly. I've lost track of her, somehow. I can't find her even though she's hardly moved and is clearly still in the room.

"Where did she go?" I ask Harold.

"She's. . ." he starts, but he can't see her either.

charles rain and quality pie

Harold Flint and Charles Rain have entirely different theories about Missing Time. If both of them were presented with this story, if both were told about the jump or discontinuity that came after Asket unzipped, their answers would not merely be different, but would be opposite. That is, if the past is any guide, Rain would blame the Missing Time or memory loss on us, on Harold and me, and he'd point to what is now known as an established fact as the explanation. We humans have been approached, off and on, by higher intelligences from the Pleidien system since the beginning of civilization, and we have always been found wanting. There is Missing Time because we can't cognize the eternal truth that Rain is offering for $19.95.

Harold, on the other hand, would claim that our memory loss was a good thing. That is, forgetting is always a part of remembering, and recognizing that we've forgotten, ferreting out a discontinuity, should clue us in on the fact that we always forget. Nothing is really continuous from one moment to the next. The important thing about UFOs, for Harold, isn't what planet they came from or what their intentions are, but rather the enigma itself as an enigma. He likes discontinuities for their own sake, and if he were writing this, if he wanted anything more to do with the UFO subject, I'm guessing that's what he'd set on the page. If Harold were co-writing this he'd do his best to convince me to leave it there and move on. Fortunately, however, I'm on my own and I'm not going to leave you hanging.

Charles Rain was already thirty-six years old when the Pleidiens decided to allow him to remember them. In 1975 Charles had been forced to seek work as a security guard at Macy's department store to supplement what was turning out to be a dwindling income as a designer and fine artist. He had three sons, a wife who was unhappy with their living situation (she felt that five people living in a two-bedroom apartment on the Lower East Side was less than ideal), and a bit of a drinking problem. Things weren't working out for Charles and he was on the verge of giving up on his art, on his life really, when, on March 23rd, 1975, everything was resolved and solved by a deus ex machine–style intervention.

Before he actually saw them, before they landed their garbage pail lid–shaped saucers at Rain's parents' cabin in the Catskills, he heard a voice. He was sitting at the breakfast table at five a.m., drinking instant coffee, and trying to cure his hangover with greasy sausages and Tabasco sauce, when he heard her talking. It was a woman's voice, surely, but not his wife's voice, and while the voice was speaking to him, definitely to him, she was not using a language he could understand. That is, it was an alien language he was hearing, and it took a few moments before the alien words were supplemented with more direct/nonlinguistic representations.

What Charles heard was a voice from another dimension, a voice coming from what he figured, after counting up from a simple dot to the sunburst-shaped copper wall clock next to the refrigerator, was probably the fifth dimension, but it might have been the seventh. Later on, after his *Saucer Wisdom* books were published but before the Pleidiens and Ralph Reality arrived, Flint would comment on the Platonic character of Rain's claims. The important bit of what Rain wrote, the most important claim, wasn't the number of dimensions he said he'd visited or heard from, it wasn't the number of light-years that his Space Brothers and Sisters traveled before presenting themselves over the pine trees and stables at his parents' ranch, but rather it was the metaphysical claim contained in the very first sentence that Rain thought he understood at the breakfast table back in 1975.

"It is difficult to communicate with you clearly from here. Where we are, in Eternity things are different. Our experiences don't translate into the material universe," the voice told him.

This idea of Eternity, of a higher-level reality from which angelic voices could be heard and redemption could be found, was just the same old delusion that had been repeating in various guises throughout all of Western history. Old Greek philosophers wrote about the fifth dimension too, only they said it was water, or if not water then fire. Then again, maybe Eternity was a realm of pure ideas, of perfect concepts. What Rain was claiming, what the feminine voice he heard over sausages was telling him, was that it was possible to know the truth, the essence of things, directly and this knowledge could fix things. The Space Brothers, the Pleidiens, could square the circle, they could resolve the problem. Lions would lie down with lambs, war was over, and Charles Rain could quit pacing from ladies' wear to the bed and bath department. All of a sudden he had a new job, maybe even a calling.

"We feel our emotions differently, more directly, and we experience joy," the hallucination told him. And, in that moment, a cult was born. Only, of course, it turned out not to be a delusion at all, and Charles Rain did not end up as just one more long bearded mad man presiding over credulous and stunted followers, but ended up as something much more than that; Charles Rain ended up as a global celebrity and as the human CEO of the first intergalactic 501(3)c. Harold knew Charles before the landing; they knew each other before either had seen a single UFO, and even back then Harold had had the same criticism of the man who would become humanity's Space Brother. The problem was that Charles Rain was too reassuring, too optimistic, both as an abstract expressionist, and as a drinker. Charles's paintings were brightly colored nicetics created with posters and mechanical reproduction in mind. He wanted to be hung in suburban homes on both coasts, he wanted to go well with the furniture, but his work was too boring to really catch on. Rain's paintings were competent, sometimes purchased, but never quite loved by anyone. Worse, as a drunk Rain was sloppy and sentimental.

Harold drank with him at the Cedar Tavern back in the '50s, nearly twenty years before the breakfast epiphany, and even then Rain had been a fount of positive thinking. He'd once even gone so far as to try to offer Mark Rothko a hug.

It was embarrassment just to know Rain, and what was worse was that Rain had helped Harold out so often. He'd helped Harold find galleries for his work, helped him find a publisher for his first UFO book, and even helped him out in matters of love. If it hadn't been for Charles Rain, Harold would never have met the woman who became his second and now late wife.

"Hold on," Harold says. He puts his chin in his hands and looks down at the basket of onion rings and fries, the QP basket as it's called, and then looks at me and my wife Virginia. He seems skeptical about something, about Virginia especially, and then, to my surprise, he reaches out to her across the yellowed tablecloth and takes hold of her hand.

"It's not true that Rain was responsible for setting me up with Carole," he says.

"It's not?" I ask.

"No," he says. "Rain sent her to me because her sighting, her abduction, whatever you want to call it, it didn't fit with his narrative. He didn't want her around his people, but he didn't arrange anything more than an interview."

"Why are you holding my hand?" Virginia asks. "That's wrong, isn't it? Me holding your hand," Harold says. But he holds on for a moment more, looking at her directly, maintaining eye contact. Then he lets go and stands up from the table. Walking around the booth, examining the coffee stains on the white Formica tabletop, the faded red vinyl upholstery, the dirty orange carpet, he seems perplexed. When he gets all the way around he sits back down. "How did we get here?" he asks. He points to Virginia but looks at me as if he's going to back me into a corner with his next question. "How did she get here?" he asks. Looking out through the plate glass windows I see that my Volkswagen station wagon is parked near the entrance. I can spot it easily even though its forest green paint job looks purplish underneath the flashing red lights from the saucer hovering overhead, but when I mention my car to Harold he isn't interested. "We were at the Studio Art Building talking to the crazy bitch alien, I was working on the reproduction of my anti-art matches, and now we're here," Harold says. "And she's here with us."

My wife takes a sip of ice water and then places the dark yellow Vaseline tumbler back down a bit too heavily so that it cracks. Ice, water, and yellow-tinged glass flow across the dirty Formica and Virginia starts sucking her thumb. She's bleeding and her hands are trembling.

I put down my Reuben and watch her.

"Have we done this before?" Virginia asks. "That's an interesting question," Harold says. "What's wrong, Virginia?" She tells me she's feeling strange. "Déjà vu," she says.

I wait for her face to change, for the flat line of her lips to soften, or for anything that might indicate that she's past it, but her panic doesn't fade. She's staring at Harold and her mouth is held in a tight frown. She's waiting for the next thing to happen and she keeps staring at Harold the whole time.

"Is what I'm saying now a part of it?" I ask.

"What?" Virginia asks. "You've got déjà vu? So, what I'm saying now, is it following the script?" I ask. She nods.

"And now?" I ask. The malice in my voice is unintended and I regret it. I regret how I've made Harold smile and nod along. I clear my throat and try again. "Is this sentence that I'm saying right now a part of the sequence?"

Virginia shakes her head no, but I can't tell if she's answering or rejecting the question. She picks up her napkin and starts to clean up the mess she made with her water glass, but stops to suck her thumb again. Then she stands up to leave. "Excuse me," she says.

Virginia is wearing an off-white sweater dress with a high turtleneck collar and a short hemline. She twists to step sideways around a rather rotund transvestite at the diner's counter and I realize that this new outfit is provocative. She looks different, is dressed differently than is the norm. Her sweater dress is too short for one thing and I'm staring at her legs as she twists again. Not only is she exposing a lot of leg, but she's barefoot. All in all she seems exposed, maybe a bit vulnerable. When the transvestite gets up from his stool at the counter, when he follows her around the corner, I wonder whether I should go back there myself to make sure she's okay.

"Do you think she still wants me, us, to continue on with UFOs?" Harold asks.

For a moment I think Harold is confused, that he's stuck in the last scene, but as he takes a fry and dips it in the little paper cup of ketchup I rationalize. Virginia was one of his abductees, one our clients. Harold and I have that in common. I met Virginia for the same reason Harold met Carole, because she wanted to know what her saucer sighting meant. In that context, Harold's question might make a bit of sense?

"She's quite pretty," Harold says.

I don't like it. Yes, Virginia is pretty. So was Harold's second wife.

Carole met Charles Rain first. We've already established that. She met him at the Buffalo UFO conference in 1981. She was an artist too, she'd seen many UFOs in the late '70s, and hoped that Charles might be interested in the work she was doing around reincarnation. She'd been visiting channelers and psychics, was working with Tarot cards, had even tried out hypnotism, but Charles wasn't interested. The problem was that she didn't want to know about UFOs, not really. What she wanted to understand was how she might use her experiences in order to change figure painting. What Carole liked about the New Age and Ufology was the folk and outsider art that came out of it. What she hoped to do was discover a new way to paint that would be informed by what she called mythic modernity or, alternatively, retro-futurism. For Carole, imagining a future, imagining what it would mean when the saucers landed, always involved a return to the past. For Carole the idea of Missing Time, the fact that we lose some things as we remember others and how we always become something we don't want as a consequence meant that we are, all of us, reincarnated while we're still alive.

She fell in with Harold, first as his mistress and then as his second wife, and by 1983 she was using his art studio to pile up nudes layered with bric-a-brac, photographs stolen from scrapbooks, and wax paper while he interviewed abductees and went to conferences. Her theory of Missing Time was like Harold's in so much as she accepted the loss of memory, but it wasn't like his theory because it wasn't abstract. She wasn't trying to get to any kind of truth, but just liked the feeling of applying paint to a canvas, of cutting up other people's mementos and dreams, of mixing the paint and paper clippings into an orange or blue or green paste.

"How did we get here?" Harold asks again. We're still at the Quality Pie restaurant, Virginia hasn't come back from the restroom yet, and the idea of going out to the parking lot to confront the saucers hasn't been raised. Harold is about to order some coffee and tell me about Yoko Ono, about one of her performance pieces, something she did before she met John Lennon. But for the moment we're still stuck on that question. "How did we get here?"

I try to think of a good answer. I think of Rain's phony UFO photos with hubcaps for saucers, and the promises of Eternity, and figure that's the best answer. Given the choice between Harold's paradoxical metaphysics, his dead wife's aesthetics, and Charles Rain's story about Eternity, souls, and flying saucers, I figure there really is no choice to make. The Pleidiens and their saucers is clearly the best answer. Jesus by the Pepsi machine.

Harold orders a cup of coffee and then lights a Camel cigarette, he's smoking the filterless kind now, and he settles in to talk. Whenever we get together we end up having the same conversation. It might take different guises, starting out as a conversation about presidential politics or something even more mundane, say the price of asparagus at Met Foods, but ultimately he comes around to his pet subject. With Harold it's always about skepticism. Incredulity, criticism, doubt, these are his talismans, his power words. Skepticism is his religion.

"I've been thinking about Yoko Ono lately," he says. "I've been thinking about how she failed."

For Harold, Yoko Ono is just another artist, and when he mentions her, her failure, I know that he isn't talking about her singing. He isn't interested in that. He's talking about the Yoko he knew before the Beatles.

"Have you ever seen *Cut Piece*?" he asks.

I bite into my Reuben, take a sip of coffee, and wait. Despite the question mark up there in the previous line my turn to speak hasn't really come around yet.

Cut Piece is a work of avant-garde performance that is nearly as old as my wife. In it Ono presents herself in her "best suit" to an audience armed with scissors. Ono sits cross-legged on a stage and stoically accepts the attack that comes. The art of it is in the process of her disrobing, the process of her being stripped of her suit jacket, her wool skirt, her silk blouse, one piece at a time.

"Ono thought that she could develop a new kind of relationship. That she could present the truth, the truth of her being, to an audience. She wanted to get past the spectator, to eliminate the spectacle and, yes, she was speaking to the usual gender issue too, but really she wanted to keep what was beautiful between the sexes. She wanted to give herself away on that stage and find freedom that way. She was going to yield and yield and yield, like a Judo master, until it was the man or woman left holding the scissors who was naked."

I take another bite of sandwich and then move it away, hold it over my plate. The sandwich's innards dribble out. Bits of it, sauerkraut and Thousand Island dressing fall to my plate.

"Where is Virginia?" Harold asks.

"What's that?"

"Where is your wife?"

I find out. Around the corner Virginia is blocking the emergency exit outside the restroom. She's sitting on a stackable metal chair positioned so that it's up to next to the push bar for the door without actually putting pressure on it, and she's got arms folded across her lap. Her sweater dress is stretched so that it covers her knees and she's looking quite comfortable. She seems nonplussed, doesn't say anything, but just gives me a wary look.

"What's going on back here?"

"It hasn't stopped."

"What hasn't?"

"I've been sitting back here watching people pass by, walk through the frame of the entranceway, and each one of them seems familiar. Like that guy there in the leather baseball cap, the jowly man there? I must know him somehow," she said. "Or the kid with him, the one who looks like an overweight TV actor. Some sitcom kid. I know him too."

"Maybe you've seen him on television?"

That isn't it apparently. I can't quite tell what the difficulty actually is or what's troubling her because, well because everything is so immediate and present to me in this moment that I can't quite predict what will happen next, but if I had to guess I'd say that her sense of déjà vu hasn't subsided.

21

"It's gotten worse."

"It isn't stopping. Everything that we do, it's scripted out."

I tell Virginia we should just leave, escape out the emergency exit and leave Harold brooding over his coffee, but she's reluctant. She points out that the door is connected to an alarm, for one thing, and she says she needs to talk to Harold before we go. She wants to say goodbye.

"Actually, it seems to me that there is something I ought to be talking to Harold about and I'm missing it," she says.

"You want to have it both ways," I say.

"How do you mean?"

"Is everything scripted or have we forgotten our lines?"

"Both," she says. "Maybe both."

onboard a saucer

Since the landing the Pleidien saucers are always on the horizon. They serve as floating billboards for the new age as well as constant invitations to join what I still think of as the Rain cult. The discs over Earth are open for walking tours 24/7 and admission is free. The Pleidiens are dedicated to transmission, to communication, and to enlightenment.

"Isn't this what you always wished you could do?" Virginia asks Harold. "Remember the first abduction case you investigated? If you'd been able to see the saucer that Deliah encountered, go back with her to the craft and see it again, talk to the people onboard, wouldn't that have been something? Wouldn't you have wanted that? Didn't you wish you could've been there?"

This might be the wrong approach to take with Harold because he'd been convinced that Deliah, his first wife, hadn't been visited by people from outer space at all, but that she'd been evolving. When he'd first written about the saucers he'd thought they were a symptom. Deliah's visitations were byproducts of her coping with a world that wasn't making sense. She'd needed to imagine space people in order to deal with the trauma of her childhood. Not that something so terrible had happened to her when she was a child, not that she'd suffered actually in the world. The problem had been the way technology, the way urban life under electric lights and in front of a television set, had denied her any sense of concrete reality. Patricia didn't have an ordinary sense of space, of location, because she'd watched *Rocky and Bullwinkle* before she'd learned to talk. Her mind worked by imagining flat surfaces and by making unlikely connections between images that, a hundred years earlier, would never have been presented to her so rapidly: a coffee can and a mountain range, both of them the same size, or a cartoon stick figure man wearing a top hat followed by the explosion of an atom bomb.

The three of us, Virginia, Harold, and myself, are in the parking lot of the Quality Pie looking up at the light show from the saucer and thinking it over. Harold takes a drag of his cigarette, then tosses the butt into an oil puddle near the yellow line. "This won't reveal anything new. I know what they're about, I've read the book. Some of it, anyhow," he says. "I read it fifteen years ago. What I remember is the advertising copy: '*Saucer Wisdom* presents spiritual truths and a sense of wonder. Rain's story of adventure, his insights on the phenomena of flying saucers, tells the secret that's been hidden from humanity for centuries. He tells us who we really are.'" Virginia pulls on her sweater dress, trying to cover her legs with it by stretching it out a bit, and then takes my hand. "We should go in, go up there," she says.

"Wait a second," I say. "It's been a long time since I read *Saucer Wisdom*. How did it turn out? *Who* did we turn out to *be*, Harold?"

"Book club members, mostly," he replied.

The saucer over Quality Pie is lit up like a Christmas tree, covered with steel bubbles that looked just exactly as if they'd been soldered on by an incompetent New Yorker and hoaxer. I'm getting a headache looking at it. My teeth ache as I consider the idea of facing all the pretty smiles, all the cheery illustrations and graphics, all the messages of hope and love.

"Kitsch," Harold says. Then he mumbles something under his breath, something about Christianity or Christ. My wife puts her hand on his back, petting him reassuringly, but pushing him forward too.

"Who are you, exactly?" Harold asks.

Virginia doesn't answer his question, but gestures with her head toward the saucer. "If we enter the vessel the déjà vu will stop. Help me out." She reminds us that we were moved, that we jumped from point A to point C without stopping off at B.

"You just experienced it," she says. "You're abductees, right? That's what Missing Time means? And the aliens are right there. You don't have to wonder, or try to figure it out. You can march right on board and ask them."

"Who are you?" Harold asks.

Virginia just points up at the spinning disc over our heads, asking us to follow her gesture and consider the ramp and lights and aperture. We are invited, she tells us. We are all three of us invited.

And walking up the ramp it does feel like it. That is, I feel as though I am being abducted. Somehow this journey on the extended escalator, being taken up mechanically into the saucer, stepping off at the entrance into a room that is lit by track lights, carpeted with well-worn dark red acrylic fiber, it all has a fatedness to it. It is decidedly odd. My wife is behaving strangely, my mentor—the man whose biography I ghostwrote—is going along with it, completely out of

25

character, and there is a man in a sequined jumpsuit behind the front counter. He's ready to tell us all about reincarnation and space travel and behind him, on a television monitor, there are flashing geometric patterns. Red triangles, orange circles, lots of little squares, all of this fills the screen as he welcomes us and asks if we'd like to know who we used to be. "The regression lasts twenty minutes and it is entirely free," he informs us as he hands us little red paper tickets. "Although donations are accepted and suggested."

Everything aboard the saucer has been kept clean: the rack of brochures and leaflets is well ordered, and the television monitor above the front counter is in good working order. It's a quality picture. But, despite this there is something of a low-end quality to the whole affair. The inside of a Pleidien disc is something more like a penny arcade or a dollar theater than it is like a museum or gallery. There is a smell of Lysol and sweat in the air, and the loud speakers are turned up a bit high.

"The Pleidiens are happy for this contact," the narrator says.

We've stepped away from the front counter. We're in the first exhibit, watching footage of their space fleet in action, watching them out there amongst the stars, when a man in a sequined jumpsuit steps comes around the corner to collect and tear our tickets.

"We want to ask you something," Virginia says to the man.

"Me?" The man in the sequined jumpsuit has a bit of a potbelly, his hair is thinning, and his sequins are green. I realize that he is not, in fact, a Pleidien, but is a human employee. "You or whoever is in charge," Harold tells him. "We were abducted. Just now, or maybe a few hours ago. We've had an experience of Missing Time and we want to talk to someone about it."

"Missing Time," the man says. He's thinking it over. "I think I know how to help you."

The usher takes us through the front exhibit and then leads us through a round metal door that slides open silently and down a hall with rounded walls that are painted a bright yellow. There are no windows or portholes, but plenty of light coming from clouded glass panels overhead, and I think of George Orwell. There might not be day or night inside one of these saucers. The light is probably always on.

The usher takes us to an exhibit room and then scuttles off before we can object. We wait for a while, thinking he's gone to get somebody to talk to us, but when several minutes pass we find ourselves taking in the computer screens, posters, and plastic models. This exhibit tells the history of alien visitations on Earth. There is a recounting the Charles Rain story of course, but there are also several other famous UFO cases on display, cases that were quite famous before the landing.

Betty and Barney Hill, for instance, are shown on one of the monitors. The smiling middle-aged couple is pictured on their living room sofa and he's holding a newspaper. Barney is pointing to the headline "New Hampshire UFO chiller" and he looks a bit proud.

Using a dingy computer mouse (the white plastic is now grey) Harold moves through the catalog of images. There is Major Marcel holding debris from a crashed weather balloon, a stage photo that he would later claim had no relation to the debris he found on the Brazel ranch in Roswell, New Mexico. There is a publicity photo of D. B. Sweeney as Travis Walton in the film *Fire in the Sky*, and there is a photo of Whitley Strieber on *Larry King Live*, and the movie poster from Spielberg's *Close Encounters of the Third Kind*.

Virginia moves on to the next monitor as Harold plays a short video of an interview with Jacques Vallée and François

Truffaut, and after this there is a video of Ralph Reality who explains that Spielberg unknowingly worked with Pleidien movie producers at MGM. The Space Brothers were apparently quite pleased with how the movie turned out.

"Too many stories about us reflected the lower-level spiritual development so prevalent on Earth. The films about us were, up until this point, filled with fear and violence," Ralph Reality says. For some reason he has a British accent in this clip, and that seems new. I'm thinking he sounded like an American when he landed on the White House lawn. "We were elated when Spielberg was so amenable to telling a different kind of story about humanity's interstellar future."

Harold takes my shoulder as I click the mouse to switch to the next video.

"What's happening here?" he asks.

I tell him I don't know and I wonder where Virginia has gotten off to, but I've misunderstood his question.

"They've gotten it all wrong. Where's Budd Hopkins?" Flint asks. "Where's John Mack and David Jacob?"

Harold thinks this history lesson from our Space Brothers leaves too much out. Harold starts to fill in the gaps with a running commentary as we move on to the next computer monitor. "It's a reader's digest version," he says. "They don't even mention Kenneth Arnold or Allen Hynek." They've left out a lot, but it becomes clear why the usher brought us to this exhibit because the third monitor presents a list of clickable items on the subject of Missing Time and abductions.

"These dark human fantasies were, in fact, only a psychic reaction to our presence on Earth. Humanity's collective unconscious was aware of us, aware that we had contacted Charles Rain and that we'd passed on our understanding of cosmic consciousness to him. These spiritual gains made by

Rain and his followers threatened the symptomatic reality of the rest of humanity, and thousands around the world psychically materialized their worst fears as a reactive response. While these night terrors were delusional they did occur on the level you consider most important. These were real physical events that you, the people of Earth, orchestrated in an effort to restage the contact in terms you could, in that moment, understand. As you were stuck, collectively stuck, in the intermediary realm between consciousness and spirit, you needed the Greys. You needed the fear they brought with them. But, if you're willing, the possibility of moving beyond this stage is now open to you," the narrator said. The voice sounds a bit mechanical.

Another Pleidien flying saucer appeared above the holographic projector. The hologram saucer was circling around the top of a Douglas fir. We were watching one of Rain's old hoaxes, the wires holding up the saucer were especially visible in this three-dimensional rendering, but the narrator made no mention of them.

"Along with Rain there were many others who helped decode and explain our presence on Earth. And even when they focused on humanity's own delusions, even when they worked with fear rather than light, many tremendous contributions were made by what was known as the UFO community."

Next is abduction researcher John Mack. Mack is a Harvard psychiatrist who wrecked his reputation on UFOs and in the promotional hologram Mack is sitting on a panel at some convention or other. Judging from the quality of the video to hologram transfer—floating artifacts, bits of static rendered as three-dimensional balls of blue and red and yellow light make me think of foo fighters—I figure the footage is to be from the '79 MUFON conference in Seattle. Mack is talking about the mix of the subjective and objective while Harry Flint nods at him. Yep, it's Flint there with Mack and the Pleidiens take up a minute or two outlining Flint's work.

"Harry Flint's approach to the sightings, to the question of our presence, was of particular interest to us. His insistence that people consider the UFOs as a philosophical problem, rather than as science fiction phenomena, interested us greatly. His work along with the work we were doing with Charles Rain, the advancements we made with him during our visits to his ranch in the Catskills, gave us the confidence to make open contact with the human race."

Flint nudges me and points away from the display, directing me to pay attention to Virginia who is standing at the center of a star map and swaying back and forth with a look of spacey consideration on her face. She's got her thumb pressed against her front teeth and clearly isn't really looking at the constellations that are swirling about her. She's standing on a round platform marked with a string of LED lights, surrounded by holograms, with her thumb in her mouth and her other hand pulling down on the bottom of her sweater. She might be singing karaoke in some dingy club but for the fact that the music has been replaced by a prerecorded lecture about star children and the hierarchy of souls. She turns a bit as a meteorite takes shape in the interference pattern that is the hologram, moves with it and reaches out as it spins past her. She lets go of her sweater, stands on her tiptoes and the wool knit sweater is pulled up. Her bare skin, her pubic hair, is visible for a moment as she turns. The fact of her nakedness along with the length of her sweater dress seems wrong to me.

"She's not dressed," I say.

"Do you recognize the sweater?" Flint asks.

Now Virginia is standing under a holographic flying saucer covered in what look just like Christmas lights. The wires aren't visible but the image is laughable nonetheless. The saucer hovers there over her head, and then zips away toward our solar system. The saucer zips toward a three-dimensional rendering of our solar system and as the flying hubcap approaches the planets grow bigger. In an instant Virginia is standing where the sun would be and the planets are revolving around her, around the platform.

"Brian," Flint says. "That isn't your wife. I don't think that's your wife."

I don't respond to Flint but just wave back to her. She's noticed us staring and she's gesturing for us to join her on the platform. She's still chewing on her right thumb and she's beckoning us with her left hand when she really ought to be continuing to pull on the bottom of her sweater with that hand. I make my way to her quickly, taking off my tweed jacket as I move between the lines of LED lights on the orange carpet.

Virginia is right there in front of me but as I step closer to her, put my hand on her hip, get close enough to smell her, I can't be certain. It's not that she smells wrong so much as the fact that my familiarity with her physical presence is clearly untrustworthy. Putting my hand on her hip is something I'm doing and what is really familiar isn't her skin, her looks, her physicality, but my desire for contact. When she puts her arm around my waist in response, touches the small of my back, I'm even less certain.

I'm standing next to my wife inside the Pleidien flying saucer, standing there in the light show while Harold stares at us skeptically, and it seems like my knowledge of her, of this kind of moment, has turned around on me.

All of it, the cheesy holographic display, the LED lights, the smell of stale air and unvacuumed carpet, it's all familiar. I feel as though I've done all this already, like I've lived through this before.

"Your déjà vu is spreading," I say. And, of course, I feel dread as I wait for her response. I feel dread because it seems to me that I already know what her response will be, if only subconsciously.

She takes her hand away, turns to look at me, and her smile falters. "Don't let him take me away from you," she says.

Only Virginia isn't saying anything, not out loud. She looks at me with her big blue eyes, runs her left hand through her sandy blond hair, and tugs at her sweater dress. And in my mind I'm thinking about rain. I'm thinking about what it's like to sleep outside, in the streets, on the cold concrete outside a First Unitarian church, or next to a fire hydrant. I've got this impression of cold, wet air and of being invisible. The picture that I'm thinking about, that she's projecting into me, is of a woman sitting by a concrete wall and holding a mirror between her legs. The woman's whole body is hidden behind that mirror, and she is looking down so that only the top of her head is visible.

"Ufology is dead," Harold says to her. "You landed and there is no need for it now."

"Take me home now," Virginia says. I'm not sure if she says it aloud or not.

Harold steps up to her, tries to make her look at him. He leans in closer and explains further, "I am not interested."

"This was a mistake," she says. And I'm still not certain if she's talking out loud or not even though, this time, I can see her lips move. "This isn't working out right," she says.

Harold steps aside as she heads for the aisle, as she heads for the exit, but he grabs my arm as I follow her.

"There was a gap," he says, "between when we saw her at Harold's art studio at the University and when we sat down with her for dinner. We went from A to C without stopping at B. There is a gap."

"She's clearly not feeling well," I say.

Harold has something else to tell me, he holds fast to my arm as the Pleidien saucers return and the holographic exhibit restarts. He seems to soften a bit, like he has some concern in there with his anger.

"When you get home, when you see Virginia again, call me," he says.

"What are you talking about?"

Harold lets go of my arm and nods. "Just call me when you get to your condo and we'll figure it out together."

The déjà vu makes me nod an okay to him and it continues on as I walk between the lights, as I enter the more well-lit front lobby of the saucer. And I'm okay with it when she takes my hand. I'm okay with her as we walk down the ramp into the parking lot, as we talk it over and decide to take a cab back to our condo.

"Are you cold?" I ask as she shivers next to the phone booth. And, on cue, I finally offer her my tweed jacket. I've been holding onto it, the leather patch wrinkled in my clenched fist, all along. She covers herself with it as I step into the booth to call a cab.

two wives

The difference between Harold Flint and the rest of the UFO community is the difference between connotation and denotation. Harold wanted to know what flying saucers meant and not what they were. A couple of chapters from now I'll try to explain his methods a bit more and tell you the story of a trip Harold and I will take to Coney Island. We'll be under the old parachute jump when Harold gives me instruction on how to understand the connotation of having two wives, but I'll get to that later. For now I just want to explain this other thing, this difference between denoting something and connoting something. For Flint this was this difference that mattered.

Let's take a pair of words as an example. Let's take the words "bare legs" and look at the difference between what the words denote and what they connote. If I were to report to you that I found myself staring at Virginia's bare legs as we were driven back to Brooklyn in a yellow cab or that she leaned against the backseat window and curled up, putting her bare legs on the back seat and letting her sweater dress ride up past her waist, you would be making a mistake if you understood me on the level of denotation alone. That is, the meaning of those words strung together in that sentence can't be fully grasped if we just read them as isolated units of meaning with straightforward positive significance. Instead, to get the full meaning of what I'd be reporting we'd have to understand the connotations, the implications, of words like "bare" and "legs" and even take a close look at words like "ride" and "curled."

"I found myself staring at Virginia's bare legs as we were driven back to Brooklyn in a yellow cab."

"The UFO skipped across the sky like a saucer across water."

Harold would think that the connotations in the second sentence above were as important to consider as the connotations in the first, and later on, when he'll tell me to write this book, when he'll set me the task of reporting our, his and my, abduction, he'll ask me to collect all the connotations. He'll want me to go beyond figuring out what actually happened or how things are, and to consider what they mean.

Really though, I don't need to be reminded to do this because this way of thinking is de rigueur in literature departments and at New York cocktail parties, and it's this approach to interpretation that was responsible for my marriage. Virginia deployed an analysis of connotations during the lit department social where we met back in 1987. It was how she seduced me.

"Why do they call it Secret?" she asked. She was talking about the deodorant Procter & Gamble developed in the 1950s. The deodorant called Secret is Procter & Gamble's only product designed exclusively for, and marketed directly to, women.

We were at a department social held at Japas on East 38th Street. We went there to eat sushi and sing karaoke on a Friday night before finals.

I'd never tried either before and was out of my element. I fumbled with the chopsticks, put a hand over one ear to block out the sound of Frankie Goes to Hollywood and the Village People sung off key by women, mostly women, drunk on Heineken or Corona, and all in all I was determined to have a bad time. That's what Virginia was up against when she started the conversation that would bring us together. She had to work to keep me talking.

"Why do they call it Secret?" she asked.

"Because it's a terrible secret that women sweat," I said.

In 1987 Virginia had permed and dyed blond hair and, for an adjunct, was intimidating. We both of us taught composition and the American short story, were both adjuncts, but while I was ruining my reputation with Flint, co-writing books sold from New Age shelves and at MUFON conventions, her story in *Granta* had been reprinted in *The Year's Best Short Fiction* of 1985. She was nice to me, always saying hello in the halls or in the University teachers' lounge, she'd even said that she thought it was unfair that everyone was judging me, the whole department was mocking me, for these books that nobody had even bothered to read, but that news wasn't exactly welcome and I hadn't wanted pity. She was nice to me, but it was only when she got up to sing "Too Drunk to Fuck" by the Dead Kennedys, only when she kept her eyes on mine from the stage, that I figured she wasn't only being nice.

"Let me show you," she said. She put her hand on mine to help with the chopsticks. She took over, showing me the proper grip and how to be more precise with my fingers.

Looking at Virginia now, as the light from street lamps and neon signs illuminate the back seat of the cab, watching as her face is lit green then red and then blue as the cab moves, looking at her bare legs change color too, I remember what her touch felt like, how surprising it was to have her hand on mine.

It turned out that she was interested in saucers. Before the saucers landed but after the sushi I often thought that she should be the one working with Harold, helping him with his research, because while I was enamored of Flint's work and especially the work he did back in 1962 with Ray Walker, Virginia was the one who really liked the stories of contact, outer space, and Kenneth Arnold. She was the one who subscribed to *Fate* magazine while I read the *Paris Review*. UFOs were her guilty pleasure before the landing, and I was lucky for that.

"You see?" Virginia asked me. "Hold your fingers like that."

I made my best effort but I used too much pressure and one of the chopsticks flew out my hand, over the counter, and out of view. I stood up from my stool and leaned across as far as I could without lying down on my plate of raw fish.

"I can't believe the whole season was just a dream," one of the other professors, I think her name was Wilkins or Watson, said. An overly tall woman with curly red hair and big glasses with brown speckled plastic frames was determined to talk to everyone. Making her way down the counter she ended my chopstick lesson so that she, a professor of Medieval poetry, could give her opinion about the television show *Dallas*.

While they talked I stared at the reproduction of a Patrick Nagel painting over the bar. It was a poster version of Nagel's cover art for the Duran Duran album *Rio*. Nagel had created a woman's face out of negative space and simple lines. Nagel's designer paintings borrowed just as much from Lautrec and the Parisian cafés of the nineteenth century as it did from *Battlestar Galactica*. Orange and green diagonal lines broke this particular Nagel beauty into four sections and placed her out of reach, behind color bars.

This ideal woman of the 1980s stared down on me. She was confident, beautiful, and remote. Looking at her I felt I was both entirely too fleshy, a schlub, and oddly superior. I might be eating sushi, but I didn't belong in the '80s. I was either ahead of my time or stuck in a nobler age. I leaned forward to look for my missing chopstick and, with my belly pressed against the counter, I confirmed that it was still nowhere. Sitting back down I sank back into my determination to have a wretched time.

In my defense, it had been a rough couple years. The Space Shuttle *Challenger* exploded, *Saucers and Reincarnation* sold abysmally, and I didn't get accepted for a tenure track position at the University. It was, all of it, getting me down, and when you add in the fact that people were laughing at my books, that I was a joke in the department, I think you can understand why I didn't respond much to Virginia. Not at first.

"We're all such cynics," she said. Wilkins had moved on down the counter. "That's why people in the department aren't reading your books. Flying saucers, space travel, the future, that stuff seems naive, right?" She picked up a bit of raw fish with her chopsticks, dipped it into her soy sauce, and then tipped her head back and dropped the fish into her open mouth. "Did you watch how I did that?" she asked. "Now you try."

I ended up spreading rice across the black marble countertop. "I think I'll use my fingers," I said.

"Good idea," she said.

Virginia was encouraging. This all happened before the landing but a long time after John Cage appeared on Ed Sullivan to make music with a bathtub and ten transistor radios, but Virginia went along with it when I brought Cage up. I described Cage's television appearance for her, told her how jealous Flint had been when his friend Cage got on national television, and she told me about Durango, Colorado, and escaping a religious family.

"Commercial artists like Patrick Nagel and the Memphis Milano group are the worst kind of nihilists," I told her. "It's a very cold work," I said and gestured at the Duran Duran cover.

She agreed with my non-sequitur judgment. "An ice queen," she said. "How is that sexy?"

Soon enough Wilkins was back with another interruption. "Are you going to sing, Brian?" she asked.

We had to pick a pop hit but the karaoke company's catalog was like a phone book. It was in an oversized three-ring binder and the pages were falling out. Both of us spent some time flipping through it and writing down serial numbers on cocktail napkins, only Virginia spent more time than I did. She kept crossing out her choices. She'd settle in on a choice, find a better, more ironic choice, and then she'd put her hand on the back of her neck and point to a title with her other one. I'd look, read the title, and pretend to know the song and why it was noteworthy.

"That's absurd," I said. "Why do they have that one?" I asked.

"Your turn," she said and slid the catalog over to me, pushing my plate out of the way.

I spent about three minutes on the list and then, after considering Elvis Presley's "Blue Suede Shoes" briefly, held up my hands in protest, my palms facing out.

"I'm not going to sing," I said.

"Everybody has to sing," Wilkins told me. She came from across the room, and left her plate of rice and raw fish behind, in order to confront me on this point.

"Not me."

"Everybody."

"But I can't pick a song," I said.

"If you don't pick I'll pick for you," she said. "You probably want to pick."

"Nope."

"You'll be sorry," Wilkins said.

And she was right. The terrible thing about the song they picked was that I knew the backstory. "Calling Occupants of Interplanetary Craft" was performed by the Carpenters in 1978, but it had originally been written by another band in an homage to World Contact Day. Charles Rain and a few other contactee gurus had organized World Contact Day back in 1953 and the song, originally performed and written by a band called Klaatu, was a tribute and send up of their effort at psychic communication between we Earthlings and our orbiting Space Brothers.

"It seems ridiculous now. But World Contact Day wasn't that different from Hands Across America," I said as the song started. I spoke into the karaoke microphone, explaining the context of the song, lecturing to my colleagues at the bar as if they were undergraduates. "Think of it this way, both Hands Across America and World Contact Day were pseudo events, yeah? They were both aimed at media and not people, both aimed to create a story but not a real tangible or material result. Did anyone actually believe that if enough people sent a mental message to the stars, to the Space Brothers, that they'd hear us and come to visit? Of course not, but did we really believe that if enough people held hands, if we could form a human chain across the country, we could end hunger and homelessness?"

The music continued and my audience grew restless, belligerent. Even Virginia was shouting at me. I wasn't supposed to talk or explain, I was supposed to sing. I was meant to sing and the song was based on the message Charles Rain had written for psychic transmission. Charles Rain's message back in 1953 was this:

"Calling occupants of interplanetary craft that have been observing our planet EARTH. We of IFSB wish to make contact with you. We are your friends, and would like you to make an appearance here on EARTH. Your presence before us will be welcomed with the utmost friendship. We will do all in our power to promote mutual understanding between your people and the people of EARTH. Please come in peace and help us in our EARTHLY problems. Give us some sign that you have received our message. Be responsible for creating a miracle here on our planet to wake up the ignorant ones to reality. Let us hear from you. We are your friends."

When I got to the end of the song, after doing my best Karen Carpenter impression, the department was experiencing real joy. Everything had gone so well, much better than planned. I was known as a serious type, sort of hated for my relationship with Flint even if it was predicated on this flying saucer ridiculousness, and watching me recite '70s cheese was, apparently, the best thing ever.

"It's not so ridiculous," I said. "No more ridiculous than Hands Across America," I repeated.

But they weren't having any of it.

"What do you think they'll look like, when they land?" Wilkins asked me.

"They might look like us, some of them look like us. Or they might look a bit reptilian."

"Like ET?" another professor, this one a balding New Englander with a grey beard and a pronounced effeminate slur, asked. I wanted to grab him by the collar of his plaid shirt and punch him right in his sardonic smile.

"Look, I didn't write that song and Flint had nothing to do with World Contact Day. I was barely born then."

"Sing it again! Sing it again!" they chanted at me. I tried to get another drink but the waitress refused my order. She told me that I could have another beer if I sang the whole thing over again, it would be on the house even, but I couldn't have a drink unless I sang it all the way through from the beginning.

And that's when Virginia saved me. She stepped up onto the stage and blew into the microphone.

"I think it's my turn," she said. "I've picked my own song."

Virginia smiled down at me from the stage and I tried again to order another beer. The waitress relented.

"When I was a little girl," Virginia sang.

I nibbled at raw octopus that tasted like rubber and thought about Virginia's *Year's Best Short Fiction* story. I hadn't read it but she'd told me it was written in the epistolary form, written as a series of letters between a father and son in nineteenth century Ireland apparently. I wondered how this evening, how the experience of watching her sing and sway through this fog of sake and beer, might be told as a series of letters.

"'Dear Virginia,'" I started. "'I hope you won't think me too forward but when you saved me from having to repeat the message to the Space Brothers I realized how beautiful your hair looks in the neon light, how beautiful your skin is even after several rounds of sake and beer.'"

"Is that all there is to a fire?" Virginia sang.

And her voice cut through the crowd and shifted the tone of the evening. Instead of laughing at me, people listened to her.

On stage and singing the words the karaoke machine was feeding her a bit off key, she made us listen. The lyrics flashed across the otherwise blank screen as the taped music, the piano and trumpet and harp, sounded, but she transformed karaoke into something else. She sang Peggy Lee's hit so that it was received by the literature department as a challenge.

"Is that all there is?" Virginia asked. "Is that all there is?"

Arriving at my brownstone Virginia is already here. That is, there are two Virginias on Fulton Street, two wives in my loft at the old Eagle warehouse. One of them, who I figure is probably the real one, is grading papers in our designer kitchen when we arrive. This one is sitting at the kitchen island, this too-narrow worktable with a rack for dishes on the bottom and a charcoal marble tabletop, and she has her papers spread out next to this potted lemon tree we purchased from the Indoor/Outdoor Gardner on 83rd maybe a year ago. The tree looks like it isn't growing at all I guess.

Anyhow, Virginia's still wearing the country tweed jacket with buttons on the right side that she almost always wears to the University, and doesn't look up at first but just keeps marking the page in front of her, and when she does glance up at us her first look is one of mild annoyance, I'm interrupting her train of thought, but on a second look this expression gives way to one of surprised recognition. And the other Virginia, the one next to me in a not quite long enough sweater dress, is also surprised. She apparently didn't know, didn't expect, this doubling.

We enter the kitchen and Virginia in the sweater dress walks over to her duplicate at the narrow table and puts her hands palms down on top of the papers.

"Virginia?" I ask the one in the sweater. "Virginia?" I ask the one in the jacket.

"Brian?" the one in tweed asks. "Who is…" But she stops herself. Virginia already knows who this woman in the sweater is, or who she is supposed to be.

The two of them don't really look alike. When the one in the tweed jacket stands up I see that she's maybe two or three inches shorter than the one in the sweater dress. And this taller wife has slightly lighter hair than the other one, and her hair is a bit longer, down past the ears. But, despite these differences, they are nonetheless the same.

"Brian?" the taller Virginia asks.

"I can't really help you here," I say.

The two women step back from each other, walk around the table, and then meet on the north side of the room by the kitchen counter. The shorter Virginia puts her hand down on top of our pine paper towel rack, then lets it fall from their to the textured plastic cutting board underneath, and then reaches up to stroke the taller Virginia's hair. She runs her fingers through the other one's bangs and this one, the one in the sweater dress, shivers. The Virginia in tweed strokes the other woman's left arm, pushing up the sleeves of her sweater.

"Brian," the shorter one asks. "Who is this? Who did you bring home?"

"I think she's you," I say. "That is, that's what I thought before. I wouldn't have brought her home otherwise." It dawns on me now what must have happened and who this second Virginia must actually be. "I think I know what's happening," I say. "Let me introduce you to Asket."

"Asket?"

"It's a Pleidien name. That's right, isn't it? You're a Pleidien?"

The woman in the sweater dress touches her face, perhaps checking to make sure all her features are still in place, and then slowly nods.

"Asket," she echoes. "That is my name, isn't it?"

I pull Virginia aside, pull her away from this woman who seems to be but isn't my wife. Out in the hall, I try to explain it all to her. I tell her about Asket visiting the University's art department, explain our tour of the flying saucer museum and reading room. I tell her that the plan was to convince Harold to start working on flying saucers again, to get him to help me write one now that the market for such a book is huge, and Virginia nods at this, but I can tell she's not listening.

"She's beautiful," Virginia says. "I'm beautiful?" she asks.

She is, but not like that. The real Virginia is shorter, like I said, and her hair is a darker blond. Virginia's nose has a different shape, it's a little larger.

My wife takes my hand and leads me back into the kitchen. "Your name is Asket?"

Asket shrinks back a bit. She looks cold in that short sweater. "What?" she asks.

"Your name," Virginia repeats, "it's Ask...It?" Virginia is smiling very brightly now, as if she's just received a present, something she always wanted. She's circling the alien, putting her hands on her occasionally, reaching out to touch Asket's hair, standing on tiptoes so that their eyes are even. "You're a Pleidien, but you look like me. Somehow it seems like you really are me. It's like you're who I'm really supposed to be."

"I am you," Asket says. "I'm Virginia."

"But your name is Asket?"

"I. . .I guess so."

Virginia makes coffee for everyone and then opens a package of Pepperidge Farm crescent shape cookies. I decide that she's handling this very well. She presents the cookies to Asket on one of our better china saucers, watches intently as her double bites down on one, watches as Asket uses her front teeth to scrape some jelly into her mouth. She seems fascinated when the alien takes a sip of herbal tea.

We all agree that what Asket is doing isn't just an impersonation. An impersonator gives you the surface of a personality.

"When Rich Little impersonates Johnny Carson or Jimmy Stewart he just mimics their mannerisms," Virginia says. "His impersonations diminish them. When Rich Little pretended to be Johnny Carson he made Carson seem smaller. He made Carson seem shallow, less genuine than he'd seemed before. But you, Asket, you aren't doing that at all. Seeing you makes me feel bigger than I am."

Asket is sitting very politely at our kitchen table, a guest in what must seem to her like her own home. At the moment not only isn't Asket imitating Virginia, they appear as opposites.

"I wonder if she's psychic," Virginia asks. "Pleidiens are supposed to be psychic, aren't you? You can read minds, see into souls? Is that how you do it? Are you reading me?"

Asket doesn't know how she's doing anything. She says she doesn't really know what is going on, and then she mumbles under her breath that maybe Virginia is the impersonator. "Maybe I'm Johnny Carson," she says.

But we've gotten past the moment for such debates and Virginia doesn't pay this comment any mind at all. She's confident that she's the original and instead of defending herself she leaves the room. She leaves us, Asket and me, to drink coffee, to pick at the remaining cookies, and to try to make conversation.

"Are you cold?" I ask.

"A little," she says. Asket pulls down on her sweater again, and I watch as she rises out of her chair a bit so that the fabric can slide down just a little more.

"I could get you a blanket," I say. "Or maybe some pajamas?"

Virginia is back with a package of index cards and a pair of scissors with orange handles. She cuts the cellophane, removes it, and then finds a Sharpie from one of the kitchen drawers. She's determined to test her double's psychic powers, and she is drawing on the index cards with this aim. She draws stars, wavy lines, squares, and circles, until she has twenty or so stacked up in front of her on the counter.

"I'm going to test you," she says to Asket. And Asket nods. She already understands what is expected of her.

Virginia moves her pile of index cards to a spot between them, to the center of the kitchen island, picks up the first card, and takes a clandestine look. She does an effective job hiding the design and then glances at Asket expectantly. "Which one is it?" she says.

The Zener card game has been around for a long time, of course, and the idea is that if Asket can correctly guess which card Virginia is looking at, if she can do that more often than would be statistically normal, then we can assume that some sort of psychic connection is at work.

"What I expect is that there will be one hundred percent accuracy," she says to Asket.

"I don't know," she says. "I wouldn't think so."

Virginia frowns, a bit surprised by this rebelliousness, surprised that there could be a difference of opinion between them.

"What do I see?" Virginia asks.

"Wavy lines."

"No." She turns the card around and shows us the circle. "What about now?"

"A plus sign?"

"No." Again the correct answer is circle. "What about now?"

"Wavy lines?" Asket asks.

This is wrong too. It's almost as if Asket is psychic but she's purposely giving the wrong answers. The final score is much worse than chance alone would predict, but Virginia doesn't appear to notice this backward confirmation.

"There must be some kind of connection," Virginia says. She's finally found herself and she isn't about to let herself pass unexploited or unexplained.

Asket actually is psychic. She demonstrated her telepathic ability on the flying saucer, but Virginia is not psychic. If Asket is some kind of spiritual copy of her would her psychic ability be suppressed?

"Are you holding out on me?" I ask Virginia. "Have you been developing strange powers all along and not telling me?"

Virginia pauses, not sure of the nature of my query. "What's that?"

"She's your double. You're not psychic so she's not psychic," I say.

I pick up the index cards and ask Virginia if the card depicts wavy lines or a star, giving her better odds, but she gets it wrong.

She frowns at me like this is my fault and then she sticks her tongue out as she's concentrating and wants me to try it again, to pick another card.

I'm not interested in this game anymore. Looking back and forth from Asket to Virginia and back again I realize that I too have an opportunity that I'm not willing to pass up. While my wife (I assume she's the one who is my wife, that I even have a wife) can't allow herself to miss an opportunity to know herself as another, I'm realizing what it is that I'm not willing to let pass. That is, if they're both in some way or another Virginia, what I'm planning shouldn't be that difficult to arrange.

"Maybe we should try something else?" I suggest.

"Like what exactly?" Virginia asks.

"What's your earliest memory?" Asket asks.

"My earliest memory?" Virginia echoes. "That's good. Only, I shouldn't be telling you. You should tell me. What's your earliest, or strongest, memory from childhood?"

What Asket remembers isn't a memory at all, or it isn't a memory of something that happened, but rather is a memory of what never happened because her parents forbid it. She'd grown up in Durango, Colorado, a small Southern town, not far from New Mexico and situated very near Mesa Verde National Park. Mesa Verde is where the cliff dwellings of the aboriginal Pueblo people are, and what Asket remembers, her strongest recollection, is that she's never visited Mesa Verde. Her parents, who were strict Baptists, believed that the dwellings were Satanic. The Indians who lived there worshipped many gods which made them satanists or, if not actual satanists then satanic. What Asket remembers is that Virginia's parents had forbid her from visiting the cliff dwellings.

"It wasn't a big problem for me. None of the locals were very interested in the cliff dwellings. That was for the tourists. Nobody questioned why I had never been. When I was a teenager I stopped thinking about it, but at ten I felt strange about it. It was strange to be afraid of a place, of a space. There were ghosts just out of town, demons about sixty miles west on US 160. I believed it too," Virginia says.

We're out of coffee now and I consider fetching some beer or wine from the refrigerator. I think there is a bottle of white wine in there, but I find myself unwilling to leave my place at our kitchen table made from unvarnished oak and I find myself looking up at the chandelier, frozen by contradictory impulses. The chandelier is really just a bare lightbulb but it's surrounded by a disjointed web of iron rods intersecting from every angle. It more of a modernist sculpture hanging over us than a proper chandelier, but it's what Virginia picked out. Who was I to disagree with her on such matters?

"On a different subject, do you remember when Erin White got a color television?" Virginia asks. She's talking to her double and not to me.

Asket does remember. None of the members of her church watched much television and children weren't allowed to watch at all, but Erin's family let her watch. They'd purchased two color Zeniths, one for the TV room and one for the kitchen, and Virginia made sure to drop in on the White family as often as she could.

"Come on and Zoom, Zooma, Zoom!" Virginia says. She's singing the introduction to a WGBH children's television program from the early '70s, a program that most 13-year-olds might've shunned but that to her untrained eyes was decadent.

"Forbidden music," Asket says. "Do you remember the very first sound before the theme song started? The sound for the WGBH logo?" she asks.

"Not really," Virginia says.

Asket swallows hard, preparing to make the noise, and then opens her mouth. A staccato series of electronic notes, a quick repetition of ascents and descents, flow from her only to be drowned out by a rising note that sounds more like a violin than a voice.

"You really are an alien," Virginia says. "Do it again."

Asket obliges her and sings it again. What we hear is so close a reproduction of the notes that accompanied the WGBH logo as it filled television screens back in 1972 that I almost believe she has a tape recorder in her throat. There must be some kind of machine in there.

But my wife presses on, quizzing Asket on the intricacies of nostalgic ephemera. She's supposedly testing Asket but she's not stopping to consider the answers.

"What was your favorite summer day ice cream?" she asks.

"You mean from an ice cream truck? That's easy, orange cream push-ups."

"I remember. They came in polka dotted cardboard tubes and I'd lick the plastic syringe inside, get every last drop of the artificial flavoring," Virginia says.

But these memories don't prove anything except for the breadth of Asket's knowledge on American life in the '60s, and when Virginia pauses to reconsider, Asket asks if she might be excused. It turns out that she'd like to change out of her sweater dress and into one of Virginia's robes or some pajamas after all. Virginia nods at this, as if Asket staying the night was never in question.

"Harold told me to call him when I figured out that she wasn't my wife," I tell Virginia when Asket is gone.

"He figured it out before you did?" she asks. She doesn't sound perturbed or surprised, but is just noting it as a fact.

"I think I'll wait to call him until tomorrow," I say. "What do you want to do until then? Should we send her back to her saucer?"

"The problem," Virginia says, "is that I'm having a hard time figuring out something that is unique to me. That bit about the strongest memory was good, that was a good question, but even that wasn't really unique to me. All of the people who grew up in our church would have had a similar memory. Every time I think of something to ask about it turns out that my head is filled with junk. All I can come up with are details that don't belong to me. A push-up ice cream treat, how is that personal to me, to us? It's junk."

"I think we should let her stay over," I say.

"Junk. 'Junk' by Paul McCartney. The album came out in 1970 but I started listening to it five years after its release during the car trip to New York. I would listen to Paul McCartney in a Studebaker, a car I'd inherited from my aunt, outside of Long Island. It was the first time I was so far from home."

Asket comes back and she's wearing one of Virginia's robes, a black silk kimono-style robe that is also a bit short on her, only this time Asket is wearing a pair of Virginia's jogging pants. She's wearing purple sweatpants.

I miss the sweater.

"Hope you don't mind," Asket says. She gestures to the sweatpants.

"Uh," I say.

"No problem," Virginia says.

"Do you remember the Old Fashioned Pizzeria at Four Corners?" Asket asks, turning the tables.

"No," Virginia says.

"Sure you do," Asket says. "It had a player piano on the main floor and you could put in a quarter and the keys would move on their own. It played 'Charleston' and 'Yes! We Have No Bananas.'"

Virginia is nodding now. "It was a restaurant for tourists and birthday parties but it scared me. Do you remember? Do you remember what was on the second floor?"

Asket joins us at the kitchen table. She leans across and takes Virginia's hand. "There were dummies dressed in period costume on the second floor. Boaters and cloche hats. Female mannequins in short dresses and male dummies in red and white striped vests," she says.

"They were frozen in place, stuck in conversation, stuck in history," Virginia says.

Watching them from my spot under the ugly chandelier, I sense that this is all going to work out in my favor in the end. They've pushed past the formalities, gotten past polite inquiry, and to something more substantial. There is an intimacy developing here.

"It was clear they were just dolls, but I thought..." Asket starts.

"You thought that they were corpses," Virginia says.

What my wives imagined was that that they, that all of the tourists were fake too. No matter how much pepperoni pizza they ate, how many Cokes they drank, they were maybe dead already. The present was already just a display, just an adequate enough reproduction put together for some future race that, while invisible, was already there.

"They were staring up at us," Virginia says. She's gazing into Asket's eyes. "The future already existed. There was already a place, maybe a place like the cliff dwellings, where the future already existed."

"That doesn't make any sense," I say. "The cliff dwellings were from the past."

"There really is a future like that. There is a future already. A place where people are already looking back on you and I belong to that. I already stand aside from this now. I'm already outside of it," Asket says.

That's how it happened. That's the explanation for her trick, her explanation for how she became Virginia's double, and it is also how the three of us end up in bed, or more accurately, it's how they ended up climbing onto our kitchen table.

The fantasy of a threesome has been in the back of my mind for a long while, it's something I picked up from *Playboy* and *Penthouse* magazines I guess, something I've seen in films of various kinds, but actually doing it in the cold kitchen light, watching as both wives crawl onto the tabletop, shoving aside placemats, watching them fumble and caress while I'm momentarily frozen in this designer chair, it isn't quite living up to expectations. Standing next to them I worry whether this table will support all of our weight. There isn't room for me anyhow. I finally decide to simply offer a hand or other appendage when the need arises.

All in all this feeling of separation, of not quite being where we appear to be, gets more pronounced as we go along. The sense of disconnection intensifies in stages, and at each step, but I'm determined to see this through, and I grab hold of one of them, not sure which one, and take her hips in my hands.

"Wait a minute," Virginia says. She's the one I'm holding. I'm holding onto her hips, she's got her hands on Asket's thighs. "Wait a minute. This doesn't feel right. This feels grubby. I feel grubby."

Asket takes her hands, to reassure her I think, but I let go and step back. I'm confused as to what's going on. I don't quite know who is rejecting whom or what's gone wrong.

"I'm sorry, but this is beneath you, isn't it?" Virginia says.

Asket doesn't say anything but just leans forward. It's impossible to say whose mouth finds whose first, but it's clearly Virginia who breaks it off.

"I'm sorry," Virginia says. "You don't have to," she says. And she backs away, somehow avoiding me as she goes, and leaves the room. I'm left there with my pants around my ankles, there is nothing but empty air where a moment ago there had been a destination, and when I look to Asket she's pulling her kimono back into place.

"You should go after her," she tells me.

I'm sitting across from where Virginia's lying, corpse-like on top of the sheets, and examining the pattern on the coverlet, a black and white pattern that, as I stare, becomes more and more Escher-like, trying to work out how to begin. I've got the leather chair shoved up next to, but not against, the radiator and I glance out the window at the flying saucer hovering nearby.

"Are you okay?" I ask without looking in her direction.

Virginia tells the ceiling that the problem was that she suddenly realized what she really looked like, what she must seem like, from Asket's point of view. Meeting this alien was wonderful at first, it seemed to confirm something that Virginia had always hoped for but had also known was impossible, but then it had turned around on her and she'd felt sick.

"Not really sick, but sickening. I realized that I was sickening, this sort of disgusting bit of nothing. Not all together there really, but there just enough to be unpleasant."

The problem was ultimately the same one that Harold had had after the saucers landed. Now that Virginia has met her fantasy self there is nothing left to support her, nothing left for Virginia to want to be. What Virginia wants to be is waiting patiently at the kitchen table. Virginia put her tongue inside the mouth of what she wanted to be and while it had been good, it had tasted just right, felt right, it had made her realize that she herself was all wrong.

The problem was that Virginia was a nobody. She was past thirty and had no children. She was a professor, but hadn't had a significant impact on her field, on criticism. She was married but not to anyone important, not to anyone who wasn't just as small and insignificant as she was. Asket, on the other hand, was from another dimension. Asket was her, was Virginia, as she wanted to be, as she imagined herself being when she was drifting off to sleep. This was how Virginia would be if she hadn't had to settle into being anybody, hadn't had to settle.

"She's so beautiful. It's like she's living in this liminal space, with perfect light, and I'm this obscure and obscurantist tenured tacky nobody with expensive furniture and an overweight husband who wants to be Samuel Beckett," she said.

"Sorry to be so mediocre," I said. But she wasn't bothering me really. In fact, I only wished that I had a pen and paper so I could take notes. This reversal, this turn around from seeing Asket as the fulfillment of a fantasy to seeing herself as a disappointment for Asket, it probably meant something. It was the kind of thing Harold would be interested in.

"It's not you. It's not you," she said. And I expected her to sit up on the bed, maybe to offer me some sort of assurance. Instead she just repeated herself. "It's not you," she said again. "Not you. Not you."

To be honest it wasn't clear if she was talking to me at all. Wasn't clear whether she was responding to my complaint or just continuing on with her own.

"Virginia, I'm sorry. All this is beyond the usual level of weirdness, I know. And probably what we started in there, trying to sleep with her, that was. . ." I pause. Trying to sleep with her was definitely a mistake. It could compromise the book, for one thing. It's exactly the kind of thing Harold might do, of course, but that kind of thing is to be avoided. This book isn't going to play at the fringes, that's not the aim. The idea is to get real exposure, maybe go on Carson. No, not Carson, it's Leno now. "Well, as I said before I'm hoping to convince Harold to write about her, to write about them. And if that happens maybe it'll change things."

"How will it change things?" she asks. And while she's still gazing straight up at the ceiling at least I can be sure she's talking to me.

"This one will sell. I'm sure of it. People will take it seriously now. People have to take us seriously now."

"Brian?"

"Yes?"

"What people?" she asked. She finally turns over. She flips over onto her stomach, stretches across the black and white comforter, and finally looks at me. "The only people who really matter now are them."

"You don't mean that," I say. And she doesn't. If she really meant it she wouldn't be worried about what this one Pleidien, the one that happens to look like her, thinks. She'd have surrendered already. She'd have converted to the New Religion and be up there on a saucer ready to lead a reading group or a tour, ready to help get new recruits. She has to believe that the saucers represent an opportunity for us beyond this opportunity to join this junk food religion they're advertising on the evening news and through flashing light shows over the highways, suburbs and malls.

"This is an opportunity," I say. "Not for some cosmic consciousness, not for enlightenment, but for me. For both of us."

Virginia sits up straight on the side of the bed. She glances out at the light show on our front yard, watches the saucer go by, and then smacks and leans in close.

"Okay, Brian," she says. "You're right. You're right."

I nod, but I'm not convinced.

"Just don't tell her what I told you," she says. "Don't tell her why I. . .Tell her that it's not her fault. Please. Convince her."

"Convince her of what?"

"Convince her to stay."

the gap

Back in my '83 Volvo station wagon with Asket I find she's smiling at me.

Virginia didn't say goodbye this morning. She hasn't faced Asket since last night, but we all agreed, if separately, that she should continue staying with us for at least a little while longer and this trip into Manhattan is part of that plan. Taking her to the Gap so she can pick out her own wardrobe seemed like a sensible move last night, but now that we're alone together in the car I'm thinking it's not the best idea I've ever had, although it's still a better option than the two of them sharing. Dressing Asket up in the same silk blouses and navy skirts that are the mainstay of Virginia's wardrobe would likely just make Virginia even less confident, and even if it didn't, living with a slightly off-kilter set of wives would confuse me. She should get her own clothes, her own human identity if she's going to stay. And we both want her to stay. At the moment Asket is back in her wool sweater only now she's wearing purple tights as well, and she's holding her left hand up to her smile and staring at me.

"Why don't you run away with me?" she asks. "We could go somewhere where there aren't any."

"Aren't any what?"

"Saucers."

I turn on the radio, twist the dial to the oldies station, listen to Elvis Presley sing about the summer sun, and watch a saucer glide over the East River instead of responding, but when we turn onto Adams Street and Sam Cooke comes on I give in and state the obvious.

"There is nowhere to go and I won't leave Virginia."

"But I am Virginia," Asket says.

This time I don't stay anything but just let Sam Cooke sing on.

"Sorry," she says. "I'm sorry."

"Where would we go?" I ask. "Where were you thinking we could go to get away from all this?"

We're on the Brooklyn Bridge and I gesture at the windshield indicating the silver disc that's rotating and blinking on the other side. Traffic is slow as some of the cars are pulling off and parking on FDR, their drivers apparently tempted by the promise of redemption.

"We'd have to go somewhere that isn't on the map," Asket says. She isn't smiling now, but just staring out the passenger side window. Glancing over at her as she sulks and then past her at the water, at a light blue motorboat that is pushing a barge filled with aluminum and wires, I'm reminded of Harold's anecdote. I think of Jesus and a Pepsi bottle, or a Pepsi machine. This is all too mundane. There is nothing otherworldly about her at all.

"What did you do before you came to Earth?" I ask.

She doesn't answer but just keeps staring out her window.

"If we wanted to get away from the saucers we'd have to go off the map? Is that something like, what's it called, that Third Space? Isn't Ralph always talking about a Third Space? Is that what you mean?"

We're across the river now, and while I cross FDR Drive the DJ on WCBS says the Dixie Cups are coming next but when the sound of drumsticks keeping a beat starts I turn off the radio and try again.

"Where would we go?" I ask.

"I don't know," Asket says. "I don't remember. I don't remember if I've ever been to the Pleides, or what I did before I came to Earth, or anything like that. What I remember is Durango. I remember that my Tuesday class didn't do the reading last week and I had to keep talking into their dumb silence for two hours."

What I remember is that she was going to help me convince Harold, that she would help me get some saucer money. That's why I brought her to Harold to begin with.

"What about that, do you remember that?"

"Why?" she asks. "Why do you want that? What is it about you that's different from Harold? Why aren't you disappointed?"

"Harold and I are different. We've always been different. He started his career by rebelling against it, trying to destroy it even, while all I've ever wanted was in. It's not that I'm a total careerist though. I have my own small ambitions artistically. I understand the necessity to do things differently, to go beyond what's already been done, to develop a vision.

"Actually that's it. That's the difference. Harold is always trying to break the frame, to shatter preconceptions, but I'm still interested in seeing, in understanding. He wants to break every perspective and assumption, while I'm just trying to find the right ones."

Asket looks my way again. She shifts in her seat, looks at me, monitoring my expression maybe. Then she looks forward, watches where we're going for a minute.

"That doesn't sound that different to me," she says.

"What doesn't?"

"Breaking old assumptions and finding new ones. Seems to me that those two activities go together."

"They're different," I say.

"I don't think they are."

Asket is smiling again. She asks me to tell her about him, about Harold. She wants me to explain him to her.

"I've always thought of Fluxus as basically a precursor of post-structuralism," she says.

"You've thought no such thing."

"Well, anyhow, listening to you talk now I think I was wrong about that. Because, if you're going to break with a structure, an assumption, or an idea, you can't be a post-structuralist. You have to believe that there is a structure if you're going to break with it."

I shrug.

"Is this where your wife shops?" she asks.

Asket seems genuinely frightened by the choices on offer. She walks down the aisle, between the racks of khaki trousers, and skeptically examines the cotton blends in all their different varieties of beige.

"Is this where your wife shops?" She might be stuck.

I don't really know where Virginia gets her clothes. The idea behind taking Asket here, to the Manhattan Mall, was to find something innocuous. I thought that if I could buy her some comfortable and attractive clothes, clothes that were just normal and didn't require any thought, it would mean that I'd bottomed out the strangeness, but this attempt to choose without choosing is maybe pushing Asket into an identity crisis.

She settles on a pair of Levis, a red and black plaid button-up shirt, a pair of penny loafers, black socks, and a black leather belt. She takes the clothes in her arms and heads toward the back of the store and around the corner to the dressing rooms and I linger at the front counter and consider the copy on a promotional poster by the suit jackets.

"We do more than sell clothes, we sell lifestyles." Above the slogan there is a photograph of a pretty young woman wearing khaki pants and a white button-up shirt that is all the way unbuttoned. The background of the picture is completely blank. This woman's lifestyle involves spending a lot of time in very clean, well-lit rooms with white walls.

I think of making some wry comment, turn to the salesgirl to give it a try, but she's too busy putting things in drawers and stacking receipts to notice me.

"Do you think that's true?" I ask anyways. I point to the poster behind her. "Lifestyles not clothes?"

She stops hurrying around and gives me a quick glance, but then she looks at her watch and at the clock on the wall, the one next to the poster of the half-naked lifestyle.

"My shift is over," she tells me. "I'm just waiting for my replacement. Sally will help you," she says.

At that moment Sally, her colleague, turns the corner in the back of the store, around the same corner Asket had disappeared around on her way to the dressing rooms. Sally is hustling. She's clearly late. She's a pretty girl, maybe twenty-four years old, looks something like the model in the poster, only with darker hair and her shirt is buttoned. But she's in uniform. She's wearing Gap jeans, a plaid cotton shirt, and a lanyard with company nametag dangling down. Sally's sandy blond hair is pulled up into a half bun and she is apologizing even before she reaches us at the counter.

The two salesgirls exchange a few words, something about when Brad will be in, and how much cash is in the drawer, and then the first of the Gap girls is gone and it's just me and Sally at the front counter. She leans across it, puts her chin on her hand, and I feel a little awkward. I'm standing there with nothing to buy.

"Can I help you?" Sally asks me as she notices my uneasiness.

"I'm just waiting," I say.

"Oh," she says.

I shift my attention to the perfume bottles on the front counter, clink them around a bit, accidentally spray a little rose smelling liquid onto the counter, and then try to wipe it up with my sleeve.

"Are you interested in perfume?" Sally asks me.

"Ah, no. I'm just waiting," I say again. And then I realize I might need to explain further. "My wife...actually, she's not my wife really, but..."

"You're shopping for your girlfriend?" Sally asks, really jumping to conclusions I think.

"No, no. She's here, shopping for herself. Only she's not my girlfriend either. She's closer to my wife than my girlfriend. She's neither of those," I say. "I'll go check on her actually. She's in the back in one of the dressing rooms," I explain.

"I don't think anybody is back there," she says. Sally is a pretty girl, looks good in cotton, but she's a bit caustic I think.

"Be serious," I say. "I really do have a girlfriend. Or a wife," I say. "I mean, I'm here with this woman and she's back there trying on clothes."

"I didn't see anyone back there," Sally says. "The dressing rooms were all empty."

I head to the back of the store, past the poster of the nearly topless model in khakis, past some soft olive green sweaters, past the headless mannequin in a dark yellow turtleneck, and around the corner to the dressing rooms. The cubicles in this row are all open, the orange curtains pushed to the left side. I shout out to Asket.

"Virginia?" I ask the air. "I mean, Asket! Is everything okay?"

I walk slowly past the dressing rooms, glancing in each one as I go by and find they're all empty, all of them except for the last one. In the last dressing room I find a pair of purple tights and a beige wool sweater.

Back at the front of the store, by the cash register, I take a good long look at Sally. She's taking an inventory, making check marks on a clipboard, but I try to ignore this, to look past the red lanyard she's got around her neck, to forget her nametag. I want to get a good look at her eyes. I get closer to her so that I'm standing directly in front of her, just across from her at the counter, and it dawns on me that she is wearing the clothes Asket took to the dressing room. I lean in closer, try to look at the back of her neck, and I'm confirmed. I can see the price tag sticking out over her collar.

"Excuse me?" She moves back and I see that there is an anti-shoplifting RFID tag clipped to her left sleeve, but when I point this out to her she merely taps it against the magnetic detacher and tosses the tag into the waste basket behind her.

"Asket?" I ask.

She doesn't answer me but puts the clipboard down and then turns to the register and opens the drawer as if to make change.

"What are you doing?" I ask.

Asket looks a decade younger than she'd looked when we walked into the store, she's twenty-two or twenty-three at the moment. She's got her hair up in a bun and her eyes look different somehow. She seems to be looking past everything. Nothing is sinking in for her and she answers my question noncommittally. She is opening and closing drawers behind the counter, shifting about uncomfortably.

"I don't think we know each other," she says. She looks around the store now, hoping to find some excuse, some other customer that needs assistance, but there is nobody else around.

I try a different tact.

"Virginia," I say.

"Sally," she says back.

"Virginia, we came here together, remember? I was going to buy you some new clothes, some clothes that were different from my wife's clothes?"

"From your wife's clothes?" she asks.

"That's right," I say.

"And who is your wife?"

"Her name is Virginia," I say. "You've met her."

"Virginia. That's the name you just called me. You think I have the same name as your wife?"

I tell her that she doesn't really have the same name as my wife, but that she used to think that she had the same name.

"Naming things, naming people, is a tricky business," I say. "The name and the person never have anything in common."

"My name is Sally," she says.

"Sally what?" I ask.

"Sally Barth," she says without looking down at her tag, and she starts to turn away from me, pretending to have some business at the cash register, but I reach out to stop her. I knock the display of Swatch wristwatches over, they're red and yellow and green.

I reach out, grab her by her right wrist and spin her back toward me.

"Let go of me," she says.

"I'll let go of you, but listen to me. We have to work this out," I say.

"Let go of me," she says. And I pause, looking her in the face, trying to gauge what's there, to figure out what she's thinking and what she'll do if I let go. Finally I relax, let go of her, and take one half step back from the register. "Let's talk this out," I tell her.

But Sally picks up the phone and presses the button for the operator. "Just a moment," she says. "Hello, operator? Could you connect me to security? Yes, that's right. I've forgotten the extension." She puts her left palm over the mouthpiece and whispers to me that I might want to leave now. "Security? Yes, I have a man here who is harassing me. Could you please escort him out of the store?"

I consider just leaving her there, behind the counter. If she thinks she's somebody else now, if she's mimicking somebody else, then she's out of my hair, out of my wife's hair, but then I think back to the fun we'd had on the kitchen table. Besides, Virginia isn't finished with her yet, although if Asket has switched over to this new persona for good then Virginia will surely lose interest. Still, if I do leave her then I'll never figure out just what is happening.

"Excuse me," a voice behind me asks, a girl's voice. "What is this? What is going on here?" Sally asks.

The two young women look at each other from across the counter and then Sally lifts the gate and steps into the workspace, stands next to Asket. This Sally who is just arriving reaches out and takes the lanyard from around Asket's neck, puts it around her own, and then reaches out and touches Asket's hair.

"You're nothing like me really, are you?" she asks. "How is it that you're doing that?" she asks.

"Doing what?" Asket is perturbed. She hangs up the phone and stares at her new twin, maybe considering what the implications are, maybe thinking up excuses, but this young woman doesn't appear to be wanting any answers.

"Please leave," Sally says. "I'd like you to leave," she says. "You don't belong here. Whoever you are, you don't belong... here."

And that's when the security guard arrives. He's a portly man in a black security uniform, wearing a baseball cap with the word "security" written in white letters across the front, and I wait for him to look the situation over, wait for the confusion to mount, but instead he simply grabs me by my wrist, twists my arm around my back, and marches me toward the exit.

"I've got him," he says to the two Sallys, and then marches me out into the hall, down the stairs, and around the corner. He's a big guy, like I said, with red hair that's turning a bit grey, a silly mustache, and a strong grip.

"Okay, okay," I say. "Shit, I get it. I'll leave her alone. You don't have to manhandle me."

Asket follows us into the corridor and then follows us as he drags me past the coin-operated rocking horse in front of the Toys"R"Us, past the cart of celebrity memoirs with yellow and red book jackets outside of Barnes and Noble, past Sears. She follows us, keeping a fast clip, until all three of us are at and then through the sliding glass doors of the exit.

"Do not," the guard says. Then he says it again. "Do not," he says, "come back inside. If you come back inside I will call the police."

On the sidewalk outside the Manhattan Mall, sitting on the fire hydrant next to the 34th Street subway entrance, I look up at the balloon-shaped flying saucer hovering between the skyscrapers, and consider Asket's unconscious. Does she actually have one or is everything about her to be found on the surface? It's a puzzle because, while her physical appearance doesn't seem to change much when she switches personalities, she's utterly convincing as somebody new. Asket is maybe some kind of identity-less creature, possibly human but possibly not, who can capture the mannerisms of a person and replicate them, even before or without meeting the person. Otherwise how is it that Sally recognized herself in Asket? Otherwise how was it that I didn't recognize Asket as Asket when she turned that corner in the Gap?

The Pleidien saucer isn't a saucer but a bulb, it's circular on top and narrowed toward the bottom, and striped red white and blue underneath. It is designed to look like a balloon, but as close as it is I can tell that it's made out of unyielding metal, and that it's resonating with some sort of energy. I know that if I wave at it or in any other way indicate interest, I'll be taken up inside and given another lesson in ecology and spirituality. I know that I can take the tour again if I want. The aliens are watching.

But before I make any sign Asket interrupts.

"We should talk," she says. "I think I need to talk to you."

Asket is loitering by the entrance to the mall, she won't come out onto the street, she refuses to step onto the sidewalk because she's afraid of being seen by, of being exposed to, the

Pleidiens. She doesn't know what's happening exactly but she knows that the aliens are a threat, that they're to be avoided. She whispers at me, stage whispers. She asks me to meet her downstairs in the underground parking lot. I look up at the saucer, still considering another tour.

I imagine that it's difficult to be so uncertain of yourself, to be confronted by another version of yourself and robbed of your individuality and originality over and over again. To truly not know who you are, that's gotta be rough. Besides, I'm curious to see if I'd get an apology, or to know if she might think of herself as Asket again. For the moment my connection to this blank person, this mirror girl, is continuing.

We meet on the third floor down, just as she instructed. The Manhattan Mall parking lot has been renovated with text. Barbara Kruger, or somebody a lot like her, has stenciled the walls of the parking lot to make the space both more enigmatic and interesting and more navigable. The idea here is that it'll be easier to find your way back to your parked Subaru if you're parked under the words "You are a special person" or "It's all about me. No You. No Me" than it would be to just write down the number of your space and try to remember the floor.

"'You destroy what you think is difference,'" Asket reads the wall aloud when I approach her at the Mercedes-Benz.

"Are we on day two together or day three?" I ask. It's just occurred to me that we must have reached day two of our adventure together, but I suspected another gap in there between the kitchen table and the mall. "Anyhow, you lost it in there. You were somebody new," I say.

Asket, and I think she is Asket now, again, starts to cry. And it isn't the kind of manipulative crying that Virginia sometimes tries when she wants something from me, it isn't a tactic aimed at distracting me, but rather it's the kind of crying that takes a person over. It's caught her unaware and come on like a coughing fit or nausea. This is crying that she clearly doesn't want and can't control.

"What I want you to believe," Asket tells me, "is that I'm a human being. I don't know who I am, don't know what is going on, but I'd like you to believe that much. I want you to believe it because I believe it." Her voice is cracking, and there are tears she has to attend to, there are sounds that she's making that she has to subdue somehow before she can go on. She sounds like she's at the doctor's office, she's saying "ah" only she's saying it over and over again. Maybe she thinks that if she says "ah" enough times she'll be able to stop saying it. "Christ!" she exclaims.

I go to her, stand close to her under the word "difference" and put my arms around her waist. I let her dry her face on my fleece jacket.

"Ah. Ah. Ah. Ah," she says. She is still crying I think, but she may be repeating a mantra. Listening to her work it out, I realize that an action that is involuntary can still be inauthentic. Listening to her uncontrolled reaction the meaning of tears fades away. This sounds as if she's groping toward the idea of crying, groping after an emotion that is, in reality, quite far away. These aren't tears but something else. What I'm witnessing is her involuntary effort to find a feeling. She's trying to figure out what an emotion is while it's happening.

"Brian?" she asks. "I want you to forgive me," she says.

"Forgive you. What for?"

She says she wants me to forgive her for the gap.

coney island

Deno's Wonder Wheel is a nightmare of spokes and springs. A roller coaster/Ferris wheel hybrid, the green latticework and rails creak as the wheel turns. It's hard to hear over the sound of it. The Wonder Wheel sounds like it's rusted, like it needs to be greased.

"The women are on the ride?" Harold asks.

"That's right," I say. "They just got on."

"That's what you remember?" Harold asks. "That's the last thing that happened?" He's eating a Coney Island hot dog complete with beanless chili, white onions, and yellow mustard and watching the Ferris wheel cars unlatch from their position along the rim and slide inward, up and down along a snake-shaped rail. He takes a bite of his hot dog, squints at me and then raises his left hand to provide some shade for his eyes. Around us there are families on holiday, some of them wearing brightly colored clothes and smiling in preppy joy as they walk the boardwalk, the blue water reflecting their own goodness back at them, while others shift along in faded fabrics looking for shade. These are locals wearing mostly black and brown.

Harold and I belong to neither group. We're sweating slightly as we are both overdressed in our tweed jackets, but we're not looking for shade. "How do you know when it is?" Harold asks.

"There are cues, usually," I say. "What you do is…"

But I find I don't really want to complete that thought; what I want to say is that one can pick up on cues and clues. Instead I look up at the Wonder Wheel. It was built in 1920, which means that those Ferris wheel cars have been sliding back and forth along the Wonder Wheel's spokes for over seventy years now, and as Harold and I both look up to where Asket and Virginia are, to where they're turning, falling, and looping back, the history of this machine and the fact that it is still here makes me feel better.

"How do you know when we are exactly?" Harold asks again. Harold finishes his hot dog, wipes at his shirt, and now the mustard stain is gone from his jacket, or almost gone. You have to really look in order to notice it. The giant Ferris wheel is creaking ominously as it turns. Standing underneath like this, so close, feels a bit reckless.

"Did we come by car or the subway?" Harold asks.

I don't know for sure. I don't recall the subway, can't remember it, and I'm sure I would remember if that's how we arrived. The subway is as much of a ride as the Wonder Wheel. Certainly just as amusing and dangerous. The only difference is that the New York subway system is dirtier than this Ferris wheel. The difference between Coney Island and the subway is the graffiti and the muggings.

People on the Thunderbolt roller coaster, the ride next to the Wonder Wheel, are screaming for their life. Looking to my right I can't tell which faction, the joyful and clean group or the New York heavies, are the ones screaming because they're all of them speeding along the track and twisting upside down, but I assume they're the beautiful ones. I assume they're the tourists.

"The way the present moment gives you cues, tells you what you remember and who you are, is always the same. You wake up, check your watch, try to remember what you did the day before, and piece together whether you're supposed to be thirty-two or fifty-five based on what you find in the mirror, what your room looks like, and so on. . ." This is Harold's spiel. I've heard it again and again, in various guises, since our first days working with abductees. The UFO isn't in the past, it's in the present. We're not in the present, we're in the past. The present and the past are both times that we're piecing together, figuring out.

"Look," Harold says. "Here come your wives."

Virginia and Asket are a bit unstable on their feet. They're approaching from the other side of the Wonder Wheel, and as they approach the ride starts up again so that it's hard to speak over the din of its turning, of its Wonder. Virginia is shouting at me but I can't make out a single word.

"Which one is which?" Harold asks. "Guess it doesn't matter as long as you're having fun."

When Virginia and Asket reach us there is a pause. Whatever was worth shouting to me when I was out of audible range is too sensitive to just come right out with now. "She wants to find herself," she says.

"What?" "She wants to stop being me, to stop being other people, and find herself."

"Is that right?" I ask her.

"Yes," Asket says.

They are dressed alike. Virginia and Asket are both in plaid, both in tight jeans. Asket's hair looks darker now too, and she's hunching her back so as to appear shorter.

Looking out over the rail I see the beach is littered with grubby New Yorkers, some of them in bathing suits and headed for the cold and polluted channel, but most huddled in groups of three or five, here and there on the grey sand. They look cold and lost.

"And she wants to stay," Virginia says. "She wants to stay for awhile. To live with us."

Virginia uses the tinfoil her Coneydog came in to catch the bits of onion and beef that fall out of the bun with every bite. She has her orange and brown sundress tucked under her legs as she kneels there on the beach and looks out into the bay. She insists that it's okay if Asket stay with us a little longer. Asket has admitted to being a duplicate, to not being the real Virginia, and she promises she'll eventually turn the identity over to Virginia all together.

"She just needs time," Virginia says. "Something has happened. She's waiting for something to happen."

"What did you talk about when you were up there?" I ask. I'm cross-legged across from her, with my back to the ocean, and there is sand in my loafers.

Virginia doesn't answer me but finishes the dog and scrunches up the tinfoil into a ball. She's a bit cross I think. Her hair is blowing in the breeze, blowing across her face and into her eyes.

"What did we talk about?" she asked me hollowly, just echoing. "You think I convinced her? You think I want her to stay?"

"Don't you?"

"Yes," Virginia says. "I want her to stay, but I don't think she should. I think this is crazy. It's making me crazy having her around."

"What did she tell you?"

Virginia gets up, wipes the sand off her sundress, and then waits for me to stand up too. We start off across the beach, back toward the Wonder Wheel.

"We talked about UFOs," she says. "We talked about UFO photos."

Before the landing the evidence for UFOs almost always ended up being put down to being a byproduct of the mechanism that did the reporting. That is, if you had a photograph of a disc-shaped saucer floating next to a tree then the miracle was quickly seen to be a bit of trick photography. It would turn out that the disc was closer to the camera than the tree was, for instance. Or if you had witnesses who'd seen a disc shoot directly up into the sky in an instant it would turn out that what they'd really seen was an airplane or a helicopter that wasn't flying straight up, but was flying toward them at angle so that it appeared that the craft was shooting straight up.

UFOs were always an illusion created by an error in the observer.

"She thinks the Pleidiens aren't any different," Virginia says. "She thinks that we humans, and she insists that she's human too, that we've misunderstood what these new saucers are in themselves. That we haven't really seen them yet. It's all a trick of perception."

I nod along, thinking how glad Harold would be if this were true.

We're to meet up with Asket and Harold by the parachute jump at two p.m. and checking my watch I see that we've almost reached the hour, but as we near the boardwalk I stop Virginia and look out at the ocean again. Something is still bothering me, something hasn't been settled yet, or maybe it's that everything is being settled too easily.

"Harold agrees?" I ask.

"What do you mean?" Virginia asks back.

"I mean, what you're saying is that the flying saucer phenomena, the abductions, sightings, radiation, cattle mutilation, and Missing Time…" I pause again, looking out at the waves. There are people between me and the water, men and women in bathing suits and swimming caps. The beach seems crowded now, there are pretty people mingling at the water's edge and dozens more splashing about in the waves, but before, when we'd been walking, the beach had seemed mostly empty. Or was it just that I'd been keeping my head down, watching my step, and hadn't noticed before?

What I want to know is if Harold has agreed to start working on UFOs again, to investigate the Pleidien contact, to go back to cataloging the anomalies? And if he has, when did this happen? What was said to bring him around and when was it said?

"Virginia," I start. "Why did we come out here today?"

"What do you mean?"

"Why Coney Island? Why the beach and the boardwalk, what made us decide to come here? Whose idea was it?" I ask.

"Whose idea was it?" she asks back.

"Did we talk to Harold on the phone and did he suggest it? Did we just drive out here on a whim and run into him? When did we decide to make the trip, last night when I'd first brought Asket home or this morning? How long has she been living with us already?" I ask.

Virginia doesn't answer but takes a bottle of sunscreen out of her purse, opens it, and rubs some on the back of her neck. "Stop looking for easy answers," she says. "Come on, let's go."

Flint and Asket are drinking coffee under the parachute jump, sitting safely on a bench near the base of the structure without bothering to look up. She seems preternaturally pleased in the moment and she's sitting close to him, laughing at his jokes, whatever they happened to be. When Virginia and I get closer I find out that they're discussing the '60s, talking about what the art world had been like back then.

"And somebody bought it?" Asket asked.

"He produced ninety tins of his own feces, or he said it was his feces," Harold said. "He was charging thirty-seven dollars a can and said the price was set based on the price of gold. I don't know how many he actually sold."

I gesture to Harold, indicating that I want to talk to him in private, and he stands up from the bench and announces that he has to get back to the University. He has more shit to package, he says.

He takes his glasses off, turns in the direction of the subway station, and the two of us start off down the boardwalk.

"Are you going to start working on UFOs again?" I ask him.

"It's always the same with you. No matter what's happening, whether you have two wives or just one, whether there are flying saucers in the skies of Earth or not, it's always about the writing," he says. "Always about your little career."

"That's not fair," I say. And it wasn't.

After all, from the beginning it was always about the writing. That's why he'd sought me out to begin with, and that's why we'd remained something like friends. It was about the work, about the writing, from the start.

When I started with Flint back in 1984 I was a typical young literature professor, a product of American letters in the late '70s. While I'd come out of Iowa, the top and most conservative MFA program in the country, I'd broken with Iowa-style realism. My nonacademic writing, what little there was of it, was purposely unreal, self-referential, and littered with the kind of political observations you'd expect from someone who vaguely remembered opposing Vietnam and who was working on opposing consumerism, corporations, unions, activism and its banalities, the university system, traditional gender roles, monogamy, the State, and, in the end, even literature itself.

All I knew for certain was that "the center didn't hold." "Western Culture," whatever it was, "had arrived at an impasse" and it was my job to describe the moment and to let people know that something was crazy in America. What Flint liked, the reason he'd approached me, was a short story I'd written for the *Evergreen Review* entitled "Red Rubber Ball." It told the story of a man who was preparing to be the best man at his schizophrenic brother's wedding, and who was trying to convince his brother not to have the song "Red Rubber Ball" performed during the ceremony. The schizo brother insisted that the song should be performed because it was, despite being bubblegum pop, a holy song. He was convinced that the smell of summer, of a rubber ball and asphalt, always accompanied the music. The schizophrenic felt sure that the one-hit wonder band Cyrkle had purposefully created an incantation of youth and, beyond that, of eternal play, he thought the message of the song was the same as Jesus's message: "Truly I tell you, unless you change and become like little children, you will never enter the kingdom of heaven."

Of course, the wedding was a disaster. It turned out that the woman the brother was marrying had epilepsy and that the song inspired her to seizure and rage, but being right provided the narrator very little joy. What Flint had liked about it, why it convinced him that I would be a good match for him and would understand his UFO research, wasn't entirely clear at the time, but somehow the story had reminded Flint of what it felt like to connect. The idea that a silly pop song, that the secret meaning in the detritus of our consumer society, might redeem us even as everything seemed to go wrong, was just the kind of thing that Walker might have enjoyed contemplating.

For me, it wasn't until I met Harold Flint, it wasn't until I went to one of his abductee parties, that I really understood what I'd written. It wasn't until I started working with him and saw my first UFO home movie, participated in a session of hypnotic regression, saw scoop marks, implants, and doctored or invented government files, that the emptiness and the strangeness of everyday life became something tangible for me.

"We don't really know what's going on," Flint said when we first met. We were on our way upstairs to an abduction group meeting he was leading at the Jefferson Market Library in Greenwich Village. He was talking about the saucers, but I'd been taken with the Gothic architecture of what had been a courthouse, surprised by the stained glass windows and religiously ornate doorways, that I thought he'd been speaking much more generally. "We might be lab rats for energy beings or part of a breeding program for little aliens who live on the moon," Harold had said back then, before he'd introduced me to Carole. At the time she was just the pretty young woman he was helping out. She'd had a UFO sighting a few years earlier and she'd come to him. I remember her vividly, she had frizzy curly hair, like Virginia had had back then too, only she was maybe a bit sexier than Virginia, a bit taller, a bit older too maybe, and more aristocratic in her posture. She was an artist but not a desperate one, when she spoke she had that almost English-sounding accent that used to go along with money on the East Coast. She was waiting in the periodicals section in the purple sunlight by a stained glass window. She was reading a copy of *Telos* magazine and she smiled benevolently at Harold and me as we stepped up next to her, but rather than introduce me to her Harold continued with this sophomoric prattle.

"We don't really know what's going on," he'd said. "We might be lab rats, or dream characters, or somebody's idea of a joke," he said.

Nothing has changed much since then. He's always liked the sound of his own voice, I think, and what he's saying to me now as we walk along the boardwalk at Coney Island isn't very different from what he told me that first time we met. "You get confused easily," Harold says to me. "And you get things wrong. It wasn't the story about the red rubber ball that made me want to work with you but quite the other way around. You didn't write that story. I did." We're back at the parachute jump, at the steel latticework of the old amusement park ride, and I look up at the structure and when I look back down, when I glance at Harold, I find he's frowning. Apparently he means it. "I've only written a little bit of fiction," he says, "so I remember every story very well, certainly well enough to be certain about taking credit."

"You're serious?" I say. "You approached me, came to me, because you admired that story. Or that's what you said. I took it for empty flattery at the time, actually."

"If you wrote that story does that mean that I'm the one who came up with how to recover 'lost time'?" I ask. He's clearly gotten everything turned around in his memory. The truth is we both worked on altering the practice of constructing a Happening that could provide a framework for an abduction or sighting, but the original idea of the Happening was from Fluxus.

While other UFO researchers were convinced that screen memories were essentially false, that these strange recollections of owls or birds, absurd memories of strange men in black suits or other strange costumes, were implanted by the extraterrestrials, Flint was convinced that these absurdities were just as real as the saucers or anything else. Rain and Mack and other researchers used hypnotherapy to uncover "true memories" under the screen images, but we took a different approach. We worked with abductees not to help them remember something new, but in order to help them come up with some interpretation, some sort of meaning, for what they could remember. If this meant that they decided that they'd been visited by an angel or a squirrel, or that they were remembering something from another life, that was all fine with us.

Our way of investigating saucer reports was to construct Happenings. That is, we'd have the witnesses reenact their UFO encounters symbolically. We'd interview these witnesses, find out about their personal history, their tastes, their neuroses, and then we'd get them to create something that summarized their experience. In Carole's case Harold ended up helping her take her memory of flying saucers and transform the memory into sounds. She'd remembered the men descending the escalator from the saucer as being faceless. She'd remembered the aliens, blond men in jumpsuits, holding up large blank sheets of orange paper, they held them up at arm's length and at shoulder level, so that as they approached her the rectangles of orange construction paper blocked her view. She couldn't see their expressions, or their heads, at all. And, for her, the sensation of headless aliens had been expressed as poems first, and then as a song she'd recorded in Harold's studio. "We need to get Asket to interpret her experience?" I ask him.

"Is that why we're here?" Harold asks me. "Isn't that backward? Shouldn't she be helping us to remember? Shouldn't we be the ones trying to interpret?"

"But, there is something going on with her and Virginia," I say. "Don't you think we need to start with there, with them? Maybe not with Asket only, but with both of them?"

Harold turns around and looks back at the two women who are a ways off now. They're sitting on the bench and that's so far behind us that I can't tell which one of them is which. All I can tell is that one of them, probably Virginia, is braiding the other's hair.

"You want this, don't you?" Harold asks.

I do. I want to start working again. It's ridiculous to turn our backs on the project, on this quest after the meaning of UFOs, now that they're here. Why stop just when it's all gotten so much easier?

"I understand why so many people, so many Ufologists, are disappointed. These aliens aren't living up to expectations. The Pleidiens are tacky and sad, sure, but why should that bother us? I mean, why should you and I care about that? Did we have expectations ahead of time? Were we expecting to be inducted into the Federation of Planets or something? Did we ever think that these sightings were anything other than strange and sad? All along this appealed to you because you thought the UFO mirrored the basic mental instability inherent to humanity. Wasn't the point to get beyond the appearance of the saucers and get to that instability?" I ask.

Harold crosses his arms and scrunches up his mouth so as to indicate that he won't interrupt me but also that he isn't pleased by what I'm saying. He clearly doesn't agree. "I've reached the end of my side of this conversation," I tell him. "Go ahead."

Harold uncrosses his arms and then, surprisingly, answers me. He agrees with me.

"Yes."

"What?"

"Yes, the point was to figure out what was happening in people, to figure out how people were thinking. It's always been self-referential. And, yes, I think it's time to start working on another UFO book," he says. "Only we shouldn't focus on the aliens, we shouldn't interrogate this woman who looks like your wife. We don't need to do any of that."

"What then?" I ask.

"We'll start with us," he says. "And when I say 'we' I mean you."

"Me?"

"You can do it, can't you? You can arrange a Happening for both of us? You can set that up?"

"Well, I think I have to teach tomorrow," I say. "What day is it again?" I take a look at my digital watch, see that it's April 12th and that tomorrow is, indeed, a Monday.

"Just find the time. Set up a Happening for us and then, after that, we'll get started on the next book. That's what you want, right? That's why you brought her around, that's why she's still around, why she's living with you. It's why we ended up at the beach today. The aim of all this is to get this started again. I'm sure you can handle it, Brian. You've done well so far."

I nod at this and then stop as we've reached a point where a few planks are missing. There is an open space underfoot, and rather than step across the gap I'm stopped by it. I pause there, glance toward the ocean, looking past the green trashcan at the edge of the boardwalk and out again at the beach, and then I look down again, into the opening. It's dark down there, so dark that I can't find the sand, can't see the ground from where I'm standing.

Harold, meanwhile, has traversed this gap and moved on. I'm left behind, just watching him get smaller as he approaches the vanishing point.

"Okay," I shout after him. "I'll get started," I say. "I'll set it up for us."

7 happenings and abductions

In Rain's book *Saucer Wisdom* his descriptions of the technology onboard the Pleidien mothership give the impression that the equipment the aliens use is terribly antiquated. Published in 1978, three years after his first contact, the book describes mainframe computers, furniture made from molded plastic, transistor radio sets, and many other gizmos and gadgets that one would not expect an advanced hyper-intelligence to use. According to Rain the Pleidien computers used punch cards and magnetic tape, the various chambers inside the craft are described as lit by fluorescent lights, and the Nordic-type alien women in jumpsuits, intergalactic secretaries apparently, sit behind aluminum desks while working on electric typewriters.

Rain's UFO experiences read like something from a B movie. Think of Gerald Mohr in *The Angry Red Planet* or Ed Wood's *Plan 9 from Outer Space*. It's as if the Pleidiens filled in the gaps in reality that their presence created using the same stock footage from NASA or the Soviet space program that Ed Wood used to fill in gaps in the *Plan 9* production budget.

No reputable person could believe anything that Rain described back in 1978. It was just too ludicrous. But now we know Ralph Reality's mothership is real, and since it's real there is this lingering question from those old days:

Why are our saviors using technology that our parents would have scoffed at twenty years ago?

My theory is that the machines onboard aren't actually used, at least they're not used in the way we might expect. The Pleidiens don't need these machines to calculate orbital trajectories or fuel expenditures, they don't need to worry about flight plans. What they need are props. They want to communicate the idea of modern technology and, apparently, they want to invoke a sense of nostalgia at the same time.

Nostalgia runs through the entire Pleidien aesthetic. For instance, in chapter two in his book Charles Rain describes how Ralph Reality took him to what they called the Eternity Chamber and what's notable in this passage is that the device that brought on Rain's first full-fledged psychotic break or, more charitably, his first "insight" was invented in the late nineteenth century. The Eternity Chamber was nothing more than a re-purposed Mutoscope from 1890. Shaped like a wheel the thing stood on an iron tripod and included a viewfinder. To operate the Eternity Chamber one stepped up to it, looked into the viewfinder, and turned a crank on the side that spun a reel of photographs inside the machine to create a moving picture.

Rain watched a Pleidien saucer appear to move back and forth across flip cards inside this device and his Pleidien minders explained what was happening. They warned him that he might experience a sense of loss as his essence was absorbed by the machine and translated into pictures. After turning the crank again Rain found the flying saucer disappeared and his own image took its place. His life was reproduced as a series of stills. His life flipped past. Rain watched it all happen again, one card at a time, and his brain's impulses were wirelessly recorded, analyzed, and stored on the mainframe computer. They told him that his personality, his very person, would later be taken from the mainframe and transferred into the Akashic record.

"It was a spiritual technology," Rain wrote. "The Pleidiens promised me that, when the process was finished, I would be a new person. They'd record everything, remove it from my brain and store it for me. I would clear out the memory without losing access to it and have space in my brain for them, for their culture, their language, their ideas and insights. I would be able to speak and understand. I would be able to carry their message and prepare the world for their eventual arrival. Watching the photographs inside the Eternity Chamber flip by, seeing my mother again, watching my baby sister learn to crawl, I felt an overwhelming gratitude. I was there, on the ship, orbiting the Earth, and yet I was also far away from myself. I was reliving my childhood, and I was beyond my childhood. I felt my body dissolve and soon I was out in the stars and galaxies. I was connected to everything, no matter how small or large."

After publication of his book Rain constructed his own Eternity Chamber. Ralph Reality and the rest of the crew gave Charles Rain permission and blueprints, but despite their help Rain's version didn't live up to their original version. Charles didn't build a Mutoscope but something more like a voting booth, and inside, behind the curtain, he set up a table and a broken television set. People came for miles around in order to experience the promised spiritual transformation, to buy an epiphany made possible through alien technology, and Charles showed them static. Back in the mid-'80s Harold and I interviewed a few members of Rain's contactee group and while they all believed in Rain, believed in his program, nobody reported anything as grand. But none of them complained. They, all of them, tried to feel something.

"The day I tried it the TV set was on the fritz and instead of seeing myself I watched a few minutes of local news. Even so, by the time my time was up, I had received a message. It was as though God was speaking to me through the weather forecast, through the curved lines and triangles on the map of United States. Maybe I couldn't understand what God was saying, not with my mind, but I felt something. I knew God was talking to me. I knew it in my heart," one older woman, a high school teacher from Minnesota who had grey hair that she kept up in a bun and who smelled of clove cigarettes told us. Her testimony was typical.

Charging ten dollars a head Rain could afford to quit his day job and work full time on preparation for the landings.

What this proved to us, to Harold and me, is that it's possible to miss or ignore inconsistencies in the world. That is, most of us see what we want to see and only question a given circumstance when it makes us feel bad or sad. For instance, when I flipped through time, I first found myself making love to two different versions of my wife in one moment, stroking first one and then the other of them as they writhed on the kitchen table, and then, in the next moment, found myself eating a snow cone on the boardwalk at Coney Island. . .

Anyhow, Harold and I have our own technique for recovering Missing Time, and it has nothing to do with Mutoscopes or any other alien technology. What we use to remember, to find out what an abduction or sighting means, is a technique developed in Fluxus. What we stage in order to remember the aliens is a Happening.

Right now, for instance, I'm setting one up for later. I'm strewing objects in the studio art building, in the studio Harold's been using along with his students, with the hope that he and I might encounter these later and that these objects will help something happen. A Happening is when there is a dislocation or break in the usual flow of daily life, a dislocation of a kind that can't be ignored. What I'm hoping is that something new will be born from a Laser Tag set, a pack of Black Jack chewing gum, a Rock 'Em Sock 'Em Robots game, and a Mister Microphone. Harold says he's willing to start again. These nostalgic trinkets are the best that I can come up with. It seems to me that these are the tools we'll need. I store the toys in a paper bag from Kroger's and open the pack of gum. The taste of anise is just what I need to settle my nerves.

Back in the mid to late '50s, back when Harold was just past his teen years, Buckminster Fuller and the Occult were still taken seriously, at least among artists and poets. That is, despite the great distance, the great emptiness that we'd discovered around our little world, despite the fact of our insignificance, there was still a glimmer of hope for meaning, for art. The Occult no longer made sense, but it did give artists a way to look past the surface of things, to find a greater reality even as they found themselves surrounded by the cruel vacuum of space.

What people like John Cage and even Harold Flint liked most about Buckminster Fuller was this idea that had been around for a long time and that was expressed most directly in the movie *The Day the Earth Stood Still.*

The line was spoken by Michael Rennie at the very end of the picture, during the bit when Rennie delivered his warning to the people of Earth. He told them:

"We do have a system, and it works." Anyhow, Harold saw his first UFO while he was at Black Mountain College in North Carolina. Black Mountain College was an art school steeped in Fuller's mysticism, an alternative school most notable for producing influential poets and artists like Robert De Niro Sr.,

Robert Rauschenberg, and John Wieners, and that's where he was when he saw his first saucer land.

Harold was helping another artist—a delinquent kid named Ray Walker—build a geodesic dome out of twigs and branches, when a Pleidien craft hovered over the rectangular college, flashed its lights, and made him go partly mad.

He said later that it was a help. Harold had reached an impasse in his art at the college, but when this pinball-style contraption, a sherbet ice cream cone covered in colored lights and emitting electric trills, appeared in the sky his whole life was reset. Harold and Walker didn't fit at Black Mountain and were rebels among rebels. They didn't fit well behind the walls of democratic experimentation, and Harold doubted whether pinecones, manual labor, and abstract expressionism were helping him. He'd fallen in with Walker not despite, but because of Walker's insistence on working in the realm of bad taste. Walker was everything that Flint wasn't: dramatic, undisciplined, and gay. Walker loved comic books and movies, and this thing called Pop. Pop Art. When the saucer appeared Walker saw it first. "Lovely," he'd said. "It's Las Vegas."

The geodesic dome they were building was falling to pieces, the twine they were using to bind the sticks together constantly unraveling, but Walker seemed to enjoy it. He said it was fitting and good that Fuller's system should fall apart, but Flint was frustrated. He was attending Black Mountain not only because it was a smart move for an artist to be there, not merely because Willem de Kooning and John Cage were teaching there, but because he wanted that system, the system that worked. The idea was not just to learn to paint, sculpt, or to write powerfully, but to be made complete. The aim was to fully develop as a human. Flint wanted to be part of something bigger than himself while remaining free while Rain would settle for the latter on its own. Before he saw the saucer Harold was most interested in Mondrian and the Russian artist Lissitzky, in the promise of pure formal or geometric abstraction. He thought he wanted purity, but when he found it he couldn't bear it. "It's Las Vegas," Walker had said. They stood on the dirt path down the hill from the rectangle, looked up into the afternoon sky at the ice cream cone spacecraft, and watched and listened as this spinning top above them distorted the sky. They watched as the lights blinked, as the air wavered, as the sound shifted from one low note to another, and they slowly became confused. Harold found he could read Ray Walker's mind. What happened during his first UFO sighting was that the ideas in his friend Walker's head, images from New York bath houses and *Look* magazine, bare-chested men and cigarette logos, flashed in the background of his mind. He was looking up at flashing lights, at an unreal merry-go-round, but the real motion was happening in the brain of his companion. He could feel it, this flux of Walker's mind, and he couldn't help thinking along with that flow. Harold thinks this psychic flash is more important than the physical fact of the extraterrestrial craft. He credits the flash, this momentary telepathy, for setting him on a new path creatively. This moment was the reason he left Black Mountain and why he later joined Walker and others as a part of Fluxus. Even after Walker committed suicide in 1966 and Harold moved away from the pranks and jokes that were Walker's preferred form to formulate his own conceptual work, this psychic connection was still what lay behind everything Flint did. To connect, to know, this was what Harold always aimed at, and when he started working with UFOs and UFO experiencers he asked his subjects, these UFO experiencers, what they thought the saucers meant. He didn't want to know what they were, didn't care where they came from, but wanted to know what they meant to the people who saw them. He asked the witnesses to paint or draw what they'd seen and then expanded the range of art practices involved and had them collage, sculpt, make short films, record audio tapes. When none of this worked he turned to the Happening.

A Happening is associated with theater but it isn't a play. In the '60s a typical Happening would be a non-narrative performance that incorporated other forms of art and that aimed at spontaneity and audience participation, but in the '80s Harold's Happenings were private affairs. He'd hold them in his apartment, in his loft studio. He'd set up various art objects and tools, usually an easel and paints, a reel-to-reel tape recorder, a tambourine and recorder, add some odds and ends like tinfoil, confetti, and some kind of paste, and then ask his subjects to tell him the story of their encounters without mentioning anything that happened.

"Metaphors only," he'd say. That was his primary instruction. While researchers like Budd Hopkins and Allen Hynek were busy trying to find consistencies in the physical evidence, working to catalog correlations between the different eyewitness accounts, Harold set out to make sure there was no actual data.

The problem with a Happening is that it can lead you anywhere, sometimes far, far away from the subject.

For instance, take Harold's relationship with Carole. It was, like most relationships between men and women, set upon the foundation of a conflict in perspectives. Both of them were artists, right? And they'd both had strange experiences with UFOs, but while Harold thought of himself as a skeptic, a materialist and anti-theist, Carole believed.

She came to him the same summer I met him, back in 1984, and at first she was just another abduction case that he and I took on as a project. By this time Harold had left Fluxus behind. His art was more philosophical and less playful, not that he had ever found it easy to be less than serious. For Harold a joke is just a peculiar kind of contradiction. A game is just a system that people act out in order to keep their minds occupied.

In the early '80s Harold was more and more like himself I think. He studied the works of Escher and Duchamp and he drew Necker cubes, broken lines, and rabbits that looked like ducks or vice versa. What he liked about this kind of work, about the cubes specifically, was that the problem of perception, the problem of what is inside and what is outside, was so perfectly illustrated by these cubes that were really just flat lines. Harold hoped that he might be able to develop an art or a practice that would help illustrate how our memories and what we called the present were also flat. He thought life itself was like a Necker cube. He thought the whole world was a cube, or if not exactly the same as a cube, then the same kind of problem.

When he started the abduction research Harold also started studying psychology and psychoanalysis. For him the problem of memory, of trying to figure out what had happened to an abductee, was the same problem as trying to figure out whether a Necker cube was protruding out from or indented into the paper. That is, discovering what really happened at a UFO sighting or during an abduction was a matter of sifting out the ideas and images that were really projections from the present, but conversely the problem of figuring out the present, the problem of what was really happening now, was also a matter of filtering. A person had to filter out what he remembered, get rid of his expectations, in order to figure out what was really in front of him.

Actually, for Harold, neither approach would work.

If you don't let yourself fall for the illusion the Necker cube stops being interesting. If you don't get fooled at least a little bit then all you'd see would be flat lines on a page. The trick was to try to see it both ways, not to eliminate one illusion or another, but to see both illusions at the same time. When it came to memories, came to UFO stories, the trick was to see the past inside the present while also seeing how the present was inside the past.

The way Harold brought the two times together, the way he tried to demonstrate the way the past was always only in the present and the present is always just an experience of the past, was by making art. That is, not by making art himself, but by forcing the abductees to make art.

"It's a balloon," Carole said. She looked directly into the camera, smiled at the lens, and then held up the rather intricate and polished sketch she'd made of a hot air balloon. The balloon was colored red white and blue in stripes that stopped at the midway point, while the top was flesh toned.

Harold lowered the Super 8 camera, took a glance at what she'd drawn, and was disappointed to see that she was being so literal, that she wasn't playing by his rules. He frowned and then hid himself behind the camera again. He scanned the room and filmed everything: the brick walls and cement floor, the full-length mirrors and oversized worktable, the stainless steel chair, and then finally the abductee, this woman with hair cut short like a man's wearing a turtleneck and jeans.

It turned out later that Carole wasn't drawing the UFO she'd seen. She'd cheated. What she drew, her balloon, it hadn't had anything to do with UFOs or with what she saw. The experience of seeing a flying saucer had not been in her mind at all. She'd figured that since she was barred from drawing or speaking about her UFO experience directly she would push it from her mind altogether. Her Happening, as it was called, would just be her reaction to Harold.

"Where is it?" Harold asked. "Where is your balloon exactly?"

"Well it's all by itself, isn't it? The balloon has drifted so far, always in the same direction, uncompromising about that, so now it's alone. The balloonist and the balloon are nowhere. See?" She pointed to the empty space on the paper, to the blank space on the page, the blank space that surrounded the bulb and basket.

Carole drew a few more balloons for Harold and then he had her record her voice on a reel-to-reel tape recorder. "One, two, three, four," she said. "Five, six, seven, eight."

Carole was an artist too. I think I've said that already, and she'd been to Happenings before, thought of them as primarily social events, basically parties dressed up and made to seem important. And when Harold asked her to put his loft to her use, when he'd told her his plan, she'd thought he'd been coming on to her. She wasn't sure what she wanted to do about it either. She'd spent her time trying to make up her mind what she wanted.

"You want to see what I'm doing?" she asked him. Harold zoomed in as she leaned across the worktable with a yardstick and a drawing pencil and made arrows. Actually what she drew were Müller-Lyer illusions: parallel lines with v's on each end, lines that were of equal length but that appeared to be of differing sizes depending on which direction the greater-than or less-than signs were pointing. She drew a few other simple perspective challenges too. One with equal vertical and horizontal lines, only the vertical line appeared to be longer even though it wasn't. She drew a Necker cube, this time with the vertical and horizontal illusion filling the space inside the box.

"Tell me a story," Harold said.

Carole decided not to give him what he said he wanted. Her approach to art was always one built on a certain frustration. That is, when she was involved in the avant-garde, when she hung around John Cage's crowd, her art struggled toward something realistic and representational. At that point she wanted more than mere abstractions. But when she worked with more conventional types, when she was expected to create some kind of narrative in her work, what she produced was always spare. When she was supposed to make stories she would always eschew representation and produce purely formal works. She just didn't like giving people what they said they wanted.

So when Harold asked her for a story she made up her mind not to give him a story at all, but to give him something else. She decided that she knew what she wanted to do about the man behind the Kodak Super 8 camera, what she wanted to do with his clumsy advances.

Carole picked up a piece of paraffin paper from the table and held it in front of her, blurring her image with the nonstick wrap, blocking her head from view. Carole held the paper in place, turned so that she was looking slightly away, closed her eyes, and instead of a story she started to sing. The song was written by Dan Daniels but had been made famous by Peggy Lee. And maybe Carole didn't have a perfect singing voice, but she could carry a tune and sing with conviction.

"I remember when I was a little girl, our house caught on fire," she sang.

The song was "Is That All There Is" and by the time she was done Harold realized that while something was happening, what was happening was not a Happening. He zoomed in closer, tried to focus the camera on her face and failed because of the wax paper.

Carole would claim that the flying saucer people brought them together, but the truth was much simpler than that. Carole met Harold and saw what it was he needed, saw what was bothering him, and rather than solve his problem for him, to give him some kind of answer, she offered her own trouble over in exchange.

Come to think of it, it's a strange coincidence. Both Harold's affair with Carole and my relationship with Virginia started that way.

I wonder, when it comes to men and women, is that all there is?

Turning onto 5th I'm stuck in traffic. I'm surrounded by rust colored sedans and Chevrolet taxi cabs, and we're all moving very slowly.

Neither of my wives care that I've started, that Harold and I have started, working on flying saucers again. It was her goal originally, it was the whole reason Asket came to us, and now it's why she's living in our house, but apparently writing about UFOs is the last thing on anybody's mind.

Virginia cut Asket's grapefruit for her this morning. She made a special effort to separate every segment from the yellow skin. She sprinkled a thick layer of powdered sugar on the reddish orange fruit flesh and Asket appeared to be delighted by this.

Virginia is still mesmerized, enraptured, by Asket. Even though her Virginia personality has faded, even though all that's left is a vacuous and naive Asket persona, Virginia treats the alien as if she's something precious. I guess she figures that Asket might reveal some new truth about her and she wants to be there if and when that happens again.

Anyhow, when I left them they were sitting at the breakfast table and giggling over stories and memories and neither of them had bothered to get dressed. They just sat around all morning in nearly identical terry cloth robes (Virginia's was orange while Asket's was dark yellow) and eating grapefruit and some sort of healthy-looking cold cereal. They were eating Wheaties or Total or something like that, smiling, and it was like my life had become an advertisement from some alternative dimension where everybody's lesbian. Virginia kept touching the alien, tapping her shoulder or stroking her arm, while I hurried about collecting my notes, double-checking my schedule.

There's a taxi keeping pace with me to my left and the driver, a man in a black cotton turban and with a grey beard, he's looking at me like he blames me for the delay. The grey sedan behind me is revving its engine. Do they think I've stopped out of whimsy or malice? I turn to look at the driver through the back window, to make eye contact, when I spot the saucer. It's hovering directly over the taxi behind me.

The UFO is following me. Am I the target? Everyone thinks there's going to be another conversion, that the saucer is going to open up and that I'm going to climb on board and leave my car behind and block traffic. They've all slowed down in preparation for my quick departure, but I'm not going anywhere. I honk my horn to indicate that I'm ready to go, to tell everyone to ignore the saucer and keep driving, and eventually the lanes start to clear.

I turn on the radio and twist the dial over to WBAI. They usually have saucer reports around this time, letting people know how many saucers we commuters should expect to see in the skies and whether or not to expect delays due to any impromptu landings. The eight o'clock newsreader, a guy named Freund, doesn't actually complain about these roadside conversion ceremonies, not usually, but unlike the CBS guy, you can tell how he feels about it. When one of these lollipops blocks traffic to the Brooklyn Bridge or causes Houston to back up, Freund's voice gets deeper. He slows down, almost spitting out his words.

"Today's spiritual surrenders shouldn't make many of you late to work," Freund says. "But, Hoboken Avenue is jammed by a landed saucer at the intersection of Hoboken and Monmouth. It's easy to avoid, but take note."

The saucer that's tailing me isn't especially big. Must be a scout ship designed for just a few occupants, something built exactly for this, built with the aim of following automobiles. It's eased off a bit. The craft is about two car lengths back and about ten or a dozen feet up, but even in the September morning light the orange spotlights on the front of the craft are visibly lit, and when the taxi pulls ahead, as the traffic clears, I can hear the UFO as it moves along. It's making that humming noise that they do, a noise that increases in volume and rises in pitch as we increase in speed. The UFO speeds ahead of us, over the taxis and Chevrolets that are inching along 5th, and then cuts to the left. The craft's lights are out now and it appears as a grey disc, looking more like the top of the Seattle Space Needle than anything like a craft, but by some miracle it is floating overhead and no strings are visible. It crosses to the left, into Central Park, and then stops and as it crosses the road the traffic stops. A few cars start to turn off the road to follow the alien craft, and many more, maybe a dozen drivers, simply abandon their vehicles and stumble out into the road and to the sidewalk. These believers are taking a chance. A woman in a pea-colored pantsuit, a man in a leather jacket and khakis, a few teens in ripped jeans and plaid, cross the road on foot and I turn on my hazard lights and open the driver side door of my Ford Taurus. I turn off WBAI, unbuckle my seat belt, and mingle with the saved.

The flying saucer's lights come back on and the craft changes color from black, to green, to red. The reassuring buzz of the craft nearly drowns out the protesting honks from 5th Avenue and by the time we reach the steps of the Metropolitan Museum of Art the traffic noise and sound of alien machinery have combined into something like music.

The red light spills across the steps of the Met and I pause at the bottom step, refusing to ascend, as the saved start to climb and undress under the red light of the craft. The woman in the green pantsuit's pale skin is covered in goose bumps and she shivers in the morning air. Half undressed she crosses her arms and tucks her hands in her armpits for a moment before unsnapping her polyester pants. What I'm watching is a light baptism and it is the only part of a mass surrender that I've ever witnessed before, or even seen on television. My understanding is that some of the converts have probably been attending reading groups and saucer meetings, while many are coming round to the new religion only now, in this moment. Some require a slow revelation, they need to think it through, while others can simply join through levitation alone.

One by one they are lifted up into the craft where, I imagine, they'll wait in line for a turn on the Pleidien tech. Each one will reenact Charles Rain's experience with the Eternity Chamber, each one will have their soul converted and stored in the Akashic record. After this each convert will be fitted with a sequined jumpsuit with green sequins, green being the color of humanity, and then some will be set back down on Earth. These returns work at conventions and in reading rooms, while the rest are kept out of sight on the saucers. Maybe some are taken to the Pleides system and integrated into Pleidien society?

Watching them shedding the ways of this world, their naked bodies turning green and then red and then orange as the lights change, I wonder if, one day soon, there will be nobody left on Earth who will want to visit the Metropolitan Museum. I can't imagine that those of us who have been saved, the humans deemed worthy to visit the Pleidien homeworld, will have any interest in what the Met has to offer. I expect that Greek statues, Egyptian ruins, and the works of Jasper Johns will seem quaint to the new humans. There can't be any value in this history, nothing worth keeping from our attempts at being our own salvation. Why bother remembering these failures once victory has been found and no further attempts are necessary?

The old ways of creating permanence that are on display in the Met, these ways of representing supposed truths that have already failed, who will have any time or interest in this history? Certainly not these followers of the saucers. Certainly not these intergalactic groupies of Charles Rain.

In the first week after the landing Ralph Reality campaigned hard for humanity's vote. He did the Sunday shows, appeared on Letterman and Arsenio Hall, and ended up on the morning news programs as well. He was a guest on the *Today* show with Bryant Gumbel by Tuesday in that first week. And before the weekend he'd been on *Good Morning America*.

Ralph Reality repeated the same few examples to explain what joining them, what accepting their message, would mean. He always spoke of Magritte's painting *The Treachery of Images* in order to explain just what the Pleidiens were offering to correct and overcome.

"This is not a pipe," he said. "That is, on Earth, there is a separation between your concepts and the world as it is. But in the Pleides no such disconnection exists. In the realm of the spirit what is and what can be believed or thought of are the same. On my homeworld Magritte would have to say "Ceci est une pipe."

"Are you saying that in the Pleides, on the Pleidien homeworld, there is no difference between thinking about something and being or doing something?"

The second example Ralph Reality always used came from an old motion picture, a somewhat popular movie starring Gene Wilder as a chocolatier. "Living there people are free," Reality said. "That is, if they truly want to be."

There is nothing erotic about this scene. As the commuters become contactees I just watch them but I don't feel anything, certainly nothing sexual. They've stripped away more than just their clothes on the steps of the Metropolitan Museum. They've surrendered on some level that's hard to articulate.

I don't want to end up like them, and I take a step back. I'm not, never have been, attracted to this idea of surrender. I want to hold onto my alienation, at least for a little while longer.

When I get to class I find that every inch of the chalkboard is covered over in notes and scribbles: layers of mathematic formulas, doodles, titles of texts, statistics, and more. The physics department shares this ancillary building with literature and they've been struggling lately to catch up with the Pleides.

I pick up a piece of orange chalk as well as a dry eraser, but the eraser is full of dust and rather than take anything away it just leaves its own wide mark. There is no space left, no way to write anything legible. I put down the chalk, and turn toward my students. Forget the blackboard.

"Here's a question that will be on the exam," I start.

My students in Present Tense: Contemporary Writing are better than most. Sure, everyone is looking for an easy "A." After all, what could be easier than studying popular novels, movies, and even television programs? But, the course is both a seminar and a workshop which means that many of the students want to be writers themselves. I can usually rely on such students to pay at least a little attention, if only because they're longing after an affirmation of their supposed talents. They listen closely to every word in hopes that they'll catch me accidentally praising them. I'm unlikely to do that, but I do attempt, from time to time, to praise their tastes. For example the question that will be on the exam, the question I'm starting with, is: "Why was Kurt Vonnegut's character Dwayne Hoover wrong to take Kilgore Trout's novel *Now It Can Be Told* to be literal truth?"

I'm not just asking this to flatter them, of course. I'm asking because I'm hoping to figure out an answer, a better answer than the one in my prepared notes.

A kid in the front row raises his hand. "Because novels are fiction?" he asks.

"Okay," I say and I turn to write this answer down on the chalkboard, which is my usual practice. When a student gives me an answer I don't want, I write it down on the chalkboard. I note it rather than merely rejecting it. That gives the impression that I at least want to believe that everyone's opinion is valid and interesting even as it demonstrates the opposite. But, of course, the blackboard is covered in equations and other strange markings, and rather than writing anything down I return the chalk to the ledge again.

"Anyone else? Why was Dwayne wrong?" I ask.

The world has gone wrong. I've got two wives instead of one, there is the issue of Missing Time, and there is this pending offer to take me to a Third Space, to Ralph Reality's space that's off the map. What I need, though, in order to write about this, is a premise, some unifying idea or, if not a full-on idea, then at least a sound bite. Something cute to catch the reader's attention.

There is something grubby about the room we're in, probably due to the fluorescent lights. In the other parts of the campus a clean and airy aesthetic dominates. Beige walls and oval benches work together to provide students and faculty with the impression of being in the moment and relevant, but this building has none of that. In this older wing of the University there's nothing but dingy tile, wooden desks, and what looks like a layer of pixelated chalk dust.

"The reason Dwayne Hoover ought not have believed Kilgore Trout's novel was because the message it gave was self-contradictory. That's a clue, now can anyone guess at what I'm talking about?" I ask.

"Kilgore Trout's novel *Now It Can Be Told* is written in the second person. It's written as a guidebook and letter from the creator of the universe to the one creature in the entire universe who has a free will. It's a book that lets the reader in on the secret that he or she alone is the only free and independently thinking thing ever made.

"'You are the only one who has to figure out what to do next—and why. Everybody else is a robot, a machine. Some persons seem to like you, and others seem to hate you, and you must wonder why. They are simply liking machines and hating machines,'" I read the passage from one of my shuffled 3 x 5 index cards. "So what's the problem with that?"

"The problem is with God," a girl in the back row says without raising her hand. She's an awkward-looking girl, a bit gaunt.

"That's on its way to it. What is it that Vonnegut, or in this case Trout, says about God?" I ask. I look around for another student, for somebody who might have figured it out, but nobody else is raising a hand. "Vonnegut has Trout claim that God is just a machine. He's like everyone else in the novel, right? God doesn't have free will either. Only you do. Or, in Vonnegut's book, only Dwayne does," I say. "But where does Dwayne get this magic if not from God? If God is just a machine then how is it that a machine, admittedly a very powerful and large machine, could create something that He knows nothing about?

"What Dwayne Hoover should have figured out was that he was only a 'free will' machine and by that I mean that he was a machine that was programmed to believe that he had free will," I say. "Of course, Hoover couldn't do that. He couldn't think correctly, because that's not how Vonnegut made him."

The question for the class, the point of the lesson, was to ask what it meant to be a character, to tell a story, in a world without authors, in a world where God was just a machine. That might be a way in to this new book too. If God were just a machine what kind of machine would he be? Would he be a flying saucer?

"Authors try a variety of tricks," I tell my class. "They tried a lot of things and are still trying. Some of them tried minimalist writing, like Beckett. Some tried the baroque approach, like James Joyce. Authors who thought of themselves as machines wrote books without punctuation, some of them went so far in their effort to deconstruct their own work that they cut holes in their novels. The idea was to print the book with holes in it so readers could look ahead and see what was going to happen next."

I turn around and write on the blackboard, I write the name "Dwayne Hoover" in big blocky letters, but as hard as I press and as large as I make the words, what I end up with isn't legible, so I say it out loud. "Dwayne Hoover. The modern author is like Dwayne Hoover, solipsistic and, because of this, self-contradictory."

What I really want to know is what happens to people once they're onboard the flying saucers, what happens to the people who surrender. That would be worth reporting on. People would buy a book about that.

We know that some of them come back to Earth and sell crystals and souvenirs, but what about the others? I wish I had some way of knowing. I wish I could punch a hole in this grubby room, in this story of an academic lecture, and look through it to a flying saucer. Maybe I could look back in time at the Metropolitan Museum of Art and the red lights on the saucer there. And while I'm poking holes I could poke a hole in the saucer too. What would I see?

Actually, if I could cut a hole and peep through it I wouldn't look back at the flying saucer this morning at all. I'd look at the present. What I really want to know is how Virginia and Asket are doing. Virginia doesn't have to teach today so she might be taking Asket around our neighborhood in Brooklyn, they might be looking for a good book at Three Lives & Company or maybe going for a drive on Adams Street, they might be headed to the bridge again on their way to Manhattan, but probably not.

What I imagine is that they're still at home, still in their terry cloth robes. They're drinking coffee, or maybe wine, in our quiet and tidy kitchen.

What would it be like to punch a hole and read, not ahead, but at parallel with this moment? I try to piece together what the sentences would be like. I write them down on the blackboard.

"Asket is vibrating in our breakfast nook," I write this on the blackboard.

Asket is vibrating in the breakfast nook, vibrating like an alcoholic or an epileptic, only she doesn't seem to be aware of it. Virginia thinks that she can hear a slight hum emanating from this woman. She hopes that she does hear a hum. Virginia would very much like something new, some other kind of strangeness, to happen.

The kid in the front row has this skeptical look on his face. He's had it the whole time. He hasn't been taking notes, hasn't been paying much attention at all. Instead of listening to the lecture he's been flipping through the big fat paperback that he's brought along. He's got a copy of *The Plejaren Prophecy*, the newest book by Charles Rain, and now the kid is raising his hand.

"Yes?"

"I think the Pleidiens have an answer for all this."

"You do?"

"Listen," the kid says. "'You ignore the signs of extraterrestrial contact because you took them to be dreams, to be unreal. But now, today, the contact experience is the most real thing there is. What the Pleidiens are doing as they rotate and glide over our cities, that is a real thing. It's time you treated the day to day, all the little errands and various doings of your individual lives, as a dream.'" The kid stands up and steps up to the front of the room, he steps up beside me at the chalkboard. He points to the book, to the passage he's just read to me, and I look at where he's pointing, trying to be polite. I nod at him without really knowing what I'm agreeing with.

"Everything has changed," he tells me. "You're teaching us about Vonnegut and Beckett," he turns to the other students, "as if these problems haven't already been solved." He opens the big book and reads some more. "'On the Pleides there is a world of total synchronicity, a world where each thing that happens, every big event, every small and private moment, is meaningful and in harmony.'"

When I stop and think of it Asket really is humming. What's happening is that Asket is vibrating so fast that she's emitting an orange light and a humming sound. And this is happening because, outside our brownstone, just beyond the front window, there is a flying saucer. The words "you are invited" scroll along the outer edge of the vehicle, round and round, and it's as if our front step is the front steps of the Metropolitan. People are gathering around and taking off their clothes, mingling together in the street like it's the Age of Aquarius, and Virginia is sitting very still, silently waiting. She's holding her half-finished glass of red wine, grasping at the collar of her terry cloth robe to hold it closed now, and watching Asket hum.

"I've read that book already," I tell my student, "and despite those words the problem of the novel continues." I point out the boy's seat where he ought to be sitting, but he stands his ground.

I press on. "That book you've got wasn't written by aliens but by Charles Rain and, if you take the time to study it, you'll find that Rain's only echoing theosophy. Charles Rain has been shilling a watered-down version of theosophy for over twenty years and the saucers haven't changed that. The ideas the aliens are bringing us have been here all along. It's just another old solution that the new writers already doubt."

How is it that Virginia doesn't notice that Asket is undressing her? She's sitting at the breakfast table, her wine glass turned on its side, and twelve-dollar-a-bottle red is spreading across the Formica table, dripping through the seam of the leaf, and onto her legs. But Virginia isn't reacting. She's just listening to the hum from the saucer while Asket pulls her terry cloth robe aside. Asket climbs underneath the table, putting her hand down in the cool puddle of red wine, and then reaches up to remove my wife's underwear.

"The question on the exam," I repeat. "Why was Dwayne Hoover making a mistake?"

My wife is naked and the vibration from the craft is migrating. At first it seems to pass along the floor, move from where Asket is kneeling to the spot under where Virginia is sitting, it moves into the legs of her chair and then up into Virginia herself. It's my wife who is vibrating now, and as Asket removes Virginia's white Adidas tennis socks, Virginia starts to hum. The sound consists of one repeated note that is modulating between B flat and G. Asket is no long vibrating. She's slowing down, she's finding her way back to the everyday, but Virginia is whirring. She is glowing orange and spinning, speeding up, faster and faster until, in a burst of orange light, she is gone. I imagine it like something from a television show. I imagine my wife's abduction as accomplished through double exposure and stage lights.

I want to tell my students about it, to warn them that the utopia the Pleidiens are promising is already here, and that it is nothing but a contradiction. There can be no kitschy salvation but only cornball destruction. We can't trade our humanity, our individual wills, for this fast food version of the spiritual. We can't let these Pleidiens, these sci-fi angels, be our future for us.

This is what I want to say, but there isn't space for it. I've run out of room because of all the holes I cut into my classroom, into my story. I look at the student who intervened, look at his empty desk, and I can hear it humming.

hypnotic suggestion and body snatching

There are three flying saucers hovering over my block, directly over my brownstone, and they're blinking madly. To get to my front door I'll have to walk under this light show, I'll have to pass under another opportunity to surrender. I'm beginning to think that these encounters aren't entirely a matter of chance. I pause at the corner, look down at my loafers, notice the way the concrete is turning pink and then blue under the saucers, and remember why it is that I've never liked nightclubs.

I think it was Immanuel Kant who said that if we were to gain direct access to reality, to have an extrasensory perception that allowed us to know the world directly, to see past the surface of it to the reality underneath, that we'd lose ourselves, our freedom, in the process. It seems to me that the enlightenment on offer costs too much. Knowing ahead of time what's going to happen robs me of a choice, or it almost does. I can apparently cut holes in this story of my life, see more than one scene at a time, but I can't choose how things should go. The only choice I might still have is a reactive one.

For instance, when I find that Virginia really has gone, that my vision in class was authentic, I'll have a choice then. Asket will open the front door for me, right as I get to the top step, before I have a chance to find my house key. She'll be teary eyed and she'll tell me that Ralph Reality has taken my wife. She'll put her arms around me, cry on my shoulder, and ask me to forgive her. And then, maybe, I'll have a choice to make.

"What's going on?" Asket asks. I'm on the front step, considering stepping inside, and she grabs me, takes my face in her hands, and makes me look at her. "Why did you do it?" she asks.

This isn't how the conversation is supposed to go. Stepping inside and turning on the front hall lamp, apparently Asket has been waiting in the dark all this time, I look around at the clean wood, at the artwork Virginia collaged together in 1977, at the skier Suzy Chaffee holding an Escher-style triangle instead of a ChapStick, and I wonder if that work has always been there or if this is new.

"What do you want to do?" Asket asks. There is, apparently, an opportunity here. There's a choice to make. I try to list my options:

I could call Harold. I could go out for a drive, or visit the corner market under the assumption that Virginia hasn't disappeared or surrendered but has only stepped out for some milk or some Chinese food. I could interrogate Asket, try to find out what she knows, or we could step back onto the stoop together and let the saucers take us. But none of these options are very attractive.

"We can't go to Harold," she says. "He can't help us."

She's sure about this. Just as sure as I am that I can't trust her. Now that Virginia is gone Asket looks more like her, seems to be her. She puts her hand in mine and then brings my hand to her mouth, touching my fingers to her lips.

"Please," she says. "We can't go to Harold. Not yet."

One thing is certain, Virginia has been kidnapped. That's something to hold onto under the circumstances, that's the fact that I can react to, act on. The Pleidien enlightenment, the meaning of their invasion, the connotations that come along with it, none of that matters any longer. My wife has gone missing, been taken. She's been abducted.

"We need to know what's going on," I tell Asket.

"Not from Harold," she says. She moves closer to me, puts her arm around my waist, and then reaches out to turn off the lamp.

"We need to know who you really are," I tell her. I turn the light back on again, glance back over at Suzy Chaffee and her triangle, and then say it again. "We need to know who you are."

Looking out into NY traffic, the green and red and rust-colored Toyotas, yellow taxis, and forest green Mercedes-Benzes, listening to my wife's duplicate hyperventilate as she looks out of the passenger window at the chaos, I'm driving fast, crazily. Weaving in and out of traffic, I'm speeding along because I know we'll get there. This is just a ride.

We're going to see Charles Rain because I figure he knows the Pleidiens the best and more than that, he knows about the end of the world.

Back in the '70s Charles Rain's brand of Ufology contained the kind of doomsaying that was popular after Nixon. He told us that society was sick because even his readership, people more interested in crystals and personal transformation than politics, knew that the power structures and institutions that manage our affairs were corrupt. Every right-thinking person felt a pressing need for change. Nowadays the common wisdom is that it was the preceding decade when the world was contested. People think the '60s were when revolution was in the air, but people in the '60s had confidence in the system, in society, in one's neighbors, but by 1977 these same people felt that what was needed wasn't a movement so much as a miracle. What needed to change wasn't some system out in the world but something more fundamental. Our task was to change ourselves, to pull ourselves up by our bootstraps.

"The Pleidiens understand us. They know how limited we humans are, they know our struggle for self-transcendence, and they want to help."

These opening lines from Rain's 1979 book *Directives from the Stars* set the tone and direction of his work, of his marketing efforts, for the next decade. All of those books written before the saucers landed were more about getting in touch with your daily life and changing your lifestyle than they were about aliens and extra-dimensional travel.

"The Pleidien leader told me that I need to learn to listen to the Earth, to feel what's right, and to let go of my obsession with self-talk. 'Self-talk,' he said, 'is a kind of self-doubt,'" Charles Rain wrote.

Still, before the landings, Rain warned us of catastrophe. He told us that we needed to find a better way to live if we hoped to survive the coming ice age, massive heat wave, overpopulation, nuclear wars, and most importantly of all, our collective identity crisis.

We are going to Charles Rain, going to his home to see him personally, because while he might be under the influence of the enemy, he knows the truth.

Sitting under oval-shaped hanging lamps in the corner of his spacious living room, across from a large clean white modern bookshelf containing a plurality of shelves of various shapes and sizes, a combination of squares and rectangles filled with vinyl records, hardback books, potted plants, and framed photographs, I reach out for the brick wall to my left, feel the cold stones there, and then glance at the artwork. There is a painting of red, yellow, and blue squares set together in a pattern that is very similar to his bookshelf's arrangement.

"Mondrian?" I ask.

"Not an original. I painted it. Copied it, back in the fifties."

Asket is sitting next to me, shivering on the metal chairs, looking at the bookcase like she's been given an assignment of counting every title, and when Charles pulls up a chair to join us at the round oak table she starts.

"Are you still working on abduction research?" Asket asks.

"Didn't you know that?" Charles asks. He's still got his long grey beard, the beard that once evoked Eastern mysticism but now reminds me more of the rock band ZZ Top. He's an old man now, older than Harold even though they're really just about the same age, Rain may even be younger, but he seems old. When she asks him about abductions his mouth becomes a firm line. "Of course I'm still researching. There is more reason to research the phenomena now than ever. We've had everything confirmed. It's happened."

We don't object to this but Asket takes a sip of the espresso he'd brought her earlier and shrugs. The alien looks exceptionally pretty tonight in Virginia's clothes. She's wearing some brand of designer jeans and a blue and white Indian print blouse of thin silk. She looks pretty, but vulnerable.

"Do you still get reports of abduction?" I ask. "Even with all these people surrendering? How do you separate that out?"

Charles folds his legs and leans back to examine us both, nods half to himself and half to me, and explains that, while most of his group, his abduction group, have converted and accepted the new reality, a few are still in the dark and they need more conventional, more terrestrial, help. Then Charles says something I don't expect, something that is certainly not canonical.

"I'm not convinced that the Pleidiens are the only ones visiting us."

He's been spending a lot of time rereading the old documents, especially the BUFORA files, which contain cases featuring different kinds of aliens.

"There are things going on, in this reality, that aren't quite what my brothers think they are," he says.

"How do they think things are?" I ask. "Just what is it that they're doing on those saucers?"

Charles smiles at me enigmatically. "You already know the answer?"

Asket shifts in her seat, takes another sip of espresso, makes a face, and then puts the cup and saucer down with a clatter.

"I want you to hypnotize me," she says.

"Yes. I think I can do that," Charles says.

"No. You don't understand. I want you to hypnotize me now."

In Charles' furnished basement he has Asket lie down on a couch while he and I sit in nicely designed wood folding chairs underneath one of his more famous paintings. Charles' work is all about circles and squares, orange and green circles and squares that have always reminded me of television test patterns. Looking at his work I feel as though the network is about to sign off for the night. 3...2...1...

"I want you to relax," Charles says. Asket just blinks at him and then she sits up.

"Don't you have a pocket watch or something?" she asks him.

"I just use my voice for this," Charles says. "I want you to concentrate on my voice."

"Okay."

"Are you relaxed?"

Asket's face loses all expression as she shuts her eyes. Her breathing slows and her hands settle down, she stops fidgeting. Watching her go into the trance I think about how Virginia, my other wife, is long gone, perhaps in outer space now.

"Are you relaxed?" Charles asks.

"Yes."

"Do you know where you are?"

"I'm lying on your sofa under that insipid painting," she says.

"What's your name?" Charles asks. He turns to me and puts his finger on his nose, like he's being awfully clever to ask her this. As if this might settle something.

"My name? I'm Carole. Carole Flint," she says.

Charles doesn't respond to this right away, but it does get his attention. He turns away from his painting of circles, he'd been looking it over perhaps to reassure himself about its merit, but now he's looking directly at the woman who says she's Harold's wife.

"Could you say that again please? What's your name?"

"I'm Carole Flint, the wife of Harold Flint," she says. "Only, something happened to me."

the alien in the art class

It shouldn't have surprised her, but it did. After the aliens landed on the White House lawn Harold Flint apologized for his work with abductees and contactees, retired from the field, and returned to making art. What disappointed her was that Harold hadn't been prepared for it. The arrival of the Pleidiens shouldn't have been a shock. She'd told him they were coming. She'd told Harold everything when she went to him back in 1983. He must have been only pretending to believe her because now the fact that they'd arrived brought him nothing but embarrassment.

Patricia had given up on the aliens years earlier, around the same time she'd given up on Harold, and she was, like him, focusing on art, on painting, but while Flint's return to art was hailed as an event worthy of a MOMA retrospective, her return only meant that she'd filled out some forms at the Mt. Scott Community Center and started teaching art history again. She had experience teaching from when she was in graduate school. What was different this time was that her students were middle-aged employees from the tanning salon next door and a few friends she'd met in her Jazzercise class. Most of her students had signed up as a kind of charity.

She reached the end of SE Reedway, the point where the asphalt ended and there was only a small dirt alleyway lined with blackberry bushes and a canopy of birch leaves and Charles fir pines that blocked the sun. The Community Center was just a little ways ahead.

(I'm confused. Is she telling us that she's Harold's wife or this other person? Of course, given that it's Asket, she could've been or could be both people. Imitating both.)

Today she was going to lecture on Suprematism before her students tried their hand at figure drawing. The idea was to emphasize expression over technique, to counter the values of realism with something else, with pure geometry and simplicity, in order to maybe mitigate the feelings of inadequacy that most of her students would feel when they saw the results of their first efforts. She knew how disappointing and frustrating it was for most students when they discovered how disconnected their hands were from their minds. The movement from idea to work was very difficult and most weren't willing to put in the effort. What she wanted was to keep those people, the people who couldn't and wouldn't learn to draw, in the class. She couldn't let anyone drop out because if her attendance level were any smaller she would lose the class. She would tell them that, yes, a simple black square could be art. And, yes, there was more to art than technique. Absolutely.

At 66th the alley ended and Patricia had to turn right to Ramona. At the corner she paused for traffic and took a moment to examine the stop sign. Was an octagon a pure form? She couldn't remember if Malevich or Mondrian ever employed the shape. The color was primal enough, but did a stop sign express a "pure feeling" in the Suprematist style? It was a question that might draw her students out for ten minutes or so.

The real reason she'd been thinking about Harold was because there was a Pleidien in her class. He turned up in his sequined jumpsuit, sat quietly in the back, and just observed. While most of them, these aliens, acted like Jehovah's Witnesses, always ready to educate and enlighten and save your soul, this one just wanted to participate in human affairs as they were. It was as if Klaatu from *The Day the Earth Stood Still* had decided buying Bobby Benson an ice cream cone was plenty enough for him. It was as if Klaatu had taken a room in Aunt Bee's boarding house and then decided to stay, maybe take a desk job, learn to sew, take an art class now and then.

There was a Pleidien in her class, but he didn't look like the rest of them. He was the only Pleidien she'd ever seen who was even slightly overweight. And Johnny, he asked her to call him Johnny, was balding as well. It was difficult to take him seriously in his ill-fitting jumpsuit. She couldn't remember if he wore glasses or not, she tried not to look in his direction much.

The topic she had to focus on was Suprematism.

(I don't want a lecture on art history. I want to know what happened to Virginia. But, apparently, I have to be patient.)

Once class started Patricia opened her 1964 Enlarged Edition of *Modern Artists on Art* and held the book open so that El Lissitzky's *Beat the Whites with the Red Wedge* was visible. She'd just finished explaining how this art of pure abstraction was still used to tell a story, and had already mentioned Lissitzky.

Johnny raised his hand.

"For humans even pure abstractions, say mathematics, contain emotions?" he asked. "A triangle can be angry?"

That was right. Lissitzky had taken the pure feeling, or what might be thought of as pure being or the ontological ground of existence, and brought this to bear in the world. For Lissitzky the Soviet Union, a State that was destined to emancipate humanity from the illusions of Capitalism and the West, was merely the living and political example of "pure feeling" acting in the world.

Johnny nodded solemnly and folded his hands on his rather large belly. "Pure feeling," he said. "That's something we understand."

Patricia's art class was held in the basement of the Community Center, in the same room as the clock repair class, and the students were crowded in close to her desk, pushed together in order to accommodate the work benches and grandfather clocks, the toolboxes and step ladders, that had been set aside an hour earlier. The Pleidien was in the front row, maybe a foot away from her, and whenever she looked in his direction she felt it. She felt dizzy, anxious, like something had touched her.

"To get an idea of what 'pure feeling' is we're going to try an experiment," Patricia told the class. She was just going through the motions, her eyes still on Johnny. She didn't really know what she was saying. "We're going to see things differently."

She'd brought along the spectacles in her backpack. She'd carefully packed them, wrapping them in tissue before putting them in a paper sack inside the backpack. Now she took the spectacles out briskly, hardly paying attention and setting them down haphazardly on the desk.

"These are on loan from the Children's Museum," she said. "Everyone be careful with them."

They were alternate vision spectacles. The lenses in each set of frames were shaped differently—some bifurcated, some compounded, some with blinders—so that wearing them gave you a view approximately like the vision of different animals. Looking through these glasses meant seeing the world as a bee sees it, as a horse sees it, as a chicken, or as a bat sees it. The idea was that, after taking a look out from these different perspectives, the question that Lissitzky and Malevich were posing would be easier to understand. Once you'd seen the world as a bee the question of pure seeing, of seeing in the abstract, would be a bit more visceral.

Wanda from the tanning salon tried on the horse-eyed spectacles and a line formed behind her, but Johnny in the front row didn't move.

"Aren't you going to join us, Johnny?" Patricia asked.

"I don't need to," he said.

"Oh no?"

"Pleidiens don't only see things with our eyes. We go beyond that, go beyond even pure seeing, or this pure feeling that the Suprematists were after. These are the wrong words," Johnny said.

"I feel like I'm going to bump into something," Wanda interrupted. "Like I'll lose my step if I try to walk." Wanda was about forty-five and wore low-cut polyester blouses that revealed her softening but not yet sagging breasts. She held her hands out in front of her face and waved them back and forth. She was wearing the bat-eyed lenses.

"Everything is fractured," one of the girls from Jazzercise said. She too was waving her hands in front of her face and turning about. She had on bee eyes and she turned too quickly and smacked Johnny on the top of his head. "Oops."

"Maybe the word is ontology," the alien said. "That's the study of being, of essence."

After everyone but the Pleidien had tried on all the different kinds of spectacles Patricia announced the break. An artist's model, a friend named Shelly who was willing to pose nude for half the usual rate, would be arriving and Patricia reminded everyone to focus on the quality of the line, on shading. She gave the class fifteen minutes to use the restroom upstairs, to step out for a cigarette, or to mill about without purpose while she gathered up the spectacles and cleared a space in the front of the room for Shelly. She placed a sheet over her desk, and then set about placing graphite pencils and drawing paper on the students' desks.

Johnny followed her as she moved about the classroom setting up. When she'd set down the last pencil, when she returned to her desk and leaned against it in anticipation, he spoke to her again.

"You've tried the bee glasses?" he asked.

She had.

"You've tried all the different ways of seeing?"

Patricia said she hadn't tried all the different ways, that she always saw things in the same way basically, but she'd tried a few different filters. She explained that her original filter, the human filter, was impossible to remove.

"I don't know," Johnny said. "Maybe I could help you with that. Would you like that?"

Johnny told her that if she would place her hand on the top of his head, precisely on the spot where the young student had given him a smack, he could allow her to glimpse the Pleidien way of seeing. He could link up with her eyes and let her see the world as he saw it.

"Is this like a Vulcan mind meld or something?" she asked.

"Not like a mind meld. I won't see through your eyes. It'll be a one-directional link," he said.

"Very reassuring."

The Suprematists' geometric patterns, their black squares and red ovals, even their crosses and people, were reductions. After the Russian revolution Malevich went to the extreme of painting a white square on a blank canvas so that the shape was just visible, so that the form was barely there. The aim was to get out of the way of feeling, to let what was sweep through the mind and come to be on the canvas.

"Everything which determined the objective ideal structure of life and of 'art' ideas, concepts, and images all this the artist has cast aside in order to heed pure feeling."

Malevich wrote this in his Suprematist manifesto, and something like this pure feeling is what Patricia experienced as she stood in the basement of the Mt. Scott Community Center with her hand on top of the Pleidien's head. Even if feeling was the wrong word that's how she thought of it.

Johnny's hair was a bit greasy, but soon this sensation passed and instead she simply saw what was, the toolbox and concrete floor, the desks and chairs, the canvas tarps thrown over piles of equipment and rubbish. These things weren't distinct but one. It was not that the things of the world disappeared, but all imposed understanding dropped away.

She couldn't say how long she stood like that with Johnny, seeing and not seeing, but after some passage of time this reverie was interrupted.

Shelly, the artist's model, arrived. Shelly was a pretty black girl, about twenty-four, five years younger than Patricia. She was the kind of well-put-together woman who made Patricia feel unattractive and awkward. In her olive turtleneck and pencil skirt she practically shined, every inch of her ensemble fit her perfectly. They'd met at the art museum where they both volunteered as docents, but when Patricia first saw her she'd assumed that Shelly was a VIP, some donor's granddaughter maybe.

"Patricia?" Shelly asked.

"Oh, hey," Patricia said. Johnny stepped back, returned to his desk, while Patricia leaned against hers. She put her hand down on the bed sheet that she'd draped over the hard wood and took a breath.

"What was going on there? You okay?"

"I'm fine. You ready to be turned into art? Or, more accurately, ready to be drawn as a Disney princess with the requisite emphasis on tits and ass?"

"You have my check?" Shelly asked.

She did. Patricia apologized again, in advance, for the twelve identical drawings that were sure to come from this lesson. They were all of them bound to be crude and unnatural, focused on the model's nudity rather than her form. All of them barring one, that is.

Johnny wouldn't draw anything like a human figure. The Pleidien didn't understand representation. All of his efforts produced Pleidien symbols—squiggles and gestures that Patricia knew was something like a language only not. The Pleidiens were too spiritual for written languages. Still, each time Johnny had drawn curly lines, his hand moving mechanically and precisely in this or that arc or with this or that flourish.

"Shall we start?" Shelly asked.

"We're on a break, but in a few minutes…" Patricia looked around to see that her students were back at their desks and that they had their pads and pencils at the ready. "That is, the restroom is through that door and to the left."

Johnny's hand was already moving. The shape he was working out was very much the kind of thing that Malevich would have appreciated. What he was sketching was a telephone pole or maybe a cross.

(Charles wants more information about Johnny. "What is Johnny doing now?" he asks. Asket turns her head a bit to the right, as if looking at Johnny even though her eyes are closed.)

Johnny was getting up from his desk. What Patricia saw was that Johnny was approaching the front of the room and that he had a creepy smile. He waved to her but Patricia didn't respond. Then he came to the front of the room, beside Patricia, and he reached out and unbuttoned the top button on her blouse and she still didn't say anything. She found that she couldn't say anything because Johnny was saying something. Or, more to the point, Johnny wasn't talking but he was standing on her desk, looming over her. His gut was at eye level, and he had his arms out, extended like he was conducting, like he was about to instruct an orchestra.

She was to take off her clothes and switch places with Shelly. Johnny was telling her to move, to step out of her jeans, to be ready, and when Shelly entered the room in her terry cloth robe, when Shelly reached the desk, she took Patricia's discolored panties, the pair that had turned a light purple and green in the wash, and put them on. Shelly took Patricia's blue jeans, her socks. Shelly took all of it. She stood where Patricia had been standing and took her place.

"Can you see me?" Johnny asked.

The students in the class were sitting completely still, just as they had been, none of them moving, apparently not even breathing, and Patricia was naked in front of them.

"It's time for a change," Johnny said. "This has gone on long enough in this direction and now you should change."

And Patricia found that she agreed with him and that she could move again. She lifted herself onto the desk and, with her back to the classroom, looked over her shoulder.

Patricia was an artist's model.

No, that wasn't it. The artist's model wasn't Patricia at all. It was Shelly who stepped up to the desk, sat down so her legs were in front of her, her legs spread and her sex revealed to the chalkboard. It was Shelly who glanced over her right shoulder to look, coquettishly, back at the students. She was a bit vain, but maybe a little saggy, Patricia thought.

Johnny returned to his seat, looking like nothing more than an overweight suburbanite.

"Okay class," Patricia said. "Let's try to be original here. Think about the Suprematists and pure feeling."

"Is this right?" Shelly asked. And she felt she was asking about something more than her posture, about something more than the butterfly tattoo on the small of her back. "Is this okay? Are we okay?"

"Sure," Patricia assured her. "You look great. Okay class, go to it."

The students built their sketches as blueprints. Shelly looked back at them over her shoulder and her pale skin was covered in goose pimples.

The students, all of them, took Patricia's instructions to heart and rendered Shelly in the Suprematist style. She wasn't a woman at all, this model. She wasn't Shelly, but was just an abstraction, a pure line on a page. She was pure feeling, identity without form, and the students drew triangles and squares. They used colored pencils, tying the feeling they were sketching together with red lines and green circles, and all of their drawings were the same.

When everyone was finished Shelly turned around and slid off the desk. She grabbed her robe and covered up, and then silently walked between the desks to the door. Her head was a triangle, her midriff an oval, and her legs were just thin lines.

(We aren't really getting anywhere. Maybe Charles put her too far under? This isn't a memory at all, but a dream maybe.)

After art class Patricia found Shelly loitering around the front of the community center. She was waiting for her by the double doors, nervously glancing into the entryway, through the pane glass doors, when Patricia, having exited from the basement door, came up behind her.

"Hey there."

"That didn't go right," Shelly said.

"Sorry," Patricia said. She stepped past Shelly and to the front door to lock up. She had a large ring of keys and struggled to find the right one.

"You have a minute?" Shelly asked.

"Who me?" Patricia asked. "Actually, I'm in a hurry. I'm sorry though. Sorry you didn't enjoy the class. We'll talk about it at the museum?"

"Where are you going, exactly?" Shelly asked.

Patricia didn't know. She felt like a blank tape, a videotape that had been demagnetized, and she didn't know what to say to her friend. Shelly looked tired. Were those bags under her eyes?

"Patricia? What's going on?" Shelly asked.

She found the right key. It was the one with the green rubber key tag. Patricia turned it, checked that the door was secure, and then looked back at Shelly and gave her an embarrassed smile.

"Did you turn on the alarm?" Shelly asked.

Patricia found the key again, ran her fingers through her straightened hair, licked her lips, and then stepped back inside. She wanted Shelly to have the impression that she would be right back, she had that impression herself, but once she was behind the closed door, standing in the dark lobby of the Community Center, she didn't move. She stood there in the dark for ten minutes and then for another ten, and then another.

"I don't want to see that girl, that model, ever again," she said into the relative darkness.

The trouble with testimony gleaned from hypnotic regression is twofold. First, there is no evidence that a person's memory is improved through the use of hypnosis, nor is a person less likely to make a mistake or misremember when hypnotized than when fully awake and relying on conscious recollection. Second, a hypnotized person is suggestible. This is why hypnotism was popular as a sideshow act and in vaudeville during the late nineteenth century, it's why hypnotism can be used as a way to treat people with various addictions, and it's why abductees and contactees generally tell stories that reflect the worldview of the researcher. The hypnotized person remembers what the researcher wants them to believe, quits smoking at the hypnotist's request, and will cluck like a chicken if you ask them nicely.

What Charles Rain asks this woman whose name we just learned might've been Patricia and might've been Shelly, and who claims to be Harold's wife Carole, is to remember what happened next. That is, he asks her to tell us what happened to her the day after she changed, after her body became somebody new and she hitched a ride in a new body.

"I can't breathe," Patricia says.

"You can breathe. Right now you can breathe," Rain says. He's a bit panicked.

Patricia is coughing, waving her hand in front of her face, like she's waving away smoke, and Rain moves toward her. He gets out of his leather chair and kneels down next to her on the couch, as if the closer proximity will help him, as if he can make her listen.

"You're with us now. The air is clear here. You're here with Brian and me, in my studio."

"Why did everyone have to smoke? Why did everyone have to smoke in that little café?" Patricia asks. Her eyes are still closed and she's still waving her hand back and forth in front of her face, but she's not coughing anymore and she's changed tense.

"What café is that, Patricia?" Rain asks.

The Telecafe was a small espresso bar near Mt. Scott Community Center, located just a couple of blocks away from where Patricia lived in SE Portland, and Patricia tended to treat it as her second living room. She went to get a latte and bagel there around 8:30 a.m. on most days, before she caught her bus and went downtown to volunteer for the art museum, and the morning after her body changed this was where she went. She woke up at seven a.m., the usual time, waited for the bathroom down the hall from her apartment to be free so she could take a shower, and then got dressed up as was usual in a tartan-patterned black and red wool skirt, cashmere sweater, and sneakers.

"I didn't know for sure whether I liked how I looked," she says. "It was sort of fashionable, but something seemed wrong about it."

But even though something seemed wrong about her reflection, even though she didn't like the way her clothes felt on her, she grabbed her purple plaid-patterned purse and house keys, and despite how odd she felt she went on her way. She was off to work even if she wasn't being paid.

When she got to the Telecafe she started coughing. She manages to tell us about how annoying the cigarette smoke was, how stuffy and unpleasant she found her environment to be, without reenacting it for us. She's got a bit of distance from her memory now, and she's able to articulate what she remembers without interruption. The words are coming from her in a good flow, like a story she might have told before.

Most of the clientele of the Telecafe are in their early twenties, almost a decade younger than Patricia, and most of them are smokers. They're sitting at their various tables, some of them square tables, some of them circular, not one matched set, drinking lattes or other espresso drinks out of pint glasses, and smoking. There is Robert, a kid she's talked to before about Damien Hirst and Carl Jung, and he's smoking a Menthol. The girl across from him, she looks like she's out of a fashion magazine, a bit like a flapper, and she's rolling her own cigarette. Almost all of the patrons of the Telecafe are smoking cigarettes, and even though Patricia chooses a spot to sit down near the door for the ventilation, she still finds it difficult to breathe. There is so much smoke she can't taste her bagel. She's coughing and coughing, and wondering why she likes this particular café.

Out on the sidewalk Patricia was deciding not to return, marveling that the ramshackle cafe ever became part of her routine. The latte was lukewarm, the bagel was clearly store bought, and there was so much smoke, and she was thinking about her bus schedule when she absently opened up her mini-purse and started rifling through it. She pulled out her pack of American Spirit lights, tapped one out, put it in her mouth, and lit it. Then she remembered.

The reason she liked the Telecafe was precisely because she was allowed to smoke there.

"There is a saucer over 11th Street," Patricia says.

"You're here with us now," Charles reminds her.

"There was a saucer over the Telecafe. I wondered if the people onboard, the aliens up there at the controls…were they watching me?"

Patricia's short-term goal was to be recognized for her good work as a docent and hired on as either Events Manager or as part of the education and outreach department, but her long-term aim was to be a curator, and the Barbara Kruger exhibit was a good example of why she felt her judgment and taste would add value to the museum. She would never have had scheduled a Kruger exhibit, not after the landing. Walking between the red and white banners that together made up the entirety of Kruger's gimmicky exhibit, taking in her imperatives and observations printed in massive Helvetica letters, Patricia was a bit embarrassed. Kruger's work had no heart to it, it was all in the head, and at a time when people felt unsure, dwarfed by events, the last thing they wanted from an art museum was to be reminded of their own alienation.

"You are not yourself," Patricia says. That was the slogan for the exhibit and the promotional poster depicted a woman's face reflected in a shattered mirror. The model in Kruger's collage was a set of shards and fragments, her smile broken and her eyes closed so that what had been a moment of joy looked instead like inner torment.

FORGET EVERYTHING. The words were six feet tall printed in all caps against a blank background, taking up the entirety of the Northern Wall.

Before she started her first tour she stopped in the employee kitchen and looked for more coffee. She had a headache and hoped that more caffeine would solve it. The employee kitchen was the only room in the museum that wasn't well lit, and she was relieved to sit in the relative darkness in a plastic charm set on rollers and examine the human-sized cupboards and perfectly serviceable sink. She put nondairy powder into the Styrofoam cup, poured cold coffee from a pitcher that had crusted to the heating element in the coffee machine, and then reheated the mess in the microwave with the hope that the powder would dissolve rather than remaining as a dry lump at the bottom of her cup.

"Will a microwave melt Styrofoam?" she asks us.

"I don't think so," I answer.

Charles gestures to me to be quiet with his right hand, making a slicing gesture at his own neck, and then leans forward on his leather sofa. "Does anything happen in the break room?" he asks.

Patricia doesn't answer but just bites her lip and furrows her brow. She says she's trying to understand something.

"What are you trying to figure out, Patricia?" Charles asks.

"One of the other docents, he's a college student, an undergraduate, he's going over his notes for Kruger's art and he keeps saying the word 'hyper-real.' I think I know what he means, but maybe I don't understand it. It's just a buzzword. Sounds smart but isn't, don't you think? I'm going to stick with pointing out that Kruger wants to critique the museum itself, to question the aesthetics of power that we find in the museum. That's what her artist statement says," she says.

"Does anything happen in the employee break room?"

Patricia asks again if Styrofoam will melt in a microwave and then, when Rain refuses to answer, admits that she doesn't want to go back to the exhibits. She's afraid of remembering. She describes how she's spilled some coffee on the counter, to the left of the sink and right in front of the microwave. The cup has melted a bit after all, the cup is hot to the touch, and she spills a little of the coffee on the counter and then puts down the cup and fetches a sponge from the back of the sink. The sponge is back behind the faucet, and it's dry. She turns on the hot water.

"The coffee on the counter, it's thin coffee, and with the cream in it I realize that it's the same color as my hand. Wiping up my spill I realize that I'm tan, dark. I'm darker than I think I ought to be."

"What color ought you to be?"

"I don't know. Not coffee and cream colored," she says. "Pinkish I think."

"Do you still remember what you told me about yesterday?" Rain asks. "Do you remember what happened in your art class?"

The term "hyper-real" does mean something actually. It's the idea of something that is taken to be real but that can only exist as a fiction. It's like a map of a dream, a map wherein one mile equals one mile. Something that is hyper-real is more real than real, not because something hyper-real exists but because reality doesn't exist. Patricia remembers this now. The other docent, the graduate student, he was explaining the concept to her when she noticed that she was spending her morning as a black woman.

"'It is no longer a question of a false representation of reality (ideology) but of concealing the fact that the real is no longer real, and thus of saving the reality principle,'" the grad student told her, quoting Baudrillard. He had longish black hair that hung down in his eyes, was wearing a plaid shirt and button fly jeans, and spoke without real inflection. Everything he said sounded like a question, like he was befuddled even as he was explaining it all.

"Does anything happen in the employee break room?" Charles asks. He's clearly impatient now, wanting to get to the good bits. I expect him to ask her if she might be forgetting something, like maybe there was an alien in the room with them, or maybe she had an out of body experience. Rain likes for there to be lots of big effects in his stories.

The grad student thought this concept of unreality, of hyper-reality, applied to Kruger's work because her work created the idea of a justice and equitable world that didn't exist. Her work was about the kind of society that could only exist in critique, only exist in comparison to something that's gone slightly wrong.

"Your moments of joy have the precision of military strategy," Kruger's poster read. What Kruger was positing, sneaking in, was the idea that there might be a joy, an enjoyment, that wasn't precise or specific, but that was generalized, polymorphous, and free.

"I'm not who I think I am," Patricia says. "I realized that. It took some time, but I figured it out."

UFOs and skepticism

The hypnotic session lasts for three hours and includes a lot of repetition, going over the basic facts again and again until we finally come up with something new that's even more absurd.

First off, to reiterate, Patricia had switched bodies. The woman who had been an artist's model became convinced that she was Patricia and the opposite happened as well. But then, after this switch what Asket, or maybe Patricia, figured out while at the Portland Art Museum, what the work of Barbara Kruger inspired her to remember, was that her real name, Patricia's real name, was Carole. Patricia was really Carole Flint.

Apparently before that art class, before the aliens even landed, Patricia had seen a UFO, and then, while trying to remember that encounter with the help from a prominent Ufologist, she'd switched bodies with his wife. . .with Harold's wife. And, what's worse is that this story involving Harold is something I remember. I've heard part of it before. That is, we did work with a contactee named Patricia. She'd auditioned for Harold and me back in 1986 and we ultimately decided not to work with her, not to include her in the book.

Harold nicknamed Patricia the Rainbow Woman because she'd come to Harold with this story about seeing a UFO at a Rainbow Gathering. We were especially allergic to what she had to offer us at the time as the book we were working on was entitled *UFOs and Skepticism*, but before we rejected her Harold spent several weeks working on her case. He'd examined her drawings, staged a Happening and, if I'm remembering correctly, gotten into a bit of trouble with this girl. Something about a visit to a hotel room.

"I went to his lecture at the Blue Stockings bookstore. He spoke about how Ufologists needed to stop seeking explanations and accept the experience as something that is opposed to all explanations. He thought he was being smart, but I knew. I knew he was lying," Asket says.

What happened was that Patricia participated in group sessions for several weeks, all the while repeating her story about the Nordic types who visited her during the Rainbow Gathering.

Back then, before the landing, Patricia was in her late twenties and floating around Haight-Ashbury as if she believed she would never reach thirty. She would work as a temp sometimes, usually as a secretary or in data entry, and on the weekends she helped out with a 'zine called *Processed World*. That was how she first heard about Harold. The people around that little 'zine were all big fans of Fluxus and mail art.

"Johnny invited me to the Rainbow Gathering. I was about to turn twenty-five, I had enough money for the trip, and we wanted to see a UFO," Asket says. "You were there," she says. She opens her eyes at this point, sits up and looks at Charles Rain.

"Relax," Rain tells her. "You're still relaxed," he says.

Asket closes her eyes again and lies back down on the couch. "What?" I ask.

"Was this back in '83?" Charles asks her.

"It was 1983."

"Then, yes. You're right. I was there," he says.

"You had a really long beard then, even longer than your beard is now, and you didn't stay in the woods but went back to the road, drove to a hotel."

"That's right," Charles says.

"Do you remember me?"

"No," Charles says.

"I look different. I look different now. I am different."

At that time Charles was lecturing a lot, going to Esalen, New Age conferences, and really anywhere that would pay a speaking fee. At that time part of the package, one of his promises, was that he would bring the UFOs with him.

"'Not everyone is able to see them,'" Asket says. "Your brochure said that not everyone could see the UFOs, and that sometimes people forget. But I saw them. The aliens showed up, just as advertised. Just as advertised."

The Pleidien craft looked right, it was exactly the kind of silver disc that she'd hoped for, but it didn't sound right. Patricia had expected to hear music. She expected the kind of music one hears emitted from a wind-up ballerina or a snow globe. She wanted to hear tinny notes produced by a metal comb or maybe organ music from a country fair.

"It didn't sound like a carousel," she said. Charles nodded. "It didn't have any sound at all."

The Christmas tree lights dropped down from the sky, everything went silent, and the Pleidiens put spiritual thoughts into her head. Looking at the saucer Patricia realized that the theory of reincarnation was true, that she'd been born many times. She realized that the Earth was in trouble, that humans needed to let go of fear and love each other, and so on. . .

It was exactly the junk food version of the UFO experience that Harold hated most. And Patricia's manner was exactly that of the airiest of West Coast airheads. He'd frequently complained that the dumbest parts of the '70s never ended, and this girl was a prime example. He'd wanted to get rid of her, had no interest at all in her story. That is, he had no interest until she asked him about his own UFO experience. She asked him a question she shouldn't have known to ask.

"Why did you tell them to leave back then? Back in the '50s?"

"What's that?" Harold asked back.

"Why did you do that? They wanted your help, they wanted you to be the one, but you said no."

Harold brought Patricia to his studio, set her up with paint and canvas and videotaped her Happening and when that didn't work, when he couldn't get anything more from her that way, he asked her to go to Budd Hopkins. They'd go together, she'd get hypnotized, and they'd find out what she'd really seen. But she wouldn't go. She just told him the same details over and over again, and wore him down that way, letting him grill her for information, letting him ask her the same question in as many different ways as he could think of, but always offering the same nonanswer.

"What did they look like?" he'd ask.

"They looked Swedish," she said.

"What color was their hair?"

"Nordic types."

"How did they talk, what language did they speak?"

"I don't know if they talked at all."

Or:

"How long were they there?"

"I just remember lights were white, green, red, and blue."

"Did they take you aboard?"

"It looked like a Christmas tree, only it was floating."

But most of all, what Patricia told him was this:

"They want you to know me."

"They want me to know about you?" Harold would ask.

"No. They want you to know me."

"They want me to know about you?"

"No. That's not it. They want you to know me," she'd say.

"Okay. Okay. But why? What is it about?"

"Why did you quit? What was it that you were afraid of learning?"

What was new to me about this story, what I didn't know before, was that Asket, or Patricia, whatever her name is doesn't matter. . .she met Carole. There was a confrontation.

"Harold went to her hotel at two a.m. on a Thursday night. And I followed him there," Asket says. "That's what I remembered. That was what I learned after the art class, after I switched bodies with Shelly. That's what I learned at the art museum that next day."

"What did you learn? Tell us exactly."

"The Pleidiens sent Patricia to him so they could switch us, so that Patricia could take my body and I could take hers. Only part of me went with her, or maybe more accurately, a part of me stayed with my body."

"Say that again? Who are you?" I ask.

"I'm Carole," she says. "The saucers made us trade. At the St. Vincent Residential Hotel, after the two of them, Harold and that girl, when they were finished fucking, I confronted them. And somehow, during that fight, we switched. I became Patricia."

"This," Charles says, "is fucking crazy."

Asket doesn't respond to this but just lies there on the couch, waiting for the next question. She looks like she's fast asleep, deeply asleep, and I wonder if she'll remember. I suppose that depends on what Charles Rain decides.

"You want her to remember this?" I ask.

"What do you mean? Remember what?"

"Remember that she was once married to Harold, for one thing," I say. "I think we should let her remember."

Charles nods, but it's clear that this isn't a point of interest, not to him. And looking at him with his chin in his hand, glancing over at Asket on the leather chaise watching her breathing, seemingly asleep, I realize that I'm no better off than I was at the start. We haven't asked her one thing about Virginia, about what happened, about where she is.

"Asket?" I start.

"We should stop now," Charles said.

"Wait a minute, I have to ask about Virginia. Where is she, Asket? Where did Virginia go? Did she surrender?"

"I don't remember," Asket says.

I regret calling Harold, regret agreeing to meet him at the Cedar Tavern, and most of all I regret telling him about Asket's hypnosis. The reason I regret this is that Harold is sitting at the bar drinking whiskey and Coke, brooding into his snifter, and I'm stuck talking to Charles Rain about, of all things, "American Cinema." He emphasizes the word *cinema*, the word must taste especially good in his mouth, but the only movies he knows anything about are big Hollywood sci-fi epics from thirty or more years ago. I count the liquor bottles, both the bottles and their reflections in the mirror, drink my own whiskey fast, and notice how the neon light behind the bar reflects onto the ceiling, while Charles tells me his theory about Stanley Kubrick's movie *2001*.

"He's a contactee," Charles says.

"Kubrick is?" I ask.

Harold is sitting on the other side of Rain, looking into his shot glass as if he's found money in it, and refusing to meet anyone's eye.

"If you've seen *2001* then you know why I say that," Charles explains.

"I would think you'd say it because you knew. Maybe your Space Brother buddies told you?"

"Oh no. We haven't discussed Kubrick, but that ending, with all the colors and the planet forming in the darkness, the oceans of light, I've seen all of that. I saw it in real time. Saw it for the first time in 1963 and not on a movie screen. Kubrick came very close to the truth there. Such a masterful representation. He must've seen it too," Charles says.

The reason we're talking about Stanley Kubrick is because, next to the mirror and right above the bar counter, there is a poster of Jack Nicholson from *The Shining*. I made the mistake of asking Charles if he'd seen the movie when there was a gap in his conversation, when he reached the end of his dissertation on *Forbidden Planet*.

"What did you think of the *E.T.*?" I ask.

"Haven't seen it," Rain tells me. "Any good?"

Harold interrupts finally. He picks up his shot glass, slams it down on the table, and then turns to us both and tells us we're idiots.

"How can you believe her?" he asks. "It's ludicrous."

"Uh…" I say. "You'll really need to be more specific."

It turns out that what's bothering Harold is the body switching. More specifically what bothers Harold is the fact that Asket claims to have remembered switching bodies. "Why would she think of herself as Carole?" he asks. "She knew, remembered, that she was really the black girl, that nude model, so why would she pursue me? It's nonsense. She's crazy."

Both of us agree with him. That is, we both agree that the story Asket told us doesn't make any sense, and if it weren't for the fact that she came to us in red sequins, if it weren't for the Missing Time, the imitation of my wife and the counter girl at the Gap, if it weren't for the fact that the UFOs have already landed, we'd agree with him.

"If this woman had come to me before the landing I too would turn her away. She might have spiritual insight, but her mind is too disordered. That story. . .there would've been nothing to do with it before," Rain says. "But she didn't come to me, she came to you, to your studio, last week, and then your friend here came to me."

Harold falls into silence again, just stares at his own reflection while the bartender pours him another whiskey and Coke. He frowns at himself and sits perfectly still on the bar stool, and I get the impression that he isn't thinking about anything, but just working on his rage. His rage is a physical object inside him and he's churning it around so that, when it's well mixed, he can spit it at us again.

"Why did you go to him?" Harold asks. "That's another thing that doesn't make sense. Why would you trust him? If the aliens are doing something other than selling books and video cassettes, if they have something more sinister in mind for us than occasional traffic jams and tithing for the moon, then wouldn't Rain be the last person you'd want to consult with?"

"I thought of that," I say. And I had thought of that, you remember. I've explained all that already, right?

"They don't talk to me," Charles says. "Not anymore. I get checks from them but they don't consult with me."

Harold knew that as well as anyone. It was one of his secret joys, and he clearly enjoyed making Charles say it out loud.

"They don't mind if you drink?" Harold asks.

"There is not stricture against alcohol," Charles says.

It's true, but it's also true that none of the Pleidiens drink. They don't have a rule against it but they do say that, once you reach enlightenment through their program, the desire for any kind of drug will disappear. That's one of their big hooks. Their success rate for treating alcoholism and drug addiction is something approaching 100 percent, or so they claim. They get a lot of people to surrender with that one.

"Yeah, why is it that you drink, Charles? I thought that wasn't a good vibration activity."

Charles doesn't say anything but just takes a sip of his lager. He gulps it down and then waves to the bartender, asking for another. Harold smiles at this. He's beginning to lighten up a little as Charles Rain's mood worsens. Charles turns on his stool, turns his back on me and faces Harold who is quietly laughing. The neon light reflects off of Harold's glasses and he tips his glass back and forth making the ice clink in his glass. His every move communicates smugness and superiority.

Rain turns on his bar stool and I'm worried. I don't want to watch. After everything, all the strangeness, the possibility of a bar fight still makes me want to avert my eyes.

"You want to know why I believe her, Harold?" Charles asks. "I believe her because I know. I know the truth."

Harold is shaking his head, still amused. None of this matters to him anymore. He's moved away from anger and into mockery, and none of it matters—not Asket, not Virginia, not me, and certainly not Charles Rain.

"What do you know, Charles?" he asks.

"I know that she was right. The Pleidiens did go to you first. You were their choice. Back in in 1957, during your sighting, that was them," Charles says. "That was them. They went to you. You were supposed to prepare the way for them. You were supposed to write *Sacred Saucer* and *Reincarnation in Space*."

"No," Harold says. "No I really wasn't."

"Maybe not. Fine, not those books, but others," Charles says. "You were meant to do it better. I'll admit it. You were supposed to write books that were better than those books, but you didn't. You told them no. You turned it all down."

"That's not exactly true," Harold says. "I did write better books."

But Charles has none of this. He accuses Harold of cowardice, of turning his back on his destiny. Harold just sneers.

"There is nothing so backward as the idea of fate or destiny except, maybe, the idea that these Pleidiens have something to offer humanity that can't already be found on the Home Shopping Network."

"That's not a denial," Charles says. "That's an explanation."

"Why haven't you started painting again, Charles? Now that the cosmic mission is complete, why not take that up again?" Harold asks.

"Do you deny it?" Charles asks.

"Oh, that's right. You can't return to painting because your paintings are as atrocious as this new religion you started."

"Do you...deny it?"

Harold empties his glass and then holds it up over the bar and soon the bartender is back. Harold swallows this round down in one go, and holds the empty glass up again.

"Do you?" Charles asks.

Charles clearly thinks he's got Harold by the balls with this question. Harold is a coward who couldn't face those lights from Kubrick's movie *2001*. Rain will admit anything, admit that Harold has the better mind, that Harold has the better understanding of the alien, the absurd, the control system, but Harold has to admit that Rain is the better, braver, man.

"Do you deny it?"

Harold is opening his mouth, about to deliver yet another insult, when I realize that I don't want, really can't allow, this to continue.

None of this is helping. My wife is missing and I'm here at the Cedar Tavern watching yet another round of what amounts to a thirty-five-year-long rivalry. Jack Nicholson and I have been silently watching, him from his frozen two dimensions and I from mine, but it's time to break free of this stasis and intervene.

"What does any of this have to do with Virginia?" I ask. "And why aren't you more interested? So what, it doesn't make linear sense, but she says she was once your wife. That is, Asket says she was Carole. She was, is, your dead wife," I say.

Harold looks at me, puts hands over his face, starts to reply, and then covers his mouth with his palm. I think for a moment that he's ashamed. I think, for just a moment, that he's listening to me.

"Wait a minute," Harold says. "That's what this is about. They're going to switch us, Charles. They sent her, this perky alien, so that they could switch us."

Charles looks like he might've grown pale but it's tricky to tell in this light especially with his beard covering so much of his face.

"Do you deny it?" he asks again, but his voice falters on the question mark.

They're ignoring me. For them the question is a game. It's more of the same pretend stuff that their careers are founded on, but I can't play along. My wife is gone. Asket has lost sight of who she is. And all of this is happening because of the Pleidiens. And what about Harold's wife? Did she die, was she killed, by these aliens?

"They're trying to take us apart," I say. "They want to deconstruct us, take the human race down, bit by bit."

"Do you deny it?" Charles asks.

They're not going to help me. These two are useless and I ask myself, why am I sitting around in a bar, why have I continued on with this routine, when I know that the Pleidiens are set on destroying, on deconstructing, the human race?

The thing is, I teach this stuff. I've shown my students *Rosemary's Baby*, both versions of the *Invasion of the Body Snatchers* movies, *The Manchurian Candidate*, and so on. I teach classes with names like "American Film Paranoia" and "The Affect of the Invasion," and in every class, at every screening, I always raise the same point:

The Paranoid style or aesthetic is a conservative one because the structure of a paranoid film demands naiveté. These movies require their characters to act as if they have faith in society. They have to have a sense of fair play, a compulsion to believe in justice, to believe in following the rules. In fact, the paranoid style makes such strong demands on a story, sets such strict limits on its characters, that there are often scenes that strain at the limits of credulity.

"You don't have to do this," Asket says.

I've got her by her elbow, by the sleeve of the woolen tunic she's wearing, it was Virginia's originally. When she tries to wiggle free of my grip I hold on tight to the seam and pull her closer to me.

We're standing on the circular concrete lawn of the Federal Building. The structure looks more like a cheese grater than anything, but I do feel a bit like an FBI agent standing here. I'm wearing my only formal suit, a dated cotton and polyester three piece with a pinstriped vest. I imagine I'm Robert Culp or some other middle-aged TV tough guy as I squint against the sun.

I really have to do this, no matter how naive it seems. Think of the 1978 version of *Invasion of the Body Snatchers*. In that one Donald Sutherland's character turns to the authorities repeatedly. He turns to the powers that be even after he discovers that most everyone in the city has been replaced by pod people. Sutherland knows that the mayor's office has been infiltrated. He knows that the police are covering up for the pod people, but when he finds his own duplicate in his backyard, when he discovers a gruesome half-formed monster version of himself, he calls the cops.

"This is a mistake," Asket says. The Federal Building's companion, the Court of International Trade, is a smaller glass and steel cube. Looking at them both—the small cube and the taller cheese grater—I feel as though the '70s never ended. The ugliness of the arrangement, the bare physical fact of these institutions presented without any ornamentation or facades, is absurd. What we're approaching is only a dingy memory of authority, which is why we're both of us acting as though we're in a movie. None of this has any more substance than that. This plaza, it's called Foley Square, is cut off from the rest of Manhattan by concrete buildings that are mostly parking lots. Standing at the entrance I feel like I've already broken some rule, already done something rash. I've squeezed in where I don't belong and now I'm seeing the pipes and electric wires that are meant to be hidden.

"We can still walk away," Asket says.

In a paranoid story even the characters that are cynics or nihilists have to at least occasionally act as if they have faith. At pivotal moments the structure of paranoia demands that the heroes act out of character.

In *Planet of the Apes*, for instance, Charlton Heston's character claims that humanity itself is a mistake. Heston starts the movie with the premise that interstellar space travel and the consequent time travel involved negates all human meaning and human authority. He says that he's glad to be disconnected from the values and norms that gave his life a shape before. And yet, even he is shocked to find a society ruled by apes. Even he can't face the reality of the destruction of human society. By the middle of the movie it turns out that Heston doesn't believe what he says. He can't believe it. The movie won't let him believe it.

"Time bends and space is boundless. It squashes a man's ego. He begins to feel like no more than a mote in the eye of eternity," Heston says at the start, during the scene in the space capsule. And yet. . .and yet he's still shocked, terribly shocked, when he discovers a world filled with damned dirty apes.

Asket tells me that she can't promise me anything if we go inside. She can't vouch for what she'll do or how things will turn out. Once we're past security she'll offer me no help at all if things go wrong.

"They know we're coming," she says. "This isn't what you want to do."

"It'll be okay," I say.

But it won't be. Every step of what's to come is planned out in advance, and they, the FBI, the Pleidiens, whoever, they won't be making any mistakes. There is no chance of a success. Not this way, not if I go at them directly.

"If we walk into the Federal Building we'll be walking into a trap. They're prepared for us. What they haven't prepared for is what happens if we walk away," Asket says. "We could go to Harold. Isn't that what you promised me from the start? That's what I want."

"Are they going to shoot me?" I say.

"No."

"Then what will happen? What are you so afraid of?" I ask.

"We can still leave," she tells me.

"No. No. We can't," I say. And it's true. It's true even though I know better.

Past the double doors of the cheese grater we find an FBI man waiting for us under the exit sign. He's a black man with a shaved head and a furrowed brow, and his blue suit and clip-on badge both hang straight on him. He's perfectly prepared for us, ready to show us around, and bring us up to date.

"Mr. Johnson," he begins, "it's a pleasure to meet you. I've read your books."

Asket steps past me, stands next to the FBI agent, and opens her eyes wide as if to remind me that she'd warned me off this. She was right, obviously.

I reach out to the agent, offer my hand to him, and prepare myself for his grip.

"You've read my work?" I ask.

"Yes, *Missing Time*," he says. "Very helpful material. You and Mr. Flint do fine work. A bit creative for the Bureau, of course, but helpful."

The agent, his name is Cokely, tells me that they are prepared to take a statement from me, that they've been hoping I'd come in. In fact, they've been trying to recruit my colleague Flint for quite awhile but have been holding back from contacting me. The job of national security has changed dramatically, obviously, but they still need civilian help, and there has been an effort to bring MUFON, and really the whole field of Ufology, into the fold now that the saucers have landed. Still, they've had to go slow.

Cokely swipes his badge across a plastic rectangle by a steel-framed door and there is a click. Passing from the exterior hallway to the back office the light changes. The bright track lighting of the lobby is gone and then we find ourselves in dim, stale rooms. Fluorescent lights make these back offices seem dingy, pale, and ordinary, and amidst the metal desks, push button phones, and IBM clones, I involuntarily relax.

"We can talk over here," Cokely tells me. He shows us to a cubicle on the far side of the vast room and we seat ourselves on metal folding chairs while he parks himself behind his small desk and keys a few commands into his machine. We wait for him to start, listen to the hum of his computer monitor and the keyboard clacking in the otherwise silent space, but nothing happens. He keeps typing, on and on, while we wait.

"Mr. Cokely," I say.

"Just a moment," he replies.

The agent is stoic. His brow still furrowed, his typing loud as he hunts and pecks his way across his beige keyboard, but otherwise he's emotionless. This is all routine. Any sense that I might have had that this agent was in public relations evaporates as he finds one letter and then the next on his keyboard. I try to watch his hands, to see what he's typing, but his hands are fast.

"Mr. Johnson," the FBI agent addresses me. "Why have you come to visit us today?"

Why have I come to visit him today? Not him, but them. Why have I come to visit the FBI today, of all days? What did I hope to accomplish?

"The Pleidiens," I start, "cannot be trusted."

Cokely doesn't respond, but waits for me to say more. I have his full attention and he cocks his head and waits.

I tell him about Asket, the Gap, Missing Time, and how my wife has gone missing and he types it all in, or I assume he's typing in what I say. I tell him that the Space Brothers are undermining us. They're trying to undo us somehow.

"They are changing us," I tell him. "I think they're changing us. I don't understand it all, but Asket's story is that one of them changed who she was. She switched around with another woman. She became an artist's model, and before that. . .well, she says she used to be Harold Flint's wife."

Asket shifts in her chair and when I glance over at her I see that her face is reddening. I'm embarrassing her.

"Well that's what you said at Rain's. That's what you said. I thought you remembered," I say. Asket doesn't say anything, but looks away. She turns her head away and glances over at the cubicle. She's pretending not to have heard?

"Mr. Johnson," Mr. Cokely says. "I want to show you something."

The FBI agent produces a wave machine from a desk drawer. It's a clear plastic rectangle filled with blue mercury and positioned on a chrome base. The agent sets it down in front of me and flips a switch. When he turns it on I hear the sound of the ocean.

"Have you ever read *Meditations on First Philosophy* by René Descartes?" the FBI agent asks me. The wave in the rectangle is undulating slowly, irregular but predictable, and I nod slowly.

"I have," I tell him.

"What did you get out of it?" he asks.

"I think," I tell him and look up from the wave machine to meet his gaze. "Therefore, I am."

"Right," he says. Only he draws it out. "Riiigghhttt."

It turns out that Cokely really wants to tell me about Descartes. He wants to explain it to me, but not the cogito part, but the section about wax:

"'Perhaps it was what I now think, viz. that this wax was not that sweetness of honey, nor that agreeable scent of flowers, nor that particular whiteness, nor that figure, nor that sound, but simply a body which a little while before appeared to me as perceptible under these forms, and which is now perceptible under others. But what, precisely, is it that I imagine when I form such conceptions? Let us attentively consider this, and, abstracting from all that does not belong to the wax, let us see what remains. Certainly nothing remains excepting a certain extended thing which is flexible and movable,'" he says. Then he reaches out to the wave machine and puts his hand on top, feeling the movement of the plastic rectangle as it slowly seesaws up and down. After a few seconds of this he stands up, walks around the desk, and approaches Asket. He walks around her, and takes hold of the metal backrest, and turns her chair.

"Who is this?" he asks me.

Asket smiles at me, then she leans forward and takes my hand. "Who am I, Brian?" she asks.

"I don't know who she is," I tell Cokely. "I can't keep track."

And this is when the bad thing starts to happen, this is when they spring their trap. Another woman, another version of Asket, appears at just this point. She steps from behind the cubicle wall, walks up to where the agent is standing, and puts her arm around his shoulder. This version of Asket is shorter than the one I came in with, but she's wearing the same stupid sequined jumper that Asket donned at the start. One difference though is that this one has on purple mascara, the kind of mascara that trapeze artists, stage actresses, or call girls might wear in order to emphasize their eyes even at a distance.

It's Virginia, of course. Not Asket at all.

"People are like wax," she says.

There is nothing in her stance, in the way she moves, or in her manner of speech, that is the same as it was. I don't really know who she is.

"We are constantly changing as we age. We gain or lose weight, our skin loses its elasticity, we might imbibe chemicals or drugs, cut our hair short or grow it long, and yet through it all we think of ourselves and each other as constants. We give each other names, ascribe personality traits, develop all manner of ideas about one another."

"Is this your wife?" Cokely asks.

"Maybe."

"Is this Virginia Johnson, formerly Virginia Keenan?"

"I don't know."

"There is nothing you can point to, is there, Brian? No way that you can find one fixed quality in her and say 'this is my wife.' The pattern has changed. That's what a person is. A person is a pattern, a way of going, and that's what we recognize and call 'wife' or 'friend' or 'FBI agent,'" the agent says. "But these ideas aren't the same thing as the people who we give the name, these ideas aren't bodies, they aren't our arms or brains or any physical part of us."

"These ideas are our spirit," the woman says.

The woman who I'm sure is my wife steps up to me, takes my hand, and gives it a squeeze. She puts her other hand against my cheek, and I feel nauseous. This is all going wrong.

Mr. Cokely returns to his desk and puts away the wave machine while this woman who might be Virginia continues to explain. I glance over at Asket now and find she's smiling. She's staring at this shorter version of herself, this New Age bimbo, and smiling at her like a morning talk show host smiles. Asket is nodding along.

"Descartes showed us that the concept of wax was empty. The concept doesn't match up to any one empirical fact but was an idea about a collection of empirical facts. People are the same. People, the idea of a person like your wife, are concepts. They are ideas we use to speak about sets of empirical facts," this woman says.

"Think of it this way," Cokely tells me. "What's your favorite song?"

"My favorite song?"

"Or your least favorite," he says. "It doesn't matter."

"Chopin's 'Prelude,'" I say. "'Number four.'"

Cokely looks pleased with this choice. He tells me to imagine that I've gone to the store and purchased Chopin's greatest hits on vinyl, to pretend that I did this thirty years ago, in 1962.

"You purchased a recording of John Browning," Cokely suggests. "And you've played the record a hundred or a thousand times over the years. You've tried to take care of it, always stored it in its sleeve, but despite your best efforts the record has become scratched. About a minute in there is a deep scratch on the record and it skips. You know what I mean?"

I nod.

"Now," he asks, "would you replace the record? Would you maybe buy a copy of Chopin's 'Preludes' on compact disc?"

I get where he's going with this analogy, but it still seems wrong to me.

"No, wait. Listen. If you were to buy Chopin's 'Preludes' on CD, a remastered compact disc of the same John Browning performance, would you be listening to the same music when you got it home?"

"It would be the same pianist?" I ask.

"It would be the same recording. It would just be a digitally remastered copy of the same original magnetic tapes," he says.

"Then, yes. It would be the same music."

"But," he says, "the music would sound different. The music would have a richer tone, it would be cleaner. These new compact discs can store more information than vinyl records, with less information in the low frequency range, but more in the high frequency range. And a CD, it won't scratch at all. There wouldn't be any hiss. Are you sure it would be the same music?"

"Yes."

"But the object would be completely different, it would be a different size, it wouldn't be grooved. The CD isn't the same body, the same physical object, at all. But it's the same song," he says.

"It's the same song," I agree. "But, Mr. Cokely, you're not listening to me. I came here today because my wife is missing."

"Your wife is missing?" he asks. He glances at the woman in the sequined jumpsuit and then looks back at me.

"Listen, people aren't songs. People aren't piano music." I feel like doing something physical, maybe grabbing this woman who looks like Virginia, maybe dragging this man, this agent, out of his chair and shaking him. Asket is still smiling blankly as if somebody has put her on pause. I can't even tell if she's breathing.

"Virginia," I say.

"I'm not Virginia," the woman tells me.

I turn to Asket. She is still smiling, still vacant.

Cokely nods at the woman who says she's not my wife and she steps over to the edge of the cubicle and around the corner. When I stand up to go after her Cokely is on me, pushing me back down in the chair and holding me there.

"Wait a minute," he says. "Hold on a minute, Mr. Johnson. You just hold on a minute."

"Virginia!" I shout. Then I shout her name again. "Virginia! Virginia! Virginia!" I shout out to her, but of course she doesn't return. She's gone now. Somehow I know it. She turned the corner and then disappeared.

"Mr. Flint," Cokely says.

"No," Asket says. Her smile falters. "This is Johnson."

"Mr. Johnson," Cokely says. He has me pinned on my chair, his face is right up next to mine so that we're nose to nose, he's spitting my name at me, and again I involuntarily relax. It dawns on me right now how I can break out of this. They think they've got a tight hold on me, that they've got this all figured out, but they've forgotten something vitally important.

"Okay, okay. We're all songs. Concepts, names, they're like songs. But. . ." I say. "But, what about Christmas?"

Back in the early '60s, when I was five or six years old, I figured out what it meant to have a personality. It was during the holidays, maybe a week or two before Christmas, and we were at the local elementary school for a Christmas pageant and arts and craft sale. My mother was concerned that I not get separated from her in the crowd, she was concerned that I would get lost amidst the bubble lights and paint by number wooden ornaments. I remember watching the chorus that was on stage in the gymnasium, walking the length of basketball court with my mom, and looking back and forth at the folding tables set up as sales booths. There were fruitcakes and cookies, Christmas ornaments and lights, homemade gift-wrap, strange wooden lawn ornaments of gnomes and goblins, and all manner of hardback books with purple and red covers.

The thing was, while I was walking and looking at Christmas, at this Christmas pageant, I realized that one thing about it was always the same. I was always at the center of it all. What made me different, what set me apart from the other children and parents, what set me apart from the merchandise, the paint-by-number Frosty placard, from my mother even, was that I was at the center. I was the personality through which everything else had to pass.

"Hold my hand," my mother told me. And I realized that I had a personality. That I was friendly and funny. I was smart and precocious. I was bad even, a little bit selfish. But, the point was, that I was me. There was nobody else that was me and all the fruitcakes and Christmas pageants were set up around that fact. We might, each of us, have a personality, but I definitely did. I was there, in that moment. I was taking everything in, and I was Brian Johnson.

"What about that?" I ask. "What about the solution? The 'I think' part," I asked.

The agent frowns at me but he loosens his grip and steps back. "Mr. Johnson," he says. "You came here to warn the Federal Bureau of Investigation about the Pleidien threat. Is that right?"

"That's right."

"We at the Bureau appreciate your loyalty, your patriotism, your humanism," Cokely says. "But the thing is, Mr. Johnson, you aren't in any position to explain this to us. We at the Bureau, we understand what is happening much better than you or Mr. Flint, and while we want your help, you are not going to be the ones to explain this to us. Do you understand what I'm trying to tell you? Are you following me here?"

I don't. Not exactly.

"Let's show him," Asket says. "I think it's time we show him."

And there are hands on my shoulders, on my back, under my arms. I'm being lifted from my chair, my hands are behind my back, and I find myself walking, trying to keep up and walk in the direction they are shoving me. There are two more FBI agents now, I can't see their faces, but I can sense them behind me and looking down and to my left and right I see their blue trousers and black leather shoes.

"We're going to show you now," Asket says. She's jogging along beside me and her eyes are open wide and I think that, while nobody has their hands on her, nobody is manhandling her, she's being moved along too. "We're going to show you the truth now," she says.

One of the doors in the Javits Federal Building leads to a flying saucer. I'm not sure how this is done, whether or not there is a bit of Missing Time involved here or whether there is some sort of teleportation at work, but when we turn the corner around a carpeted cubicle wall and Cokely takes hold of the chrome door handle, I find myself in one of Charles Rain's saucers. We're back in time or seem to be. Surrounded by mainframe computers with blinking lights, we're in a room with curved walls and an oval-shaped desk, a white plastic desk with an egg-shaped chair behind it. And, in the chair, there is Ralph Reality. He's sitting there in his jumpsuit looking like Barry Gibb from the Bee Gees, only without the beard.

"Ah, Brian," Ralph Reality greets me. "Sit down. Sit down." The agents pull up a plastic stool for me and then pushes down on my shoulders so that I sit again.

Reality's smile doesn't falter as he waits for me to speak, waits for me to break the silence. The computers are churning around us, paper is falling from a slot a few yards to my left, and I focus on the rhythm of it, counting the beats as each connected sheet emerges and folds along the perforation before heading down onto what I've decided is some kind of linoleum floor.

Asket walks around the oval desk and stands next to Reality. She reaches behind her back and unhooks her dress as he opens a hidden drawer under the flat surface and pulls out a jumpsuit for her. It's a clean white polyester number with red sequins on the front and Asket pulls her dress off over her head and stands naked for a moment before stepping into these new clothes and zipping up.

"You realize now," Ralph Reality says, "that your wife is not your wife. The question is, what else do you know?"

Ralph Reality wants me to respond to cartoons. He places a pile of 3 x 5 flashcards on the plastic oval desk in front of me and asks me a series of questions about each cartoon, photograph, and painting. The first card depicts a group of seven men and women—four women and three men—divided into two groups. The first group contains four people (two women and two men) and the second contains three people (two women and one man). The men and women are all of them dressed for business, each one young and attractive, and all of them working on their careers, on bettering themselves, and on getting ahead. I can tell all this about them despite the fact that the men and women consist only of solid black shapes and negative space. That is, these people have no features, no faces. The face is supplied by the viewer. I supply each person with a face as I fill in the gap between where the solid black shape of their clothes end and the solid black shape of their hair begins. There is nothing in between.

"What are they talking about?" Ralph Reality asks me.

Above each of the figures there is an empty speech balloon, and Reality wants me to fill these in. To create dialogue for the scene.

"They could be talking about anything," I say. "There is no way to tell. That's the whole point of it. The point is that we, the viewers, don't know what these hip and important people are saying to each other. The point is that they know something and we don't."

Reality nods, apparently I've said the right thing, but then he presses me. "Okay, that's true, but make a guess. What might they be saying?"

Asket has come up behind me, she's gently stroking my back and looking down at the cartoon print with me. I glance up at her with the hope of some sign of camaraderie, some sign that she's still on my side, but all I get back is a look of sincere compassion and encouragement. She seems to be trying to assure me that I can answer the question. It may seem difficult, she's saying, but I can find the right answer. I squint at her, trying to convey some message back to her, something along the lines of "fuck yourself," but she just frowns her concern at me. All I get from her is more and more sincerity.

"I can't tell what they're saying. Probably something about which copy machine is best or how to use a fax machine," I say. "The whole thing looks very corporate."

Reality waits for a moment, maybe hoping I'll say something more, and then sighs and flips the card over so that I can try again.

The next one is a blue card with black outlines of two faces, two silhouettes of a man and a woman facing each other, pressed against each other as if for a kiss. It's a Venn diagram of faces actually with the two profiles sharing a common nose.

One of the faces is a solid black and one is a light grey, so the nose is a mix, it's a charcoal color.

The thoughts of the two heads, the images inside their skulls, are different. The man's head is full of gears while the woman has a head with a more organic tree shape inside. The thought inside of the woman's head is filled with branches and roots. The woman's thought is growing while the man's idea just keeps clicking along, round and round, repeating.

"What's this about?" Reality asks me.

"It's about language," I say. "It's about men and women and their opposed way of communicating."

"That's good," Reality says. "But what are they saying to each other?"

"They aren't actually talking at all," I say. "It's something more like telepathy happening."

Reality seems excited by this answer and he leans over his desk, toward me, and I watch his sequins flash as he shifts position under the lights.

"What are they thinking?" he asks. "What are they thinking about?"

"Are they planning something?" Asket asks. Ralph Reality looks up at her, surprised at her, surprised that she might try to lead me. His glance silences her but it's too late.

"They're not planning or talking," I say. "This is just a symbol. The point isn't what the characters say here, but what they represent. You don't read it for a story, but for something else."

The next image shows another face in profile, this time the face is set against a red background and the top of the head is opened up, a partial circle with a rounded edge set at a 90-degree angle from the rest of the head, like a toilet lid on an open toilet. From inside the head there are arms reaching up and out. The hands are open too, the hands are seeking help. There are people inside this psyche, this head, that want out. There are four people, one blue, one dark green, one white, one darker red, and all of them are grasping for support.

"What's the story with this picture?" Ralph Reality asks.

"What did you do to my wife?" I ask back.

"What do you mean?" he says. "Which one? Which wife?"

"My real wife," I say.

"Your real wife? You don't have a real wife," Reality says. "Mr. Johnson, I understand that you are confused, and that you want answers, but you really should try harder. Answer these questions. We can help you."

"I don't want to play your games," I say. "I'm not going to play your games, not willingly. If you want me to keep answering your questions you'll have to do something more. You'll have to make me answer."

"You want your wife back, is that it? Either this woman here or some other one?" he asks.

Ralph Reality starts flipping the flash cards over, one at a time. He slowly flips over one card and then the next, making sure I have time to see each image before it's replaced, but no longer asking questions. There is a photograph of a fist punching through a light green plaster wall, there is Holbein's *Ambassadors* with its hidden skull, some wavy lines, Betty Page in silk lingerie and black stockings leaning against a stool with her mouth open wide, there is Garfield the cat, another pin-up model only her head has been replaced by the head of a giraffe, and so on. . .

It's the computers, more than these images, that are the problem. If they weren't clicking and clacking so consistently, if there wasn't such a steady rhythm of beeps and printing,

I could keep up better with what's happening, with what these images mean and what they're doing to me.

Asket leans over and whispers in my ear. "Brian, you're very close to it now. We just need you to answer a few of these to know for sure."

But I don't know what the answers are, not anymore. Manet's *Olympia* flashes by, a happy family standing in line at a bank, the words "maestro" and "toaster oven." I don't know what these things mean and I don't know what the aliens want from me or what they want me to say.

another break

There is another break here in the text. It's here because what happened on board the UFO, what Ralph Reality ultimately told me, what he demanded of me, can't easily be expressed in words. There will be another break like this one, a bit later on, when Asket or Virginia or Carole (whatever you want to call her is fine) recounts her own transformation aboard Reality's spaceship. That one will hopefully be a bit more lyrical, more imagistic and concrete, than this. The aim in this later break will be to bring you the reader into the moment, to convince you that something really did happen. Something mystical and strange did happen, or will happen. But, for now, all you're getting is this disruption.

When I was on Ralph Reality's ship and he was flipping through those flashcards, when Asket demanded that I answer, that I fill in the meanings of the icons and images they were giving me, something slipped. In fact, the point of the interrogation wasn't to get information from me, but really it was this break that was their aim. I'd come in to the FBI offices determined to bring a fight, but they were ready for me and it turned out that a fight wasn't possible because every possible blow I might deliver was destined to miss the target and boomerang back. I wanted to expose them, but I only exposed myself. I wanted to fight them, but only ended up back here. I only ended up walking through Times Square surrounded by flashing messages from Coca-Cola signs, stacked monitors displaying the clean and well-scrubbed faces of casual fashion models set against primary colors, and the geometric face of the Lucky Goldstar logo. Underneath the glitter and glam of Times Square Asket is explaining why she sometimes looks like my disappeared wife even though she doesn't.

"There is a network of associations that we use to interpret objects in the world, a network of ideas that allows us to recognize that the yellow shape in front of us is a single thing, a taxi cab, even as its shape appears to change as it rolls past. Looking at the taxi from the front reveals an entirely different set of shapes and impressions than looking at the same vehicle from the side, diagonally, or from the back, but because of the way we have learned to associate certain signals we make it out as a New York taxi and not as the strange warping thing, the confusion of color and sound, that perception alone would reveal," she says. She's monologuing here and I wonder how long it's been that she's been talking. I wonder how long it's been that we've been walking and whether it would be possible to retrace our steps. There was a toaster oven on a flashcard, there was Asket's warning, her admonishment that I should cooperate, and now there is the Lucky Goldstar logo and her prattle.

"The reason you think I'm your wife has to do with the idea of your wife, the network of associations that really is your wife. It's not about what I look like," she says. "Think of this, everything and everyone on the streets of New York move to the same time signature, right? I mean roughly everyone does, and that's something you have to pick up on when you're in New York City. You can tell the tourists from how they move, from how they miss the beat, but when these tourists figure it out, when they move with the crowd, they're New Yorkers."

We're walking like New Yorkers ourselves, keeping to the beat, but we could walk slower or faster and become Mexicans or Swedes.

Asket is looking at her feet as she walks and I'm watching her legs and feet too. She's not in her sequined jumpsuit anymore. What I'm watching is how her orange and white striped skirt moves, how her hips sway a bit with each step. This isn't really how Virginia walked or walks. We're on 46th Street, on restaurant row, moving under foliage, under leaves from the small trees planted along the curb, and underneath awnings and signs that read Broadway Joe's, Galaxy, and Barbetta's.

"You're different," I say to her. "How are you different?"

"I'm a network of associations that knows about networks, about switching and moving and time signatures," she says. "I'm a Pleidien."

She moves a lock of her sandy blond hair behind her ear and licks her lips and I wonder if she's always had sandy blond hair or if, at one point, she was a brunette. She's waiting for me to ask another question, to ask about what will happen to me now that I know, or almost know, what she knows, but I change the subject.

"Let's get a drink," I say. I gesture to Barbetta's restaurant and then ask it again. "You want a drink? You hungry? Let's get lunch."

Inside Barbetta's we find candles, pink walls, and ornate eighteenth-century furniture. The chandelier above our table is a glory of ironwork and glass and to our left there is a harpsichord. The rest of the diners are dressed in blue and black business suits or red or peach-colored silk dresses but we press on and order duck and white wine and I'm pleased to discover that Asket is uncomfortable in her wool skirt, it's too informal for this network apparently. I put my hand in the pocket of my grey vest, in the top left pocket, and tap my chest.

Asket's hand shakes a bit as she takes a sip of her wine. She puts her hand to her head and looks down at the pristine white tablecloth. You'd expect, given the decor, that the tables would be a bit dusty, but they aren't.

"Explain something to me," I say. "It's something that's been bothering all of us. That is, it's been bothering Harold, Rain, and me. That first time you switched you were an artist's model. That is, you were this model and then you were Patricia, but Patricia had been Carole before. Why is it that you, the person who had been this model decided that, when you realized you'd been switched. . .that is, why didn't you try to get that model identity back? Why did you decide that Carole was the real you? I don't understand."

"I told you already. I explained that."

"Take me through it again," I say.

"I remembered that switch first. I remember being Carole and then becoming Patricia instead," she says.

"But that wasn't your memory. I mean, when you realized that you'd been that artist's model, when you recalled that that switch was the most recent one, why did you care about the earlier memory? Shouldn't the most recent switch be the one that matters? And even if it isn't, even if you have to go back to the first switch ever, wouldn't you have to talk to the woman who had been Patricia and had become the artist's model in order to find the original?"

"I can't explain it rationally," she says. "It isn't like that. It wasn't about what was original or intellectually true."

"What then? What was the basis? How did you decide?"

"It was about feelings. It was about how remembering being Harold's wife made me feel."

She'd reached out to Flint back in January, sending him a few postcards and letters and then, in early February finding him through a computer bulletin board system called the Well. She'd read about the service, found out about the group of high-tech free spirits in Sausalito who had set up some computers and modems in the basement of the office building that housed the *Whole Earth Review* when she picked up a copy of *Mondo 2000* magazine from the SFSU bookstore in December of 1991. The woman on the cover was standing in a cathedral, dressed in a brown robe that might've been burlap or might've been silk, a woman who looked like either a fashion model or a monk. And she'd purchased the magazine because the cover advertised an article on Identity Construction along with one on DMT Elves and Project Blue Beam.

The essay on Identity Construction wasn't much. Changing careers wasn't what Asket wanted to read about, but a short essay about the Well had caught her attention. This computer bulletin board connected people in the Bay Area to the internet and, conversely, connected people outside the Bay Area to these users of the Well through the internet. The organizers and managers for the Well thought of themselves as cyber-environmentalists and life hackers, but what interested Asket was the fact that Harold Flint was apparently a member.

"He'd ignored my postcards and letters," she tells me. And then, after taking another sip of wine, she waits for me to prompt her.

"You found him through this computer network?" I ask.

"We started talking in the mind/body conference, during a flame war about the split, but soon enough it was all private," she says. "He sent email."

On the Well's forum Asket got Harold's attention right away. She interrupted a conversation between Harold and some psychedelic guru in Berkeley by mentioning the name of a hotel. She told Harold that she knew him, that they'd known each other, and she'd mentioned the hotel where they had, the two of them, solved the mind/body problem in real time.

"I'm the Oregon City contactee," she told him. And that was true in a way. That is, she no longer thought of herself that way, but she was in fact stuck in that position, in that personality. Then she told Harold the name of her favorite drink and her old room number.

The fact that Harold had slept with Patricia, that he'd slept with one of his UFO clients, doesn't surprise me. It didn't surprise me then, when it happened. At least, it didn't surprise me much. At Black Mountain his collaborations had led to a number of short-lived romances with both men and women, including Walker. Flint isn't a particularly warm person, but he isn't asexual.

"I've had my own dealings in that direction," I said. When I first met Harold, when we first started co-writing, or to put it more accurately and bluntly, when I'd first been hired to ghostwrite his books, there were a few incidents that led me to wonder if he was interested. He was with Carole then too.

"You think he's tried to seduce you?" Asket asks. "Sometime in the past, somewhere in your memory, you think he made a pass at you?" She finds the idea funny.

"We originally communicated through the mail. Just like the two of you, actually. He sent along some collages and some of those collages had had a sexual component. A few were overtly erotic. Homoerotic even."

She puts her chin in her hand and her fingers over her mouth to hide a smile. "What did he send you? Describe one of the images."

One had been from a gay porn magazine. "Two body builders making love. A black body builder and a white body builder. The black muscle man taking the white one from behind only Harold had replaced their heads with cut outs from *National Geographic*. The black man had the head of goat, a ram, and the white body builder's head had been replaced by the head of a raccoon."

Asket puts her head down so that her right hand is pressed against her forehead. She looks down at the tablecloth. She's laughing, quietly laughing. "I think you're misremembering," she says. "It's very interesting to hear about though."

"It is?"

"He didn't send me collages."

"No?"

"He was, after some time, direct with me," she says. "He made it clear."

I don't know what to say to this so I return to my meal, or what's left of it. I pick through my green beans, now cold, with my salad fork.

"You're jealous," she says.

For Asket the mind/body forum was a playground, a virtual space for an erotic game. She asked Harold why, if he knew the answer to the mind/body problem, he wouldn't just come right out and tell her what it was. Why was he always just insinuating at it, hinting, but never really explaining?

In private email she wrote: "You tell me that you want to relive our nights together. Which part of you wants to do that? Your body or your mind?"

"I don't remember telling you I want to relive anything" he wrote back. "What are you? Psychic?"

When they communicated publicly at the Well he was curt and academic with her. He answered her questions about sensations and identity, about her sense of disconnection from her body, her worries about her identity, with quotes from Hegel and Plato and French philosophers like Althusser. He was a namedropper, but then he'd send her a dirty poem or provoke her with a question.

"Ideologies are fantasies that support our relationships with each other and these false pictures give us our very identities. In fact, we don't really fantasize about the world, but rather we are the fantasy," he wrote to her in the philosophy forum.

"Where do these fantasies come from? Where is the origin?"

He responded to this question privately, by email. "Our fantasies, like this one we're concocting about each other, don't have an origin. We're making it now by acting it out, or typing it out."

We order another bottle of wine and then wait for the waiter in silence. Looking down at the tablecloth I find a spot where I've spilled some wine. I feel a bit of panic about this and then let out my breath slowly. I think I'm the one who is drunk.

"For me the problem wasn't just academic, it wasn't just a game," Asket says.

"The problem? What problem?"

"The mind/body problem."

third space

Our fourth book, the one we stopped writing when the saucers landed, was entitled *The Third Space*. The idea was to take Jacque Vallée's idea that the UFO phenomenon was a kind of mythic control system and run with it. We would explain the UFO phenomenon not from the perspective of astrophysics or conspiracy theories, we'd put the extraterrestrial hypothesis aside. Instead of from outer space the aliens were from this Third Space, a space that was neither internal to people nor out there in the world. The Third Space was something humans had been creating since we'd come down from the trees. To say it was from the imagination was to miss it, but in modern society it had become primarily associated with the arts. The Third Space was where ideas were independent and freely associated. It was a realm where things were implied but could never be directly known. The Third Space was where our lives were acted out and yet, it was a place without people. None of us could yet sustain a life there.

"It's like television," I say.

"What's that?"

"The Third Space is like a television screen."

Asket nods. This was the kind of thing that she'd gone to Harold for, what she wanted Harold to explain to her. If she wasn't her body and she wasn't just her ideas, just the thoughts in her head, then what was she? She could change her body, swap it around for someone else's, but she always lost a bit of herself in the process. Part of her always came out different. Was there anything that was fixed, permanent, or real? And if not, then how was there anything at all? How could everything be a mere appearance without there also being something real? What would a mere appearance be an appearance of if there was nothing behind or beyond it?

"This Third Space," she says. "It's real?"

"I have no idea," I say.

Jacques Vallée wrote that the control system was "the means through which man's concepts are being rearranged" and that because this system works on the level of myth or imagination the visions and experiences the control system delivers are always absurd. What we added, what Harold believed before the landing, was that the control system had a goal, an end. The goal was to make itself visible. The control system was something we had built, something we were always building and rebuilding, and when we recognized that we were building this system, and that it was a system of control, we'd be free.

"That's what I promised him," Asket says.

"What do you mean?"

"I'd tried a hundred different ways to tell him what was happening, to tell him what I'd experienced, who I thought I was…"

"You thought you were his wife," I say. "But you never told him that."

"Not directly," she says.

"What did you tell him?"

"That I could help him be free."

Harold was excited by Patricia when he saw her at the convention center and she hated to disappoint him with the news that she was actually his wife. After all, the misunderstanding wasn't exactly accidental. She had traveled across the country to meet him at the MUFON symposium, and while her main goal was to tell him what had happened to her in 1986, what had, finally, happened again, she had other ambitions too, and she wasn't exactly surprised that all Harold wanted was to make sure that she had his room key.

They compared their schedules, got everything arranged, and then, assured, he left her to explore the steel struts and glass walls of the Jacob Javits Convention Center while he prepared to give a speech.

The lecture was to be about Flint's idea of the self-confirming falsehood, and, while the program notes didn't make this plain, the photograph that accompanied the description of his topic insinuated that the Pleidiens were themselves examples of this idea.

Patricia arrived around eleven a.m. when the late morning sun was nearly directly overhead. Standing in warm natural light amidst the Pleidiens and UFO enthusiasts, looking up at the latticework of steel and the stair-step pattern of glass cubes overhead, Asket enjoyed the open exposure. The bustling of the crowd under the high ceiling, the open air, the sunlight, and the television monitors mounted here and there, made her feel safe. The moment was both ordinary and ordered. The organizers, the architects, the staff members and government officials manning the booths, they knew what they were doing. Everything was under control.

It was only when she found a folding chair by the main stage, only when Harold began to speak, that her stomach flipped and her anxiety returned.

"A self-confirming falsehood," Harold said, "can only be discovered in a dream or in a hallucination."

Here's how it went: What was required for a statement to be discovered as both self-confirming and false was for one to become lucid. He gave the example of dreaming that one was in Paris, perhaps on the metro, and of hearing a Parisian man or woman say the following: "This sentence is in French." Harold made a special point of repeating this.

"'This sentence is in French,'" he said. "'This sentence is in French.' Only, of course, it isn't in French. The sentence 'This sentence is in French,' is in English. However, if you're dreaming that you're in Paris and you hear a woman dressed in the latest French fashion, whatever that might be, let's say she's wearing a beret and a nautical sweater with black and white stripes, when such a dream woman says the sentence 'This sentence is in French' you are likely, if you're dreaming or feverish or even if your just newly arrived in Paris and surrounded by a cacophony of the French language in a public space, you're likely to think to yourself, that sentence is self-evidently true. And, in fact, if you understand the sentence as something spoken in French then it is self-evidently true. Just as 'This sentence is in English' is self-evidently true right now."

To Asket, Harold seemed unreal. Up on stage he reminded her of nothing so much as a character in a horror movie. He was the character who realized that the monster aliens were on the move, that they were taking over. He was talking slowly, deliberately, about optical illusions, but what she heard was, "You're in danger! Something terrible has happened! You aren't who you think you are! Can't you see? They're after you! They're here already. You're next! You're next! You're next!"

And then, in the middle of this, it happened.

She knew it would happen, that it was happening all the time, but it made her sick to watch it happening to someone else, to see it happen to Harold. Toward the end of his lecture, when Harold was finishing up describing the problem of time (the notion that one moment really does follow the next and how this might not always or ever be true) one of the men in the front row stood up and walked onto the stage. He was about four inches taller than Harold, but they were dressed in nearly identical clothing—khaki pants, blue button-up shirts, tweed jackets—and all this man did, all he had to do, was exchange his tie for Harold's tie and take Harold's glasses. The slightly taller man handed over his tie and then he stepped up behind the podium. The taller man, the taller version of Harold, waited while the other Harold exited the stage and found a seat, found the seat the taller man had been occupying. Then he, this new Harold, reshuffled the notes and the lecture started over. The new Harold started from the beginning.

"'This sentence is in French,'" he said. This Harold looked out, into the audience, and Asket realized that he could see her. He'd found her out there and was watching her. His desire for her had moved into this new version along with the rest of Harold's personality.

After witnessing Harold's switch she wasn't sure if she still wanted to be with him. It was unrealistic to expect that he would be an original, that he wouldn't be as susceptible to the Pleidien influence as any other human, but she had secretly held this hope. She had assumed it. Harold would different.

She had forty-five minutes until she was to meet Harold in his hotel room, just that much time to decide. Her original hope of regaining her life, of landing on something original, of returning, was, she realized, dashed now. She couldn't listen to the speech anymore, couldn't bear to watch this new version of Harold even though, as he spoke, he seemed more and more like himself to her, so she stood up from her folding chair, clasping her metallic mini-purse in front of her like a shield, and made her way to the back of the audience and then into the another section of the convention center.

If Harold had been authentic he would have been the only authentic thing at the Javits Convention Center. Everything else at the MUFON conference was a duplicate, a copy. While MUFON had been vindicated, Ufology as a business had been decimated. The kind of merchandise she associated with the field, the self-published channeled books, the blurry UFO photos, the used copies of abduction research in paperback, and every single trace of the Greys, all of that had been consigned to the dustbin. In place of these there were copies of Rain's latest book, *The Plejaren Prophecies*, commentaries on his book, and signed photographs of Ralph and Charles Rain. More than that every kiosk and all the merchandise tables were manned by Pleidiens or by surrendered Earthlings. It had turned out that, after landing, only one alien corporation was ever going to profit from the fact that flying saucers were real.

Asket stopped at a kiosk, pretended to examine the merchandise, the plastic reproductions of hubcap-shaped craft, the glossy covers of *Star Insight* magazine, while she considered what it would mean to give herself physically to a man who wasn't himself. It wouldn't make a difference, would it? She wasn't herself either.

Asket looked at her hands on the glass counter, tried to stand still against the jostling crowd, and looked down at her arms. She couldn't remember what color her arms should be.

"You're white now. Your arms are pale," I say.

"Are they?" Asket asks, but she doesn't notice or even look down to check. "What I saw helped me decide. Next to the grey plastic boom box there was a stack of neatly folded white jumpsuits with purple sequins and I asked the clerk, a woman who, as it happened, was wearing an identical jumpsuit, what the purple sequins signified."

The Pleidiens are a liberal race but they did have rules and one of them was that no human was to wear the Pleidien jumpsuit with the traditional colored sequins. They insisted on this, not for their own sake of course, but in order to protect humanity. For the time being they wanted to maintain a distinction. Mankind was not ready to live without distinctions. They didn't want to confuse anyone by erasing such an important difference before we were ready.

Asket purchased a green slushy in a Ralph Reality memorabilia cup and admired the blond man. There he was with his broad chest and blown dry hair, and she realized that the cup, for the surrendered, had a religious significance. Sipping through the twisty straw she found the apple slushy to be both too sour and too sweet at the same time, and she stuck her tongue out in disgust and was immediately embarrassed. The woman in the purple sequins frowned at her, disapproving of her disapproval. A green apple slushy was apparently some new sacrament, and even if it was disgusting she had to drink it all. When her tongue turned green and her teeth started to ache she would apparently be redeemed.

Harold greeted her at the door to his hotel room with a question. "Do you believe in fate?" he asked.

She wanted to take him back to the convention center, to get away from the dim light and stale air that smelled of air freshener and dust, but after he asked her this question he turned away and walked back into the room so that she had to follow him in to answer.

Sitting down on one of the twin beds on the far side of the room, facing away from her and toward the venetian blinds, Harold was acting out their fantasy. He was waiting for her to join him there on the polyester comforter, to sit next to him on the bed.

There was a saucer hovering outside the hotel and the red and green and yellow lights were bright enough to light up the overcast sky and to lend the small room in a Best Western the ambiance of a discotheque.

Did she believe in fate? The question went unanswered as she crossed the room and put her hand on him, stroking the small of his back and petting his grey hair and bald scalp.

Right now she is looking down at her meal, at the broiled chicken set in red sauce on a china plate dusted with green pepper, while gripping the stem of her wine glass, averting her eyes as if deciding on where to start, but the sly smile she's wearing gives her away. The memory of what happened, of what she and Harold did together, is a pleasant embarrassment for her.

"You weren't there to seduce him," I tell her.

She takes a sip of her wine and then pokes at the meat on her plate with her fork, suddenly ambivalent about her order.

"I asked him to call his wife," she says.

"You did?"

"After a time, I asked him. He didn't like the idea."

"What about his question? Do you believe in fate?" I ask.

"Like I told you before, there are moments that can only go one way. Maybe it's not down to fate but patterns. There are moments that are predictable."

What was predictable in that hotel room, what anyone could figure out in advance, was where Harold would put his hands and how the transition from separation to unbuttoned intimacy was going to be achieved. These kinds of transitions are actually always worked out in advance, and the moves, his moves and her supple acceptance, while not fated exactly, are definitely worked out in advance and according to an established plan.

Afterward she sat on the bedside table, the phone between her bare legs, her sweaty back pressed against the wall lamp's cool metal base, and she told him.

She finally told him directly, again and again, that she was Carole. She was the original Carole.

"The Pleidiens have the power to switch people around, to change their identity. They did it to me, to me and the woman you think is your wife, and it needs to be undone," she said.

"What are you saying?" Harold asked. "Are you trying to blackmail me? You're my wife?"

She walked him through it slowly, even repeating his own words back to him. She told him that she was speaking French. She told him that she was an untrue truth, and that the Pleidiens weren't to be trusted. Finally she told him that she was his real wife and that Harold needed to call her. She asked him to call his wife. She lifted the receiver from the hook, held it on her lap, let it dangle on the curled black cord for a time while they argued, and then handed it over.

"When you get her on the line tell her to meet us here. I want to talk to her in person," she said.

"You're crazy," Harold said. "What do you want to tell her?"

"I'll tell her that she's going to have an identity crisis."

When our bill comes I'm glad for the interruption. This news that my wife's doppelgänger had slept with Harold Flint troubled me even more. Somehow this troubled me more than discovering that she thought she'd once been an artist's model who thought she was Harold's dead wife. She'd slept with him not when she was his wife or his wife's double, but when she was someone like or approximating who she is right now.

She's at the restaurant with me but she's thinking about him. That's what is worse. I'm happy to leave the empty wine bottles and chandelier elegance behind, thrilled to get out of Barbetta's and onto the sidewalk, and I let Asket hail a cab while I think over what she's told me. New Yorkers keeping up with the beat and step of the city pass me as I hold my ground in the middle of the sidewalk.

Asket is stretching. She's on tiptoes at the curb and her litheness and appeal is accentuated by the tight sweater and orange skirt she's wearing. It occurs to me that she must have changed out of her jumpsuit in the saucer. These civilian clothes she's in, her Earth uniform, must have been provided by Reality. Watching her stretch and then get her bearings and scan the road for a taxi, the question of her bothers me. Just who is she? Where is she really from? It can't be that she's an Oregonian, some community college art teacher with an artist's model's body. She's got to be one of them.

"I don't believe you," I say as we climb into the taxi. Music is blaring from the radio. A maudlin pop tune called "Careless Whisper" is loud and she pretends not to have heard me.

"What are you saying exactly anyway? Carole killed herself the weekend of that convention. Are you saying otherwise?" I shout. Asket just keeps nodding along to the beat of the song, and as we turn on 5th I lean back into my seat and cross my arms. If an argument isn't possible then I'll settle for brooding.

Carole was buried six months ago, before the election of Bill Clinton. She took too many pills. She was always taking too many pills, but this time the mistake was fatal. It apparently wasn't a mistake at all. That's Harold's story. The reason he gave, that she was depressed by the landing, that the arrival of the aliens had gotten to her in the same way as they got to John Mack and Betty Hill, never made any sense, but it's even less likely that Carole would've overdosed, offed herself, over Harold's straying. Something else must've happened.

When we arrive back at the brownstone Asket immediately excuses herself to the restroom while I head to the kitchen and open our designer refrigerator, this shiny black wonder that's set into the wall. Inside there is nothing I want, hardly anything in there at all. We just have some leftover rice and a half bottle of wine. Closing the door I spot my own reflection in the black sheen of the door and feel foolish.

Why are we here? More specifically, why is she here? Asket doesn't live with me, or she ought not to live with me. Not anymore. What reason is there for her to be here, to be staying here?

"You aren't who you think you are, Brian," she tells me. She's changed into Virginia's clothes. She enters the kitchen wearing a pair of button-up jeans and a Pink Floyd T-shirt from their 1986 Momentary Lapse of Reason world tour. The ironed-on transfer is from Floyd's album cover. There are empty beds, cots, on the beach and all of them are about to be washed away.

"You've got it backward, Asket. It's you who aren't who you say you are," I say. "It's you who aren't who you pretend to be."

Asket ignores me, pushes past me, and opens the refrigerator again. She fishes out the wine, pulls the cork free with her teeth, and fetches a pair of mason jars that Virginia bought so we could jar our own jam if we ever wanted to, but of course we don't. I put them back and take down two delicate tumblers, the ones with the thumb indents that Virginia insisted we had to have. Apparently Asket is not familiar with the kitchen, not anymore. She doesn't know where anything goes.

"Did Carole kill herself?" I ask.

"No."

"What happened to her?"

"I don't know."

"Why should I believe you? Why should I let you stay here?"

"Carole became somebody else," Asket tells me. "We all switched around, that's what always happens. That's what's been happening."

I take a sip of the white wine and find it's too sweet. "This is crap."

Asket pours more wine into my tumbler and then puts the empty bottle in the sink. She keeps her back to me for a moment, pauses for effect, and then she turns back to me again. "Do you remember what happened at the FBI?"

"I was tested," I say. "You and your Pleidien friends thought it would be great fun to test me…"

"And after that?"

"After that? There was nothing. After that we went to the restaurant," I said.

"Brian, he gave you twenty-four hours. Reality said you had twenty-four hours."

I want to object but decide to drink more wine instead. I swallow down the sickly sweet stuff in one gulp and then leave the kitchen. I make my way to our mock Gustav Stickley chair with oversized leather cushions and sit down heavily. The arts and crafts movement might not have produced a socialist utopia but they knew how to make a chair. Asket sits down across from me, on the leather sofa.

"Listen," she tells me.

Harold told her he had no intention of calling his wife from the bed he'd just used with another woman, that he had no intention of calling her at all. He rolled over and sat on the side of the bed, lit a filterless cigarette and pulled on his boxer shorts. They were fifteen stories up and from where she was on the bed all Asket could see out the window was the blank dark sky. The light from the hotel room, from the bedside table lamp, reflected off the double pane.

"Harold, do you believe the mind and the body are split?" Asket asked. Harold didn't answer but he twitched. He was sitting with his back to her and his arm moved, his whole body jerked slightly. "That's your answer to the mind/body problem. There is a split and that split is a third term."

Harold didn't want to discuss it. He didn't appear to want to talk at all, but just wanted to smoke. He didn't say anything until the light from outside filled the room. Not sunlight, but a pink and yellow light spilled in. It alternated on and off as the flying saucer spun. The craft was nearer now, not quite level with their floor but closer, lower.

"They look cheap," Harold said. "They look exactly like saucers should look, so much so that we've already forgotten they're out there. They just blend in."

Asket sat up in bed, put her hand on his shoulder, and got him to turn back in her direction. She watched his eyes as he looked her up and down and when he met her gaze she asked him again.

"Call Carole," she said. "Call your wife. I want to meet her."

Harold stood up from the bed. He moved away from her and nearly stumbled on the carpet, had to catch himself with an outstretched hand or he would have smashed his forehead against the fake wood of the television cabinet. As soon as he regained his balance he crouched on all fours and felt around under the bed for his trousers.

"This was a mistake," he said. "I don't know how I could have been so stupid."

Harold was scared. Whether he was simply scared of being caught out by his wife or if it was something more than that, Asket couldn't tell, but he was definitely frightened. He was frightened of her.

"I know things that I shouldn't know," she told him. And Harold, the tough cynic, the worldly anti-artist, the skeptic, flinched. His face fell.

"Listen, Patricia," he said. "I like my life. I mean, it's not perfect, but my wife...I don't..."

"I know things," she repeated, "that I shouldn't be able to know."

The Pleidiens had contacted Harold first.

Before Charles Rain, Harold had been their favorite, the one they wanted. They'd only found an alternate when they'd run out of other options. They'd only turned to the B-movie version of contact, resorted to a security guard at Macy's and to the idea of a new religion, when Harold had asked them, begged them, to stop. They'd contacted him, they'd been talking to him from Eternity, since he was a little boy, and they made themselves known to him consciously when he was at Black Mountain College. He was a contactee too, even though he wanted to deny it. He'd received the same wisdom message, the same visions, that Charles Rain had received. The only difference was that Harold had rejected it.

"You could see more than Charles," she said. "It wasn't just a set of ideas for you, it wasn't just a fantasy story."

"What wasn't?"

"The Third Space."

Harold's encounters with the Pleidiens changed him. He couldn't see straight, he had vertigo for weeks after the first contact and every time after that, when they would land their craft or speak to him telepathically, he would have the same symptoms or worse. The problem was that for Harold the Third Space wasn't invisible, it wasn't some distant imaginary dimension, but it was active in the world. It was what gave the world shape, and it was always moving.

"Here's another thing I know that I shouldn't. Those symptoms almost stopped us from getting married," she said.

"What's that?"

"The vertigo, the confusion you felt when you were in contact with them. It almost stopped everything."

On December 17, 1979, Harold thought the world might be ending.

He'd seen the saucers the night before, but he'd been drinking heavily and thought, hoped, that they might've been a delusion. This time the flying saucers were brought on by the mix of marijuana and alcohol in his system.

The craft had been hovering over McSorley's, the men's-only tavern that his friends from Black Mountain thought would be the perfect place to celebrate on the night before his second marriage. Harold could usually hold his liquor, but after an untold number of dark beers he found himself unable to follow the thread of conversation around him. Harold couldn't figure out how to draw a bunny no matter how many times Ray explained it to him. And when Ben Walton tried to reenact a Steve Reich percussion piece with a fork and a pint glass Harold felt faint. He stared down at the sawdust on the floor of the Irish pub, and tried to ignore the undercurrent that he could hear emerging. He didn't want to understand how these disconnected conversations were combining into an entirely different message.

"Fleshy bodies…in a world that may or may not…have changed."

The people around him were unconsciously cooperating in order to speak to him in code. "A common way…to find the answers…alters your living space." The words he made out were spoken by Ray, Ben, and Joe. He was involuntarily putting them together into a new sequence. He felt sick to his stomach and dizzy, but he was supposed to stand up from the table and go out onto the street. That's what was expected of him.

"You couldn't quit doing it," Asket told him. She was still naked on the bed, sitting Indian style with her hands folded in her lap, and Harold was listening to her. "You saw a saucer that night, again, and the next day, when we were going to be married, your head was pounding. You had too many ideas, couldn't differentiate your own thoughts from what was going on around you."

"I was hung over," Harold said.

"It was all a flow of ideas, of words and concepts, and you were just another idea in with the rest. It was impossible for you to keep up, to keep interpreting. You almost didn't make it to the church we'd rented."

Harold had had to drink again, that next day, to get good and drunk, get good and stoned, in order to make the image of the saucer leave him. He couldn't tell where he was in time, whether he was standing outside of McSorley's watching the saucer land, back at Black Mountain College putting together a geodesic dome that would never support its own weight, or sitting in his Brooklyn walk-up waiting for a cab.

Eternity, for Harold Flint, wasn't something to wish for. That space outside of appearance, the disorder that supports the ordered world of our everyday life, was cold, overwhelming, and deadly in its allure and beauty.

"You were so drunk on our wedding day," she said. "I thought I was making the worst mistake of my life. But then you told me about the saucer, about what they'd done to your head, and I understood. I tied to understand. You hadn't done it, hadn't gotten so drunk, in order to hurt me," she said. "And we got married."

Harold shook his head. He shook his head and then sat down on a chair with rollers that was set up against the television cabinet. "You and I didn't get married," he said. "We've only just met, or we've only just met again, after a half decade."

"You're wrong. I'm Carole. Or, I was, at one time, the woman you know as Carole," she said. "Does anyone else know that story? Did anyone else see the saucer? Did you tell anyone else?"

"No," he said. "No."

The two of them recognized each other when they met at the hotel bar. Carole was drinking stale coffee at the bar when Harold stepped up to the counter on her left side and pointed across to Asket who was standing on her right. He introduced her as the woman from the Well, which was a little disconcerting as Asket had thought that theirs was a clandestine relationship. Carole offered her hand to shake and her grip was firm, but not aggressive. She was a pretty brunette who looked like she might have stepped out of another era. She looked a bit like Doris Day and a bit like Elaine de Kooning, and had an old school aristocratic air about her.

Before they'd even spoken Asket realized that this Carole knew. She might not know everything, but she knew that Asket had been to bed with her husband, but what was equally obvious was that she was not going to say anything directly about it. Carole's knowledge of her husband's affair would be the subtext of the encounter, a secret source of power for the wife.

Or that was how Carole saw it, but Asket had none of that.

"Patricia, isn't it?" Carole asked.

"I prefer the name Carole," Asket said.

"Are you trying to be clever about something?" Carole asked, but then she gave Asket a second look and it clicked. Carole's eyes widened as she recognized herself in this other woman.

"Oh, Christ," Harold said. "I think I need a drink."

"My name is Carole," Asket said.

"I think it is," Carole said. "It's nice to meet you, Carole."

Harold ordered his drink but before it came Asket dragged them back into the merchandise court. The best way to demonstrate what she meant, to convince them both of what had happened, was to give a demonstration.

"Follow me," she said and led the two of them out of the hotel bar and back to the kiosks and tables by the main stage. They stood back from the activity as Asket searched out a target.

She settled for a representative of the New Church, a pimply adolescent in purple sequins who had recently surrendered. The three of them watched as he wound up a saucer toy with a metal key and then set the saucer down and let it skitter across the glass counter and then stop. The toy couldn't overcome the strip of aluminum at the counter's edge. It rotated 180 degrees round and spun away, and the Pleidien convert, the saucer toy salesclerk, picked out another and inserted the key.

"Can we ask you a few questions about the new faith?" Asket asked him when they reached the kiosk. The teenager looked at them, the saucer still in his hands, only half wound, and closed his mouth. The smile he'd had disappeared and his braces and rubber bands disappeared with it.

"This is only a merchandise kiosk. There is a reading room on the second floor and saucers outside the convention center," he said.

Asket smiled at him and then moved a lock of her straightened black hair behind her ear. She leaned across the table so as to be physically closer to the boy.

"I know that you're not, what do you call it, a spokesperson?" she asked.

"A communications officer," he said.

"I know you're not a communications officer, but you're a convert? You've surrendered?"

The kid put down the toy craft and it spun sluggishly away, just making it halfway down the countertop before stopping.

"I'm a member of the New Church," he said.

What Asket wanted to know was if the boy understood the Pleidien faith well enough to go along with her. She asked him to explain the Pleidien idea of background reality which, they claimed, was the realm they accessed during interstellar flight. She wondered if he knew that this realm was supposedly both singular and multiple. She wondered if he was as confused by it, by their idea of an accessible but closed background to reality, as she was. And she wondered, suspected, that if he was confused, as confused as she was, that she might be able to exploit that confusion. She wanted to use the background reality, to test it. He would be her guinea pig.

"I've heard," she started, "that there is no difference between thought and reality. The Pleidiens say we are just materialized thought."

"I…the reading room is on the second-floor pavilion," the boy answered.

Asket took one of Rain's books, *The Eternity Factor*, and opened the dust jacket so as to read aloud from the inside flap.

"'Our Pleidien Space Brothers are here to deliver the good news,'" she read. "'You are a spiritual being. You are a materialized thought, an idea in the flesh. Hunger, war, disease and indeed all fear and strife can be eliminated through the proper understanding of this simple fact. You are spirit. Welcome to the Cosmos.'"

The boy's braces were showing again and his smile seemed genuine.

"You believe that?" Asket asked.

"It's the truth."

"And as spirit you can float free. Your body isn't a trap," she said.

"The body is a vehicle for the spirit," he said.

"Why not get out then?" she asked. "Why do you always stay in the car?"

The boy was winding up the toy saucer again, absentmindedly overwinding it actually. He put the toy down and it made a terrible grinding sound.

"Get out of the car?" he asked.

"Why not try another vehicle?"

"Another vehicle?"

Asket walked around the kiosk and stood next to the boy. She pointed out at the crowd and asked him which one he liked. "You could be any of these. Take your pick."

"What do you mean?"

"Get out of this car," she said. She nudged him in his soft belly. "Try a test drive in a different model."

The salesclerk picked out a teenager who looked a bit like a television star, like a soap opera actor. This other boy had perfect teeth and perfectly combed blond hair, and the four of them approached this kid's table. This boy was sitting by an Orange Julius kiosk drinking a strawberry slushy through a twisty straw and reading one of Rain's books. Asket asked him if he knew the doctrine, if he believed in the spirit, or if he thought he was just his body. And then, while Carole and Harry watched, she got the two teens to switch. It was really just a matter of suggestion, of getting them to meet each other's gaze and make the exchange.

First they took out their wallets and, watching each other, they made the trade. The better-looking boy, the television personality, appeared to be a bit disappointed when he looked at the ID, as if he hadn't noticed what the other boy looked like, hadn't noticed how stocky and soft the boy was, until that moment. The boy from the kiosk, on the other hand, was beaming at the other boy's photo.

"Football?" the boy from the kiosk asked.

"Touchdown," the better-looking one said, and then he asked the question back. "Football?"

"Star Trek," the kiosk kid replied.

This exchange drew the attention of a few passing Pleidiens. A man and a woman in jumpsuits with red sequins stopped at the boy's table and watched as the fatter of the two unbuttoned his shirt. The blond female Pleidien was smiling with a big forced smile, her teeth showing, and she reached out for the more attractive kid and put her hands on his temples. Once contact was made the boy's eyes closed and yet, as if automatically, he started undressing too. He started with his pants, and as he unzipped the woman put her hand on the boy's chin and pulled down so that his mouth opened.

"I was thirteen years old," the boy said.

"Thirteen," the kiosk clerk echoed.

"I was thirteen years old, too old for a babysitter, but my parents thought I needed one anyway. They were going to the movies, having an evening out together, and it was obvious that they needed to do something to repair all the damage they'd done to each other, but I didn't need a babysitter. I protested and protested, right up to the moment when Monica arrived. She was sixteen and pretty and we watched television together, some sitcoms, *Silver Spoons* and a couple of others, and then we played a game of Scrabble, but we didn't finish the game because...she started talking about her life in school, and what her sister was doing in college, and asking me if I'd ever tried drugs, and by the time my parents got back it was like she wasn't my babysitter at all. We didn't make out or anything, although I definitely wanted to, but she'd started to treat me as a peer. And after she left I wished I could drive, I wished that I was the one driving her home instead of my mother, but most of all I felt grown up and, strangely, free. I realized that my relationship with babysitters, with girls, wouldn't ever be quite the same again. Things were going to be different for me," he said.

"When I was in third grade I got separated from the rest of my class during a trip to the New York zoo. There were about thirty of us in the class, but when we got to the monkey house and everyone lined up to go through the double-glass doors I didn't. I didn't want to see the monkeys because I liked the cats. We'd already seen the cats, but I wanted to see them again. There was a mountain lion in a cage that I particularly wanted to keep looking at, and so I turned around when everyone else went forward," the salesclerk said. "I didn't expect to get away with it, but nobody noticed me. Nobody noticed when I left. And I spent the day in the zoo on my own, just went my own way. I spent a lot of time with the cats, and I spent a lot of time in the Penguin House. I had a digital watch and I knew when the buses were leaving. I knew when I had to be back at the exit, and I kept careful track of the time so that when three o'clock came I was there at the gate along with everyone else.

"Nobody realized what had happened or what I'd done. Nobody had noticed that I was missing the whole time and it made me feel invisible but it also made me feel free."

By the time the salesclerk was finished with his story he wasn't the same person anymore. That is, he and the other boy had exchanged clothes, exchanged wallets, exchanged watches. The thinner boy, not really more attractive anymore, but just thinner, put on the salesclerk's glasses and then took them off again, while the bigger boy, not fat but just bigger, seemed surprised to discover that his jean jacket wouldn't button.

The Pleidiens hummed a little tune to themselves. It sounded like something by Bach or maybe some other baroque German composer, but it was probably alien, and Asket turned to Carole and asked for her purse.

Imitating the boys Asket told Carole a story. She told her about taking cotillion lessons back in 1967. Cotillion lessons were dance and etiquette lessons for both the young women who aimed at attending a cotillion or debutante ball and the young men who, due to their parents' station, were likely candidates as these women's future escorts. Asket had no ambition to attend any ball but she'd been signed up for the lessons regardless. Her parents drove her downtown every Wednesday and dropped her off at the Benson hotel for the two-hour lessons. There she, along with a dozen or more of the other girls in their Sunday dresses, lined up on the right side of the crystal ballroom, under the gold inlaid ceiling and chandeliers, and waited for a boy in an uncomfortable-looking dress jacket and probably a clip-on tie, to cross over from the left side and ask for a dance.

What was surprising was that she'd taken to it despite her initial reluctance. She'd learned to waltz, to foxtrot, and more. And she'd even managed to secure a regular dance partner. His name was Ronnie and while he was not destined to escort anyone to a debutante ball—Ronnie was a nice boy, but not an especially handsome one in his too-thick glasses and powder blue suit—he was a fast study. Despite his limitations Ronnie could dance and they practiced together at every lesson for months. They did this without ever talking to each other, without even looking at each other off the dance floor. The cotiliion and waltz were separate from the rest of the world, from the rest of Asket's life, somehow bracketed off, and dancing there was a pleasure with no consequence.

"And then Ronnie asked me to dance at homecoming. He took my hand and put his on my waist, assuming that we'd waltz and I was mortified. He would ruin everything. If we tried this we'd be sure to embarrass ourselves permanently. I was going to be socially ruined in a high school gymnasium. But, even though the Rascals' "Groovin'" was too up-tempo for us, we didn't embarrass ourselves at all. What happened was that everybody stopped and watched. Instead of going wrong, instead of embarrassing ourselves, we got applause. They were impressed, hippies and jocks both. And I felt free. I felt as though everything was going to be okay," Asket says.

Carole began to unbutton her blouse, she was ready to switch, ready to tell her own story maybe, but before she could she was interrupted. The Pleidiens who had helped the boys with their transfer stepped in between Asket (or Patricia) and Carole. The Pleidiens stopped the transfer.

"We would like you to attend Ralph Reality's presentation now," one of the blond-haired women in sequins said. Asket couldn't tell the two of them apart. "This thing you're doing now must stop. It is dangerous for you to do this on your own. You need instruction."

"What kind of instruction?" Asket asked.

"You are to attend Ralph Reality's presentation now," they told her. They spoke in unison.

The presentation was on the main stage. It was a combination of a laser light show and a magic act. It was dark outside and the space was illuminated by lines of high-powered track lights set in rectangular patterns in the grid above them. President George Herbert Walker Bush stood on stage with the crew of Ralph Reality's mothership. Surrounded by six blond women in uniforms that seemed to be modeled on vintage stewardess uniforms rather than the usual jumpsuits, purple polyester skirts, and collarless jackets, the President looked uncomfortable. At the front of the stage a bubble machine revved up and when the President approached the podium he had to traverse a field of drifting bubbles. Bush stammered a bit as he spoke, stumbling over words like "historic," and "welcoming." When he finished he wiped his brow with his shirtsleeve and Ralph Reality, appearing seemingly out of nowhere, took the stage.

Carole and Asket were standing close together in the back, behind row upon row of folding chairs, while Harold stood further ahead of them. None of them had said anything about what had happened at the kiosk, they hadn't had the time nor the inclination to speak about it. But since then Carole had grown sullen. She clearly felt violated in some way and she seemed inclined toward blaming Harold for her unease. She wasn't looking toward the stage, wasn't paying attention to what was happening there, but was staring at Harold. She was watching the back of his head as he pretended not to notice. He was keeping his distance from Carole and Asket both.

What Asket wanted to understand was why the Pleidiens had interrupted. She was worried, wondering what they'd do to her now that they knew she'd caught onto them.

"Hello, Earthlings," Ralph Reality said. His voice carried easily, smoothly, to the back of the convention center. "I am from another star and I am, of course, happy to be amongst you today."

Ralph Reality spoke in clichés and buzzwords. While bubbles floated over his head he spoke of spiritual energy and the coexistence of objects. Asket noticed that he'd grown a mustache since his arrival on Earth six months earlier. It seemed to Asket that he might have even grown a few inches since then too, but his wide eyes and goofy smile were the same as ever. He held his hand aloft, tapped the air with his index finger, and a flash of rainbow-colored light, like sunlight through a prism only more solid seeming, flashed in a halo pattern around his head.

"There is a mediating field between each one of us," Ralph Reality said, "and each one of you can learn to touch it, to use it."

The Pleidien doctrine was simple if absurd. The universe was imaginary. This didn't mean that the world was a mere hallucination or that the whole world was all in your head, it was not a solipsistic doctrine, but rather the point was that your head was imaginary too.

There was a spirit and the goal of this spirit was to realize its own falsehood. The Pleidiens had already done this. They were a people who'd realized that they themselves were imaginary.

Ralph told the crowd that spirit is the background to their lives and that spirit is changeable, and then he gestured to one of the stewardesses who nodded back to him. This blond assistant in knee-high polyester boots stepped through the bubbles, made her way through the line of security, and mingled in with the crowd.

"The idea that one day follows the next in a chain of cause and effect is an illusion," Ralph Reality said. "The truth is that one idea follows another in a chain of associations, not in a chain of cause and effect. The history that you think you know, that history changes all the time. That pattern of cause and effect, that chain of Happenings that occurs so that each thing that is created will have somewhere to be, that changes."

And it was at this point that the crowd started to react, or more specifically to respond. For example a man in his forties, maybe six rows ahead of Asket, he started unbuttoning his IZOD shirt. He was sporting grey hair tied in a ponytail and wearing khaki shorts which he unbuttoned as well while another man, maybe a decade younger and Japanese, pulled his Hard Rock Cafe T-shirt off over his head.

The stewardess stood off to the side smiling and nodding as two young women who looked like they might be identical twins, right next to Asket, started undressing. Seeing as both of them were wearing nearly identical bib overalls and white T-shirts, from the outside this exchange seemed pointless.

"Anything can happen," Ralph Reality said. "One day a big burly man might wake up to discover that he is now a woman. The change happened to him, for whatever reason, but when it happens he won't be surprised. When he discovers his penis is gone the next morning, when he sees that he has a vagina instead, he will be neither annoyed nor delighted. It will make sense to him. He'll remember the surgery that made his transformation possible, maybe, or he'll think that he was born a girl. He'll go about creating, manufacturing, evidence for this new history. His wife, if has one, will remember too. She'll remember something different, but what she remembers will match this new reality. When he goes to work, goes out into the world, that won't bother him either. After all most of the world is indifferent to him, and in the pockets of the world where he is noticed, where he has some influence, he'll find nothing but accommodation to this new reality.

"Think of the difference between the foreground and the background in a photograph or a painting," Ralph Reality instructed the audience. "Think of how easily those two categories are reversed with just a few simple marks or a shift in perspective." He held up a poster-sized line drawing of a cube, a Necker cube. Using both hands he held it up over his head so that everyone could see. "Where is the background and where is the foreground?" he asked. "In this picture, which is which?"

The open and public way people were switching, the fact that Ralph Reality was speaking of it, made Asket feel very nervous. What she was feeling wasn't just personal anxiety, but a different kind of fear. In fact the very space and security that she relied upon in order to be personally afraid for herself seemed to be in danger. With every cheery explanation what Ralph Reality was really telling the crowd was that the people they thought they were, the kinds of values which they held dear, these things didn't exist. They, all the fathers and mothers, businessmen and telecommunications experts, researchers and science fiction fans, they were all of them erased. That is, the identities that they thought were so close to their hearts were utterly transitory. It could easily be switched around.

"Nobody, not one human being, is really who he thinks he is," Ralph said. And then, Reality did it. Then he made his big move. He staged his attack.

Ralph Reality turned to the President of the United States and he reached out toward him. He snapped his fingers. "Mr. President," he said.

"What is it, Ralph?"

"Please undress."

Up until this point in the proceedings it might have been possible for the attack, the rearranging, to remain unconscious. That is many people might have been able to convince themselves that they hadn't seen anything unusual, or if not that, then they might have convinced themselves that they were the only ones who did see it. Asket herself might have chalked it all up to some peculiar delusion on her part, but when the President of the United States unzipped and removed his pants there were gasps. There was a collective intake of breath and even a few screams.

Then the man who was leaving Ralph Reality unzipped his jumpsuit and stepped into and zipped up the President's khaki pants, and then the man who had been alien stepped over to the microphone and adjusted his tie. The screams started to spread and transform. This man who should have been Ralph Reality, who still looked like Ralph Reality, started the proceedings over from the top.

"My fellow Americans, and all of you from a-a-around this whole Earth," the man who was no longer Ralph Reality said. He spoke with the President's stammering voice in an imperfect but somehow convincing imitation. This new President seemed just as confused as the other one had been as he introduced Ralph Reality, the ambassador from the Pleides. The President of the United States gestured to the figure who had been the President but who was now wearing red sequins.

The crowd started moving toward the stage as the new President and the line of security between the audience and the stage hardened. Secret Service men in sunglasses and black suits pulled out handguns and blond-haired Pleidiens of both genders unholstered large purple plastic laser rifles, but instead of opening fire, the Pleidien guards reached into their jumpsuits, into pockets that seemed highly improbable, and produced crystal shards that glowed pink and purple. Like a bad television effect these crystals pulsated and as they pulsated there was a high-pitched squeal that filled the convention center. It was so high-pitched, in fact, that it was almost inaudible. But as crystals pulsated and the sound filled the convention center, the crowd settled down.

Asket wondered if maybe the transformation of Ralph Reality, the transmigration from Bush to Ralph, hadn't entirely worked. Was an alien-to-human or human-to-alien transfer possible? Had something gone wrong?

"Of course it is," Ralph said. "Everything is going as planned. This is what is known as the revelation of method, and now that everybody has seen the truth, now that everybody knows that we're in control, we can resume the pretense that things are otherwise. We've shown everyone here what is impossible to fully imagine. Which means that most everyone will unsee what they've seen. Everybody but you, right?" Ralph stepped down from the podium and as he did so one of the blond women took his place.

"I am so pleased to be able to talk to you all on behalf of Reality," she said. "He sends his sincere regrets that he can't be here with you today."

Ralph made his way through the crowd. He took a glowing crystal from one of the security guards and created a path for himself with the light, moving people out of his way.

"Maybe," Carole said. "Maybe we should go?"

"Yeah," Harold said. He was backing away, or trying to back away, but the Ufologists and tourists had risen from their seats and crowded around him. He couldn't go anywhere until Ralph Reality cleared a path for him.

"Don't be afraid," Ralph said as he came closer to them. "I've been so hoping that you would be here, Mr. Flint."

All three of them, Harold, Carole, and Asket (Patricia?) found themselves unable to move. Maybe it was the crystal, or maybe it was something else, but some kind of paralysis overtook them.

Ralph Reality smiled at them. He was standing so close to Asket that she could feel his breath on her neck.

"How would you," he asked, "like to take a ride in my flying saucer?"

In your typical Grey alien–style abduction the abductees, usually lumberjacks or subsistence farmers, were subjected to medical exams. That was the story, anyway. That's the kind of thing that most Ufologists were worried about before the landing. Charles Rain's abductees, however, never encountered that kind of scenario. The typical Charles Rain–style close encounter was more bizarre, more abstract, than even the worst proctological examination could ever be. The men and women who encountered Rain's Nordic types, which is what we called them even though Rain claimed to know which star system they were from, wouldn't take humans aboard their craft at all. Instead they employed some kind of energy ray and would beam information directly into the human's head. They would basically show home movies on the inside of your skull. Not home movies exactly, but long montages of super eight art house fare. Think of Stan Brakhage or Thorsten Fleisch, lots of juxtapositions, some scratches on the film emulsion, maybe some landscape photography.

Yet somehow, the people who survived these encounters always came back with rave reviews.

"I saw into the unknown," they would say. Or, "We need to change our relationship with the Earth."

One way or another the contactees always gained some spiritual insight from what they saw, even if those insights were contradictory. Some would claim to have seen or remembered a past life when the flying hubcaps hit them with their lasers, while others would get good with Jesus.

What happened to Asket aboard Ralph Reality's UFO was, to a large extent, just another contact story. It was just like that, full of intimations, chock full of spiritual truths, and impossible to dissect.

Once they were aboard Harold and Carole held hands, this supposed authentic Carole leaned on her husband, while Asket was left on her own. Reality led them through the craft, past mainframes and lava lamps, and brought them to a movie screen. This time rather than project the pictures into their heads directly they were taken to the source and they, all three of them, made sure to keep their eyes on the moving pictures. Ralph said that everything would be explained and the truth of their identities would be made clear.

"No more switching around," he said. "No more play acting."

They just had to watch a movie and it would tell them everything they needed to know.

"I hope you enjoy the picture."

But before the picture started Asket took Harold's hand and it was the current Carole who was left to the side when the stars appeared and disappeared on the screen.

The three of them were alone in a room with rounded steel walls and a seemingly magnetic movie screen erected in the middle. There was a hum coming from it, a pulsing energy. They were in a room right out of Donald Keyhoe's book *The*

Flying Saucers Are Real, a large room with rounded walls made with slotted steel vanes protruding out. There was a large eight-by-ten-foot tele-screen in the middle, a screen that was itself made entirely from steel or some other silver metal, and when the pictures appeared it seemed as if the surface of it, that the metal itself, was changing, perhaps because of heat, and that this almost chemical alteration of the screen was what was bringing them pictures. This was a movie made possible due to discoloration.

Asket felt that they were being watched as well as watching, there were windows along the top of the room, near the curved ceiling, or she thought there were, but she couldn't take her eyes away from the screen, from the story, long enough to check.

The film was about dotted lines. That is, the stars that were flashing by sped up so that soon the dots blurred together into lines. There was a grid onscreen and, while the dots had at first appeared as stars, there was now only a pattern. What had been the cosmos became rectangles, triangles, and squares.

"Do you hear that?" Harold asked her.

Asket says that the images, the simple geometric shapes, were making a kind of sound. It was the kind of sound, apparently, that they could hear with their eyes. She could hear a square, for example. What was onscreen, the simple geometric shapes, was also a voice that was explaining how it was that the world was put together into names.

None of this is the important bit, by the way. The important bit comes after the enlightenment. The important bit comes once the movie does its work and their personalities are swept away. But before we get to that you have to hear about how Asket became sexually excited by a triangle.

Her body responded to the changes on the screen before her eyes could catch up. The triangles and circles were flashing by, making noise, speaking to her, but more important than what the triangles were telling her was how they were set against a blank, black emptiness, and it was this emptiness that bothered her. After awhile she stopped listening to the voice and concentrated on what wasn't there.

Asket looked out at rows and rows of empty seats. Between the lines, where there wasn't sound, there was a massive theater with three balconies and an oval ceiling. And on the stage there they were, the three of them, only now they were naked and engaged. That is, she imagined that Harold, Carole, and her were making love in an empty theater. She imagined a mouth, a breast, a pair of staring eyes.

"There were two women on a stage as the stars kept spinning past, there was a man who looked like a small fishing boat without a sail, and the people who weren't there, the people who would arrive later to fill the seats, were urging us on in our orgy," Asket says.

And it becomes obvious why housewives in Des Moines prefer books by Charles Rain over books by guys like Budd Hopkins or John Mack. The contactee experience is more enjoyable all around.

"What was happening was that they, the Pleidiens, were changing us," Asket explains.

"How were they changing you?"

"They weren't changing our bodies around, they were changing us. Changing what we meant to ourselves, what we meant to the other."

"To the other?"

"To each other."

The three of them were watching themselves on a square movie screen inside the Pleidien flying saucer. They weren't making love to each other, but were watching themselves watch themselves on a movie screen. What had made her long to be touched a moment earlier made her lose all sense of herself as a body. The movie shifted from something passionate to something cold. What she saw was a regress. They were watching themselves watching themselves. They were the figures on the screen and they were watching themselves on the screen where they could see themselves watching and so on and so on.

"It was a bit like falling," she says. "I thought to myself that this flying saucer was not in outer space at all. It was deep underground, or it was in the past."

"Uh-huh," I say. I'm glad that I've been drinking wine.

"The main thing was that the Pleidiens wanted something from us," she says.

Watching the loop, falling into the movie screen, it dawned on her. "They wanted something," she says.

"What?" I ask.

"They wanted us to wear polyester."

Asket is getting drowsy now, and as she lays back on our overstuffed couch, that is my overstuffed olive green couch, the one I bought with Virginia, her explanations, her story, drifts away and I worry that she's fallen asleep. Worse, she hasn't gotten to anything that matters.

"Asket," I say. "What are you telling me? That they let you wear red sequins? Is that what this all leading up to? All the body snatching and mind games, all of the Missing Time, Virginia's disappearance, it's all about the New Church?"

"Carole," she says. Her eyes aren't closed. She's staring up at the ceiling fan, or at the track lighting, and I offer to get her some coffee. I tell her that she needs to wake up. There has to be more and she needs to tell it to me.

"They aren't aliens," she says. "Not from outer space. Harold's been right about that all along. The saucers are just props, it's all staged."

This isn't any kind of answer at all. The saucers can't be fake because there they are, right outside my window there is one of them hovering over the Park Slope condominiums. It's hovering impossibly over somebody's sound investment. We might not be who we think we are, she might or might not be my wife, but if anything is certain it's that the flying saucers are real.

"They're not disrupting our identities," she says. I've got her upright again. And I go to fetch some coffee, but once I'm in the kitchen and I get the coffee machine out from under the sink, once I wrench it free from where it's stuck behind the Cuisinart, I worry that by the time the water boils she'll be on her back again. Asket is willing herself to sleep out there in the living room. There is something more, but she doesn't want to tell me.

I go ahead with the coffee, boiling the water, dumping Maxwell House French roast into the Mr. Coffee coffee filter and wait for the pot to fill, and then I go back to the living room and start to panic when I find she's not there, but can breathe again when I hear her moving around in the bedroom. She's by my nightstand. She's leafing through a copy of Whitley Strieber's book, not really reading but just turning pages.

"Carole and Harold left the ship," she says. "They offered us red sequins, like you said, but Harold didn't want them. So he left."

"Ralph let him leave? What about Carole?"

"She left too, and it wasn't that Ralph let him leave, it was more that he couldn't stop them."

Carole was dead. I'd been to her funeral, it had been an open casket, but now I realized that I couldn't be sure who it was I'd seen in that box. On the other hand, if they'd been trying to get away from the Pleidiens and Carole had died that way, then why would Harold cover that up?

"They left the ship," Asket says. She puts down the book on my side of the bed, leaves it open and face down, like she's going to return and keep reading from where she left off, and I follow her out of the bedroom and back to the kitchen where the coffee is still brewing.

"Here," I say. I take a coffee cup, my Henri Lautrec mug with the kicking Folies girls on it, and slip it onto the burner. I exchange the pot for the smaller cup, and then pour what's in the pot, the little bit of coffee there is, into the ceramic mug. "They left the ship? What does that mean?" I ask.

Asket doesn't know how to explain it to me, so she decides to draw me a picture. She finds a memo pad in the drawer underneath the phone, goes to the drawer like she knows where things are kept, and then uses a nubby pencil to draw five boxes. In the first box she quickly makes a line drawing of a cloud and the right tip of what turns out to be a cartoon saucer. The ship is flying through the panels, moving left to right, but when Asket points to the line drawings to explain what they mean to me she doesn't point to the saucer or the cloud or to any of the drawings inside the frames but to the space in between the boxes.

"When Harold left the ship he went there," she says.

Asket explains that there really isn't anything in between the boxes. That she didn't mean to suggest that there was a place that Harold went to, and it was an empty place, but more that there was a person he went into. What happened was that, in order for Harold to escape Reality and get back to himself, to get back to what he knew of himself, he had to draw a new box. He had to be somebody else.

207

And then Asket looks at me. She looks at me and I remember that I'd been at the MUFON convention too, that I met Ralph Reality there, before our encounter with the FBI. I was there, by the kiosk, and maybe I was there in that hotel room with Asket, with Patricia as she called herself, too.

"What's going on?" I ask. She's sipping from my Lautrec cup, keeping her eyes on me, and I want to snatch the mug away from her, maybe smash it to pieces. Her talk of boxes is just crap, it's a distraction. It's exactly like the kind of thing I'd come up with for a communications course with a name like "After Individuality" or "Modernity and the Masses."

They did something to me, at the FBI, or maybe at the MUFON convention. And now Asket is doing something to me to. She's finishing the job with her story about Harold creating a new identity, a new person. That can't be the answer.

"Don't you remember?" Asket asks. "Reality gave you twenty-four hours. You're going to join us, get back onboard really, in twenty-four hours."

"What do you mean?"

"It's all right, baby," Asket says. She puts down the coffee cup and moves across the gap between the sink and where I am by the breakfast table. She's at my side, with her hand on my neck. "It's okay."

I push her away.

harold's happening

The Happening with Harold takes place in the University art studio and I'm chewing a stick of Black Jack while he winds a bedside alarm clock and considers the idea that his second wife isn't really dead. He doesn't seem surprised but just adjusts his tie, his stupid skinny navy blue tie, as I explain what happened at the MUFON convention and instruct him on how this Happening is going to happen.

"We're going to figure out what's really happening, Harold. We're going to get some facts this time."

But he gives no indication that he understands anything about what I'm saying. He improvises instead. He finds the laser tag gun that I left by the mannequin and points it at me.

"Sit down, Brian," he says.

"Harold, you're not listening," I say.

He laughs at this at then sits down himself, returning to his work of cataloging 1961. All the old sarcastic trinkets are lined up on his worktable and he picks up a pencil and licks the lead.

"Ten-hour clock," he says, and then writes it down.

He licks the pencil lead again and then puts it down and examines his prank clock. This is what has always bothered me about the old man, what's caused the cognitive dissonance I've always associated with him. Here he is, sitting at a table littered with absurdities—cheap little jokes like a can of 100 percent pure artist's shit and a mousetrap that's caught a tube of paint rather than a mouse—but he's got this serious expression on his face like he's working out some big mystery. How can it be that such a humorless man has spent his life producing these jokes?

"I've met with Ralph Reality and he says I've got twenty-four hours. He's 'invited' me to join them. Apparently it's my time to surrender. It's predetermined. A matter of fate," I tell him.

"They love that kind of talk. Fate, destiny, spirituality," Harold says. He puts down his notebook, sets it next to the mousetrap, and spins toward me on his stool. He clears his throat, letting me fidget in my half panic, and then he tells me how he thinks things really are.

"None of that matters," Harold says.

"What?"

"The plot, the big conspiracy, all of that is a distraction."

Harold's nihilism doesn't surprise me and under normal circumstances I wouldn't argue with him, but this time I find myself explaining the obvious to him. If it's true that the Pleidiens are changing people around, mixing people up about who they are, directing their lives for them, then they have to be stopped.

"What are you going to do? You've gone to the police, to the FBI, and that didn't help. Are you going organize a gang to attack their ships? What are you going to do? They've got the White House now. They've got the shopping malls," Harold says.

"We can expose them," I say. "We're writing a book, remember? We can nail down the facts, get the evidence, and expose them."

Harold's laughter is unpleasant. There is always a sneer tucked away in his laughter, and this time is no different.

"Who are we going to expose them to, Brian? Just who is going to listen? Let's say we get this on television, let's say we get the word out, what's to stop them from switching us all around again, starting the story over, creating another gap?"

Why have I been relying on Harold for so long? Why did I ever tie my reputation to his? What did I think he understood? What did I think he was going to help me with in the end? There is nothing behind this Fluxus bullshit, all these Happenings. His art, the whole movement, has traded on nostalgia and absurdity, but now that something real is going on, now that the saucers have landed, all he's got is a can of artist's shit and an alarm clock. He's got that and this musty art studio where he can tuck himself away at the University's expense and continue to pretend that the purity of his vision still matters. All he's got is this room filled with paint brushes stored in coffee cans, crap paintings by second-year students, and four walls. I suppose he finds this is enough. It's as good a place as any to hide in.

"What is it, exactly, that you think you know, Brian?" Harold asks. "You say that they've switched our personalities, confused us about who we really are, but is that what they did to you? Is that what they did to Asket?"

"What they did to Asket?" I ask.

When I stop to think of it Asket never did explain how she became a Pleidien or what happened to her. She really never explained anything.

Harold tells me why it is that he's working on Fluxus again. He says he's doing it, taking this inventory of all his work, because he's trying to rethink the problem.

"What problem, exactly?" I ask.

"Everything," he says. "Art, life, UFOs. The whole shebang."

In the beginning Fluxus was like every other avant-garde movement of the twentieth century. The aim was to erase the line between art and real life. It was the same as Surrealism and Dada and Impressionism and Expressionism in that it aimed to bring art down from on high and give it to the masses. The goal was to eliminate the transcendent and make art accessible. Using everyday objects, making art that was funny, making art that was small, all of these Fluxus tactics aimed at bringing art to regular people. The goal was to infuse the world, to infuse everyday life, with an artistic sensibility.

"We went wrong at the very start," Harold says. "We thought we could erase the line but what we did was reinforce it."

He points to his alarm clock, points out to me that it is different from most clocks because instead of twelve hours it has ten. The idea of this work was to exhibit something that was, in reality, impossible.

"If you try to use a ten-hour clock then what will happen, after the first ten hours, is you'll lose time," Harold says. "You won't be able to keep track of your day with it. A person using this clock would be late for everything, probably. Just consider the math here. If everyone else keeps on using twelve-hour clocks and you had one of these ten-hour jobs, you'd have to read past the surface in order to keep up. You couldn't just glance at the clock and see it read half past seven and think you knew what time it was. You'd have to keep track of how long you'd been using the clock and calculate the time that way. To know what time it really was you'd have to remember how the numbers on this clock related to a twelve-hour clock.

"What would happen is that, after the first ten hours, the decimal clock would be two hours ahead. It would read two o'clock as noon or midnight in order to keep up with the regular schedule, to keep up with everybody else. Then, after the second ten hours had passed, two o'clock would no longer be noon, but two o'clock would be ten o'clock and four o'clock would be noon or midnight. After the third day the four o'clock would be ten and six o'clock would be noon. And so on. . ."

I nod at this, tracking it out loud. "By day five eight o'clock would be noon, seven would be eleven, six would be ten, five would be nine, four would be eight, three would be seven, two would be six, one would be five, and ten would be four," I say. "Nobody could use that clock. . .but so what? What does it matter that you made a useless clock?"

"What that tells us is that time, the twenty-four hour day, can't be reduced down to mere clocks. The twelve-hour day is something more than the clocks that measure it. We'd set out to demonstrate how malleable time was and instead we made an object that proved that time, as it was, couldn't be broken up differently. Time was objective after all," he says.

"So what?" I ask.

"People are like clocks," he says. "Being a person, being Brian Johnson, that's like being a clock. You're an objective person, but only because of how you fit into the whole system. You're Brian because you respond to the name, because there is a set of behaviors, a set of movements, phrases, symptoms, attitudes, that are what it is to be Brian, and you match that idea."

"No. I'm Brian Johnson because I'm alive. I'm right here," I say. And I thump my chest with my open palm.

"We're talking about two different things. There is this idea called Brian Johnson, that's like time, and then there is the body, this thinking thing, that is here right now, and that thing, that body, is like a clock. You're Brian Johnson as measured out on this clock," Harold says. He taps my chest with his middle finger. That is, first he makes an "o" with his middle finger and thumb, and then he lets go and taps my chest.

Harold winds the clock again, his ten-hour clock, and sets it down on the table. We both of us stop and watch the second hand move. We let a half-minute tick by as if maybe we expect something to happen. As if we think the clock is going to do something unexpected.

"We could make it work," I say. "We could slow it down," I tell him. "We could set it so ten hours on that clock were the same as twelve hours on a regular clock."

"Actually, that's how it does work. We just changed the face on a regular clock," he says. "Let's forget the clock. Let's start again. You think the Pleidiens are trying to undo, unhinge, the human race."

I nod, slowly. That seems right to me.

"But, what exactly are they taking away from us? Just what are we, you and me, afraid of losing?"

They're taking our identities away from us, obviously. They took Virginia away, took away his wife, or turned her into one of them, into an alien.

"Think of it this way, if they were to erase your identity who would you be when they were done? Or if you were to get switched around, who would you be?" Harold asks.

I pick up one of the other Fluxus works, a series of homemade stamps constructed out of pornographic photos from the '50s and an old Sears catalog. Catalog images of different tools—a hammer, a pair of pliers, a power stapler—have been cut out and set atop pairs of breasts, a prone blonde with pursed lips and half-closed eyes, a bent leg, and other titillating body parts. Nipples and body hair fill each rectangle and the overall effect is both erotic and cynical. Bodies and desire have been reduced to stamps that might be separated from each other along the perforated lines, licked, and sent out to friends and colleagues in the mail.

If the ten-hour clock is only of interest because of its relation to the twelve hours that make up a normal day, then these stamps are only interesting in relation to the world of pornography and desire. But, these stamps are somehow art precisely because the fracturing of bodies, the collaging of pin-ups, has done nothing to reduce the erotic impact of the original images. A nicely shaped pair of tits or the curve of a lady's ass is alluring with or without context.

I start over. I tell Harold that we should hold a press conference. We should announce that he's returned to Ufology and that he's discovered an alien conspiracy. The government needs to be on guard, people should resist the allure of the saucers and their perpetual invitation to join the New Church. We should do something to stop this.

"I saw a film where, during an alien invasion, the heroes took over a television station. We might do that," I said. "Goddammit, we've got to do something."

"You're avoiding the question. You know something, not about the aliens or UFOs or Carole or some damned science fiction movie, but about yourself and about me. I've figured it out and you know it too, but you're refusing to think it. Who are you, Brian? Where are you from? What's your earliest memory? You don't remember, do you?"

I do remember. Of course, I remember. I remember Fort Carson, Colorado, where I grew up. We lived in a tract house there in the '60s, when I was about six years old and blond. I wore striped shirts, red, brown, and white striped shirts, and corduroy pants. I wore corduroy pants even on summer days.

"How did you get that scar on your chin? Do you remember?"

I had a Big Wheel, it was a hand-me-down from my older sister Helen and it had little flower stickers on the wheels. There were daisies and some other kind of blue flower; there were decals of flowers stuck on the indentations between the plastic spokes on the oversized front wheel. There were red, white, and blue plastic ribbons that dangled down from the handlebars. I could make my Big Wheel roll very fast, but I didn't take corners very well. I had to slow down at the corner of the block in order to make the turn.

"No," Harold says. "It was a purple tricycle. Your older sister's name was Cheryl and she gave you her tricycle. That is, my older sister's name is Cheryl.

"I had a Big Wheel; a purple Big Wheel made for and marketed to girls. I was teased about it but it went fast. I could make it roll very fast." But I see it now. Harold has a scar too. We both of us have scars on our chins, scars that run parallel to our bottom lip. Scars that are just to the right side.

"I got this scar when I was riding my sister's tricycle on a dirt road in upstate New York. We were on my grandparents' land and I tried to turn too fast, I was trying to turn all the way around and ride back and the tricycle flipped over. I landed in the tall grass, fell onto a rake that was hidden in the yellow stalks, and I got a bad cut. They had to take me into town to get stitches. I bled and bled," Harold said. "I was about six, I think."

"I was almost seven, and there was no rake, no tall grass. I hit the asphalt, face first, when I went off the curb. I couldn't make the turn."

Harold stands up from his stool and I shrink back from him involuntarily. Why am I afraid of him? He's waiting for me to do something, to admit something. But what? I don't have anything to confess. I turn back to the art objects, reach out for a small box made of blonde wood, it's about the size of a cigar box, and I pick up the pencil and his notebook, as if I'm going to continue cataloging. That's when Harold makes his move, the move I should have known was coming.

"We've got the same memory," he says. "We've got the same scars." He reaches over and picks up the Rock 'Em Sock 'Em Robots game from the worktable. The toy is just where I left it, but I'm surprised to see it. I'm afraid of it, somehow.

There they are, two identical robots in a yellow plastic boxing ring, and Harold has the blue control sticks in his hands and he's waiting for me to take control of my side of the fight.

"Come on, you have a sporting chance," he says.

But I don't.

Harold asks me how it was that I came to know Virginia. "She sang a Peggy Lee song to you. The first time you really met her. Didn't she?" he asks. "Why do you think Ralph asked you to join them? Why did he want you? All along Asket has been after me, trying to get to me, but now they want you? Suddenly I don't matter?" he asks.

"We've got to stop them," I say.

"Play the game, Brian. They want you because they want me. They're going to make you like me, replace me with you. I thought they wanted me to be Rain, but I was wrong about that. It's me they want. They want you to be me. That's their plan," he says.

"That makes about as much sense as a ten-hour clock," I say.

"You want to do something, but what you really want is to stop yourself from thinking," Harold says. "That woman Asket, she says she was my wife. But, she was also an artist living in

Seattle, an artist's model, a Pledien visitor, and she was your wife too. She was Virginia."

"She was Virginia," I say. "No. She only pretended to be Virginia."

"Right. And now it's time to stop pretending," Harold says. "Be honest with yourself. You know the truth and you just don't want to face it. Who are you Brian?" Harold asks. "Other than this word 'I,' other than this body standing here, and your stupid voice that is prattling on and on, who are you?"

"I...uh."

You're me, Brain. You've been saying, over and over again, that you think therefore you are. You've been telling all these little stories, trying to make as if you exist on your own, as if you have this history of your own and a fixed, a material, place in the world, but you don't. You're just me, a part of me, an extension of and a distortion of me, and I've been letting you run this show for too long.

"Where are your quotation marks?" I ask.

Harold tells me that he doesn't need quotation marks anymore...no, that's not right. I don't need quotation marks anymore. Let's stop this. Stop fighting this. You know what happened at the MUFON convention, you know that our identity was split. No. It's my identity that was split, and you're just a projection. Now it's time for you to stop. You can stop now. There is nothing for you to do but to stop.

"I grab the control sticks for the red Rock 'Em Sock 'Em and try to remember if there was a jingle for this toy. I know it was advertised on television, but there wasn't a jingle just a running commentary from an off-screen announcer. The joke was the announcer was treating this kids game like a real boxing match. The announcer said something like, 'They're slugging it out.

A left to the body, a right to the jaw, and. . .Pow! ZOOM! He's knocked his block off,'" Brian says.

But, Brian Johnson is just a younger version of me. He's who I'd like to be, in a way. He's more approachable, younger. He's a bit fat, fatter than I'd hoped for, but he's less worn out and less cynical. So what if he knocked my block off? It's just a game. And, if he's picking up the whole toy set now, if he's lifting it up off the table and over his head, that doesn't matter. He can swing it down as hard as he likes. He can really let me have it right on top of my head but it won't mat-

Everything "meta" contradicts itself. Metaphysics, for example, contradicts itself and so does metafiction. Here's how it works or doesn't work with metaphysics. Metaphysical theories claim to give us the tools we need in order to perceive the reality behind or underneath the universe. The claim is that we can actually see, either through reason or through some other faculty like intuition or faith, that which is by definition unseeable. That's a contradiction.

Likewise metafictional stories claim to pull back the curtain on literature. The idea is that by making the literary conventions employed in a work obvious, by reminding the reader that he or she is, in fact, reading a made-up story with its own rules and traditions, and by demonstrating that this story can't be said to have any relationship to the real world outside the text, metafictional stories hope to deliver a message about that outside world.

Bertolt Brecht wrote an essay about metafiction back in 1936, only he called metafiction "Chinese theatre."

"Above all, the Chinese artist never acts as if there were a fourth wall besides the three surrounding him," he said. "He expresses his awareness of being watched. This immediately removes one of the European stage's characteristic illusions."

Metafiction and Chinese acting both aim to lead the reader or audience member into a state of self-awareness, and both paradoxically rely on setting up an identification in order to make the reader or audience member think of himself, but, and this is the important bit, Brecht got it wrong when he said that the Chinese artist never acts as if there is a fourth wall. That is, it's true that in Chinese theater the fourth wall isn't between the artist or actor and the audience members, but that doesn't mean there is no fourth wall at all. There is a fourth wall, but in Chinese theater both the actor and the audience are on the same side of it. Both the audience and the actors are, in a sense, on stage. In a book, both the writer and the reader are characters in the story.

In a traditional European play or novel the audience member or reader identifies. That is, the reader suspends disbelief and imagines that what he's reading is actually his own lived experience. The reader takes leave of his or her own life and forgets himself in the process of reading. In a metafictional story, on the other hand, the reader is made aware of himself as a reader but she still identifies with a character, only the character the reader identifies with in metafiction is the author or the narrator.

Brecht aimed to create the proper amount of distance between the audience and the actor, to break the habit of identification, but what he actually achieved was an even stronger identification, one based on an abstraction. That is, what the audience identified with was the common experience of watching a play, and because it was based on this abstraction, based on the mere concept of sight or awareness, the identification was taken to be real.

Think about the words you're reading now and the person you assume has written these words. Who am I? So far, in this story, the first-person narrator has been the character Brian Johnson. Johnson, the experimental writer whose work on UFOs and whose relationship with the Ufologist Harold Flint led him into some confusing and troubling circumstances. He's our point-of-view character, or he was until very recently. But who am I, the person writing these words right now? Am I still that character? Or are you and I fully outside of the story at this point? Are we at least very distant from the story? How could I still be Brian now that I've realized, admitted, that the fourth wall doesn't stand between us? How can I be me and also admit that I'm just a contrivance, a device? Wouldn't it be more likely, considering everything that's happened so far, for me to be somebody else?

identity crisis

Back at my brownstone Asket is gone and I'm left to examine walls that are papered over in an arts and crafts ivy vine design that I've never liked. Sitting on a mock Gustav Stickley chair with oversized leather cushions and an adjustable back I wonder why it is that Virginia and I ended up with such tasteful stuff. Sitting here in the late-afternoon sun, watching the shadows on the stained walnut floor grow, I look around for something that is really mine, something I can claim as reflecting my taste, and all I find is catalog and magazine stuff. We were careful about what we purchased for this place because we wanted to make a good impression.

At least that's one explanation. The other explanation would be that this room is as blandly tasteful as it is, so vacant of real personality, because it reflects my personality all too well. What I would tell my students if I were to teach a class about this room is that the minimalism of the space, the way it is quaint but not lived in, is an indication of the impoverishment of its occupants. There is no dust here, no hidden-away corners, because everything that might be mine, everything that might be a sign of my private life, my private experience, is missing.

That's what I'd say if I were teaching a class, but right now, in this room, all I want is to discredit this notion. If Virginia were here I could turn to her for some assurance on this, and when I find her again I'll bring it up with her.

Sitting here alone, in this clean room with nothing hidden in the corners, I'm determined to discover something private, something that is really mine. If I can do that then I can make a plan for how to change my situation. If I can find one thing that is me, that is mine, I can start there.

But I don't start. I don't even think. I want to do something, to make a move, but instead I'm stuck in this arts and craft–style armchair, stuck waiting for Asket to come back to me, waiting for Harold to call, for a saucer to land. Anything. Maybe what I'm really waiting for are some instructions or my next cue.

"What I am doing," I say, "is having an identity crisis." It's helpful to say it out loud like that. It breaks up the flow of the text a bit. I'll say it again.

"I am having an identity crisis."

We left the story there for a bit, jumped out after it was suggested that I might be a projection of Harold's ego, but that isn't right. It can't be. Beyond the basic problem, the physical fact of our being different people, we're not the same in personality or type. We're very different. There are generational differences for instance. Sure, we both of us hate popular music, but he hates the pop music of the '60s, aiming his scorn primarily at the Brits, while I tend to despise disco.

Okay, the thing is, I haven't had much time for music since college. Not since high school really. I've been focused on books, on writing, on the UFO question. I haven't kept up on popular music nor developed a taste for music of other eras. But in high school I actually liked the music Harold hates. I liked Herman's

Hermits, Talk Talk, and that one about comic books... "Sunshine Superman." I remember being fifteen years old, stoned out of my gourd, and listening to Donovan. I listened to popular music when I was in high school. High school.

I set off to the bedroom because there is proof there. If I'm a projection, some kind of phantom, then I'm a projection that started his freshman year at Farmington High in 1967. That can't be, can it? If I was created in a flying saucer then I couldn't have been on the chess team back then, and Shelly Guerin couldn't have written her phone number in my yearbook back in June of 1971. I can picture it clearly. It has a yellow cover with a sun, it's a simple design. The sun has arrows sticking out in all directions; it's just an orange circle with arrows sticking out like oversized rays of light. The yearbook was called *Reflections* I think. No. It was called *Rollcall*. That's what's on the cover:

Rollcall '71.

I've still got that yearbook, still have Shelly's number. Maybe I'll give her a call.

Only, I can't find it. It's not on any of my bookshelves. The cardboard boxes in the back closet are filled with Christmas ornaments and research papers. All I've got are piles of government documents. I've got *Project Bluebook* back here but no yearbook.

I'd like to call somebody. Talk to somebody who will call me by my name and behave normally, but there is nobody I trust enough even for such a simple thing. Virginia is gone, she joined the other side, and Harold doesn't believe in me.

I could call a colleague, maybe my boss in the literature department, but what would I tell her? What excuse could I come up with? And what if she could tell that I wasn't real? What if she noticed?

I open the Baby Boomer Edition of Trivial Pursuit in the parking garage. The trip to Toys"R"Us wasn't very helpful. They didn't carry anything that seemed familiar, just Troll dolls, Rockin' Robots, and Teenage Mutant Ninja Turtles, but I did find this game. I managed to get in and out of the over-lit store with the box decorated in the same yellow and blue pattern the Cub Scouts use and back to the garage in fifteen minutes, but I'm still hurried. I remove the cellophane, open the box, and spill the cards onto the asphalt immediately. Some of them landing in a small pool of oil in the space next to mine, others fluttering under the back right wheel of my Volvo, but most are still in the box. I dump these cards into the paper sack that came with my purchase, and leave the game board and the rest of the cards on the asphalt. I don't even feel guilty about it.

This will be my own Happening. I place the bag in the passenger seat and pull a card from inside it before putting my key in the ignition. I read from the famous quotes category before I turn the engine over.

"'Say kids, what time is it?' Who asked this and what was the answer?"

The answer is too obvious. I'm sure that Harold knows this one. He might not have watched *Howdy Doody* back in the '50s, not regularly, but even he has to know the answer to this one.

When Buffalo Bob asked "What time is it?" the answer was "Howdy Doody time."

Turning on the radio and scanning the dial, pushing the buttons for preprogrammed selections first and finding only electric guitar noise, synthesized drum beats, advertisements for Dunkin' Donuts, there is still nothing there for me so I turn the dial so that the needle is between station and I'm comforted by the static.

I pull out of my parking space and drive the loops ramp to street level.

There really is no way to convince myself that I am who I think I am. On my own I'm useless. On my own I'm just an in-between space. I'm living in static. I have to talk to somebody. I need help.

The flying saucer over NYU Polytechnic is a bit different from the usual hubcap-shaped vehicles with their cherry and orange light displays. This one is more aerodynamic at least in appearance, more like an egg, and there are only a few blinking white lights on the underside. I pull off Smith Street and into the University parking lot just as the hatch opens up and the escalator plank emerges.

This saucer is dedicated to science. I learn this from the brochure in what I'll call, for lack of a better word, the lobby. A sequined man greets me as I pass through the hatch on the conveyor belt, and I'm handed the promotional material as I step onto more stationary ground.

"The Pleidiens are happy to share our technological and scientific understanding with humanity," the man tells me. He tells me that his name, not his real name but the Earth name he's selected, is Andy.

The exhibits on display in this saucer are all focused on aviation and, specifically, the engineering and physics involved in interstellar flight. There is a computer monitor filled with arrows and circles behind the alien tour guide, and when I look at the screen, follow the movement of the circles and arrows, the guide starts in explaining.

"This is a graphical representation of the process of energy release that we generate in our main engine. Notice that each circle has a certain polarity and flow."

I look where his finger is pointing, see a red circle orbiting a larger yellow dot, and watch as both are followed by a green line, their path traced along the upper half of the screen.

"We reverse this polarity in order to produce the energy required for faster-than-light travel," my guide tells me.

I shake my head at this, indicating that I'm not understanding, nor do I want to know. This Space Brother is a young man, his blond hair is neatly combed, his eyes open wide, his posture rigid but not tense. I get the feeling that he has never been sick, never suffered any deprivation at all, and I feel deflated. This isn't going to help me either.

"Can I ask you a question?" I ask him.

"Most certainly," he tells me.

"Who said, 'It leads everywhere. Get out your notebook. There's more'?"

This young man is perplexed but only for a moment. When he's figured out my question he smiles broadly and opens his arms.

"This is a game?" he asks. "Am I right? You're asking me to play a game?"

"Trivial Pursuit," I tell him.

Another couple of Earthlings enter the craft, a couple of guys in polyester shirts and wearing pocket protectors. They're both of them young too, probably the same age as the tour guide, only far less put together. One of them is rubbing his nose obsessively, sniffing and rubbing his nose with his shirtsleeve.

"Just a moment, gentlemen," my guide says.

My guide doesn't know the answer and just guesses that it might have been a police detective, somebody like Columbo or Magnum PI, but when I turn over the card I see that the answer is Deep Throat. Not the actual Deep Throat, but Deep

Throat as performed by Hal Holbrook in the movie *All the President's Men.*

"Ah, that's right. That was about Richard Nixon and Robert Redford?"

I tell the alien that he's half right, and reach for another trivia card. His wrong answer makes me feel like I'm getting somewhere. This is progress. But before I can ask him who said "Don't trust anyone over 30," he stops me. The alien grabs me by my shoulder.

"Mr. Johnson, isn't there something else you want to ask me? Maybe another game to play?"

Am I an alien? A robot? A split personality? How can I know? How can I know that I am who I believe myself to be?

"No, no," I say. "I don't have a question at all."

"Maybe I could ask you one?" the Pleidien asks.

"You want to pick a card?"

He doesn't need a trivia card. The question he asks me is how I know that the world is more than five minutes old.

"What's that?"

"It's from your philosopher Bertrand Russell, a quite ingenious problem really. What do you think of it?"

I tell him I know the world is older than five minutes old because of the dust on the first exhibit, the thin layer of what's probably minuscule flakes of human and alien skin on the model of a starboard engine, but this doesn't satisfy him. He says that if the universe is five minutes old that it would include the dust, it would include the flying saucers, it would include everything. All of it could have been created in a flash five minutes ago including our memories of it, if you follow the logic, fictional past.

"Isn't that what your friend Mr. Flint would say too? Isn't that the whole point of his work?" the alien asks me.

I don't answer, but fumble with my trivia card, looking at the answer, reading and rereading the name "Deep Throat."

There has to be a plausible reason to leave.

"Mr. Johnson, calm down. I'm not going to do anything to you, but understand that there isn't a lot of time left."

"Not a lot of time?"

He turns away from me, toward the other patrons, apparently through with this conversation, but I'm struck by a wave of courage and grab the man's shoulder, pull on his polyester collar, and turn him back in my direction.

"Who am I? I mean, am I somebody? Am I my own person, can I be confident in that much? I don't need to know whether I really did fall off that Big Wheel bike, I don't need to know whether I really did fall in love with Virginia in a sushi bar back in 1987, but I just want to know if I'm me. Tell me that much. Am I here at all? Is this Memorex or something?"

The Space Brother steps away and I'm left standing next to the dusty starboard engine, left watching the orange dots and blue lines on the computer monitor as the same explanation for interstellar flight repeats itself.

"This is how," the narrator explains, "we reverse the polarity of the neutron flow."

surrender

My twenty-four hours are up and I'm in Central Park for the light show. The flying saucer is here with me, of course, silently hovering over the neat and tidy lawn of North Meadow. And while I've been mentioning these "lollipops" or "hubcaps" or "saucers with Christmas lights attached" all along, I might as well take a moment, here at the end, to describe this one in a bit of detail.

This particular flying saucer looks like two sombreros that have been attached at the rim so that the two crowns are pointing in opposite directions. That is, there is a bulb on top and a bulb underneath, and on that top bulb there is what looks like a clasp. A person could easily thread a fishing line through it. To be brief about it, the saucer looks cheap, fake, and maybe even a bit flat, like it's been inserted into the New York skyline, as if the scene was set via not-too-competent photo manipulation. Yet there it is, hovering there. I can hear it humming. I'm sure that, soon enough, I'll be able to touch it.

I'm unzipping my jeans now, as is the protocol for surrender, and I worry that somebody is watching me. I look back, at the gravel trail behind me, thinking there will be others coming, more fictional characters who want to surrender, but there is no one.

I take off my boxer shorts, remove my favorite green and red plaid Fruit of the Looms, but nothing happens. The grass is cold with morning dew, and I wish that it was a bit later, that the sun was higher in the sky and I could feel it on my back, or alternatively I wish I was in a field of wheat or corn, something that would give me cover as I wait for the disc to receive me.

It's just half past six in the morning and I'm waiting for the ship to open. Maybe the problem is that I'm still wearing my watch and my socks. I unlatch the black plastic band of my water-resistant Casio W59 1V, drop it onto my crumpled-up Levi button-downs and try not to care as the watch slides onto the wet grass. I bend over and remove my tube socks, realizing for the first time that they don't match. One sock has green stripes while the other's stripes are bright yellow.

And it's these, the unmatched socks, that change my attitude. I'm not ashamed anymore. I actually hope that one of them, maybe even the President of the United States, Ralph Reality himself, is on the craft watching me. I don't have such a great body but I do want to be seen. I can accept being a fiction, but if I'm going to go through with this, if I'm going to leave the University, New York City, the whole world behind, I'd like it if somebody would pay attention.

The saucer is spinning faster now and the red lamps on the underside of the rim illuminate. Taken all together it looks as much like an amusement park ride, like something from Coney Island, a newer ride probably, as it does like a craft.

If there are people aboard watching me they're probably those clean and kempt tourists. Maybe all of them are in IZOD shirts rather than jumpsuits. If I'm just an idea, an image on a screen or a string of words in a story, then the people aboard the flying saucer aren't any more real than I am, they can't be because they're on the screen, the page, with me. I stop worrying about whether there are Space Brothers enjoying this sad spectacle. Sure I've got goosebumps and I'm shriveled up, but I'm also free.

Standing naked with my gut hanging out and my dick retracting up into my pelvis like a mollusk looking for its shell, I scan the horizon, examine the underside of the craft, and wait for some kind of sign.

The underside of the craft doesn't have a clasp or anything else attached. It's just smooth silver down there, a muted grey really in the gloomy morning light. From where I'm standing there don't appear to be any seams, but then, as promised, the underside does open. A door pops free and swings down, and a plank emerges. After all, I am invited.

Once I'm under the disc, as I approach the escalator, I find that I'm not alone after all. I don't know where they've come from, these other two nudists, but here they are. Now there are three passengers lining up in a queue. Directly in front is a black-haired woman, relatively short, and I figure she must be Virginia. She's either Virginia or Carole, or some other character who I don't know about, an actress maybe. Somebody who was paid to play those parts. I recognize her, anyhow. She's pale and covered in goose pimples like I am. And I notice that she has stretch marks on her otherwise attractively round hips.

I grab her elbow and turn her toward me so that I can see her face, and it is her of course, but she doesn't seem to recognize me.

"It's me," I tell her.

The old man in front of her turns to face me, to intervene, and it's Harold obviously. I wasn't sure when he had his back to me. He has a large mole on the back of his neck apparently, one I'd never noticed before, and his bare shoulders are slumped. The look on his face is fierce. He doesn't want me to speak again apparently, but I wouldn't say that he recognizes me either. His eyes are blanks.

Asket and Charles Rain appear at the top of the ramp waiting for us. They're dressed in sequined jumpsuits, holding pamphlets that we're encouraged to take from them. These are our instructions.

"Faster-than-light travel can be difficult for a human being," Charles Rain explains. "While the Pleidiens guarantee your physical well-being during this journey, everything you need physically will be provided, you will be responsible for protecting your mind."

Opening the pamphlet I see it's a cartoon. Rather than writing the story, our upcoming journey is told in pictures. On the first page there is an outline of a UFO and all around there are figures, just outlines of people like the icons you see on restroom doors. These figures are standing under a beam of red light, just like the beam of light we're under now, and they're queued up too. The triangle and rectangle people are surrendering, and on the next page we get to see them aboard the ship. They're stacked on each other in rows, neatly piled along the outside edge of their cartoon saucer.

Asket gestures to Charles. She makes a karate chop motion in the air and then steps forward toward us, toward Virginia, Harold, and me.

"You will not be able to protect your minds," Asket says. "That is what you must be prepared to accept. What will be required of you for this journey is an acceptance that you won't be able to protect your minds or your identity. That is, in fact, the very reason you've agreed to make this trip. That's why you're here. You're here to surrender."

"Good luck," Rain says to Harold. "Good luck. Good luck."

It's clear that Charles isn't coming with us. This enlightenment stuff isn't for him. Not yet. "I envy you," he tells me as I walk past. And then, right before I step onto the escalator he says it again. "I envy you."

Now, when two people switch bodies what happens is that one personality is transferred to another and vice versa. Nothing physical really changes, or at least that's how it seems.

"The people aboard that craft are no more real than I am," I say.

"That's right," Charles says. And Asket is beaming a smile in my direction as Harold takes his first step up onto the plank. He's moving away from us, up what is basically an escalator.

Virginia or Carole, whichever you want to call her is fine, starts to shiver and shake as she too steps onto the mechanism and drifts up. I'm right behind her, about to step aboard when I say it again, but this time it's a question.

"The people aboard that craft are no more real than I am?" I ask.

"That's right," Asket says. Her smile falters a bit.

"What about you, Charles?"

"That's right," he says mindlessly.

"And them?" I ask, gesturing up at Harold and Virginia.

"That's right," they both say. They're getting impatient with me now, I think. It's time that I got aboard the ship.

"Take that first step," Charles says and he points to the ramp.

When Asket and Carole switched bodies, or started to switch bodies, at the MUFON conference they told each other stories, they told each other their history. When the two boys, that fat kid in the purple sequined jumpsuit and the TV personality, when they switched they did the same thing.

"That's right," Asket says.

But the thing is, I have a story to tell too. Mine is like theirs. Those other stories were about the moments in life when those people—the fat kid, and the alien, and Harold's wife, and the television personality—about when they felt free. They shared how it was for them, as individuals, to feel free. And that helped. That helped the switch happen.

"That's right," Charles says.

The thing is this is the moment I want to share. This is the story I want to tell. Right now. This moment is what I have and I'm giving it to you, Charles. This very second. I'm giving it to you freely and for free. I'm giving it to you and not asking for anything back. Do you understand?

"I . . ."

Charles is wearing a dark blue button-up suit jacket with gold buttons, dark blue slacks, a light blue shirt, navy blue tie, and leather loafers. I start with his shoes.

"What size are you?" I ask him.

He's a size nine, which is a pretty good fit, and while the pants are a bit tight around the waist they're close enough for now. I can have a tailor let them out.

Charles runs up the escalator as I button up the front of the jacket. He takes the escalator steps two at a time and then he's inside the ship, right behind Virginia.

"There they go," Asket says. "That went very well I think, Charles."

"It's Brian, actually," I tell her. She just smiles.

The flying saucer hovers there for just a moment or two longer, spinning like a top and humming, and then it flies away from us. The UFO skips away from us through the air, like a saucer skipping across water.

And as it goes I wonder about the people aboard. Are they going to end up like us, like me, or am I the last of the Ufologists now that the saucers have landed?

Also available from Douglas Lain and Night Shade Books:

Last Week's Apocalypse

Gore Vidal meets Philip K. Dick in this collection of lit-fabulist stories. Douglas Lain's work has been attracting high profile attention throughout the field, and this collection features some of his finest and most controversial fiction.

The stories herein present electric messiahs, identity constructs, the Beatles, and even nuclear Armageddon as comic foils for Lain's everyman characters. He is an America where the packets of Sea Monkeys that arrive in the mail contain secret messages and the girl next door can breathe underwater. With *Last Week's Apocalypse*, Douglas Lain arrives with a punch line and a warning.

"The stories in *Last Week's Apocalypse* are like a series of short, sharp shocks. Lain's writing is unsettling, ferociously smart, and extremely addictive."

—Kelly Link, author of *Get in Trouble* and *Magic for Beginners*

$14.95 trade paper • 978-1-59780-034-1

Also available from Douglas Lain and Night Shade Books:

In the Shadow of the Towers

In the Shadow of the Towers compiles nearly twenty works of speculative fiction responding to and inspired by the events of 9/11, from writers seeking to confront, rebuild, and carry on, even in the face of overwhelming emotion.

Writer and editor Douglas Lain presents a thought-provoking anthology featuring a variety of award-winning and best-selling authors, from Jeff VanderMeer (*Annihilation*) and Cory Doctorow (*Little Brother*) to Susan Palwick (*Flying in Place*) and James Morrow (*Towing Jehovah*). Touching on themes as wide-ranging as politics, morality, and even heartfelt nostalgia, today's speculative fiction writers prove that the rubric of the fantastic offers an incomparable view into how we respond to tragedy.

Each contributor, in his or her own way, contemplates the same question:

How can we continue dreaming in the shadow of the towers?

$15.99 trade paper • 978-1-59780-839-2

about the author

Douglas Lain is a novelist and short story writer whose work has appeared in various magazines including *Strange Horizons*, *Interzone*, and *Lady Churchill's Rosebud Wristlet*. His debut novel, *Billy Moon*, was published by Tor and was selected as the debut fantasy novel of the month by *Library Journal* in 2013. *After the Saucers Landed* is his second novel.

Lain is the publisher of Zero Books, which specializes in philosophy and political theory, and hosts the *Zero Squared* podcast, interviewing a wide range of fascinating, engaging people with insights for the new millennium: philosophers, mystics, economists, and a diverse group of fiction writers. He lives in Portland, Oregon, with his wife and children.